Union Atlantic

ALSO BY ADAM HASLETT

You Are Not a Stranger Here

NAN A. TALESE

DOUBLEDAY

New York London Toronto

Sydney Auckland

Union Atlantic

A NOVEL

Adam Haslett

For support during the writing of this book, the author wishes to thank the John Simon Guggenheim Memorial Foundation, the Rockefeller Foundation, the MacDowell Colony, the Corporation of Yaddo, as well as Nan Talese, Ira Silverberg, Robert Millner, Ruth Curry, Luke Hoorelbeke, Amity Gaige, Jon Franzen, Julia Haslett, Timothy Haslett (1966–2008), Nancy Haslett, Sarah Faunce, Jenn Chandler-Ward, Andrew Janjigian, Melissa Rivard, Adam Hickey, Brett Phillips, David Grewel, Daniela Cammack, David Menschel, Joe Landau, Mark Breitenberg, Julian Levinson, Michael Graetz, Richard Eldridge, Brendan Tapley, Josh Cohen, and Daniel Thomas Davis.

 Published in the United States by Nan A. Talese / Doubleday, a division of Random House, Inc., New York, and in Canada by Random House of Canada Limited, Toronto.
www.nanatalese.com

Library of Congress Cataloging-in-Publication Data
Haslett, Adam.
Union Atlantic : a novel / Adam Haslett.—1st ed.
p. cm.
1. Bankers—Fiction. 2. Older women—Fiction. 3. High school students—Fiction. 4. House construction—Fiction. 5. Social classes—Fiction. 6. Massachusetts—Fiction. I. Title.
PS3608.A85F57 2009
813'.6—dc22 2009011875

ISBN 978-0-385-52447-6

PRINTED IN THE UNITED STATES OF AMERICA

1 3 5 7 9 10 8 6 4 2

First Edition

For my mother,
Nancy Faunce Haslett

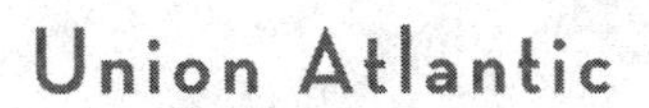

Union Atlantic

July 1988

Their second night in port at Bahrain someone on the admiral's staff decided the crew of the *Vincennes* deserved at least a free pack of cigarettes each. The gesture went over well until the canteen ran out and then the dispensing machines, leaving fifty or so enlisted men and a few petty officers feeling cheated of the one recognition anyone had offered of what they had been through. A number of them, considerably drunk, had begun milling outside the commissary, suggesting it ought to be opened up to make good on the promise. Realizing he had a situation on his hands, the admiral's staffer pulled Vrieger aside, handed him an envelope of petty cash, and told him there was a jeep and driver waiting for him at the gate.

"That place on Al Budayyai should still be open. Get whatever you can. Get menthols if you have to. Just make it quick."

"Come on, Fanning," Vrieger said. "We're taking a ride."

"But I've got mine," Doug replied, holding up his half-smoked pack of Carltons. Three or four beers had done their sedative work and set him down here on this bench by the officers' mess, where he sought only to rest.

"It ain't about you."

Hauling his gaze up from the linoleum floor, Doug saw the lantern face of his lieutenant commander bearing down on him. He wasn't a handsome guy, with eyes too small for the broad circumference of his head and a big jowly mouth. The square metal-rimmed glasses added to the look of middle age though, at thirty-one, he was little more than a decade older than Doug. Vrieger was the only guy in the navy who knew more about him than the town he came from and the bases he'd trained at, and this counted for something.

Lifting himself from the bench, he followed Vrieger out the rear door of the mess.

Outside, the temperature had dropped into the eighties, but the air was still humid and laced with the scent of diesel fumes. A mile in the distance, across the desert plain, the white needle towers and minaret of the grand mosque rose up spotlit against the empty night sky. This forward base at Juffair, a small, island pit stop in the Gulf, consisted of a few acres of outbuildings strung along the port southeast of Manama. If the tour had gone according to plan, Doug would have returned to the States from here. But who knew what would happen now?

He shuffled into the backseat of the jeep, not quite lying across it, not exactly upright either.

"Where to?" the driver asked, as they rose onto the rutted two-laner that led into the capital.

"Just head into town," Vrieger told him.

"That was some dogfight you guys were in, huh?"

"This kid sounds likes he's fifteen." Doug called out: "Kid, you sound like you're fifteen."

"No, sir. I'm eighteen."

"It wasn't a dogfight," Doug said. "No dogs, not much fight."

"Shut up," Vrieger said, leaning into the driver's face to ask if they were obeying some kind of speed limit. The jeep leapt forward. Slumping lower across the seat to escape the wind on his face, Doug closed his eyes.

All morning he'd been on the phone with a staffer at the Naval Weapons Center back in Virginia going over the *Vincennes*' tapes and then all afternoon with the investigators, the same questions again and again: When the plane first popped on Siporski's screen, what did Lieutenant Commander Vrieger do? Asked for a tag. And it came back what? Mode III. So the first time you tagged the plane it came back civilian, is that right? Yes. On and on like that for hours, every answer rephrased into another question, as if they didn't understand a word he said. Not even so much as a "must have been rough," nothing, not even a handshake at the beginning. He'd told them the truth. To every question he'd told them the truth. They'd listened to the tapes. They knew what Doug had seen on his screen and what he'd failed to report. Yet they never asked him what information he'd communicated to Vrieger, as if they knew in advance the story they wanted to tell. Back home, apparently, the Joint Chiefs had already begun covering for what had happened.

The engagement occurred in international waters. Untrue.

The Vincennes *was acting in protection of a flagged tanker.* Untrue.

As the kid steered to avoid the potholes, the jeep swung gently from side to side, while a song by Journey played on the radio. Doug had listened to the same song in the backseat of a friend's car in the parking lot of a mall in Alden, Massachusetts, the week before he'd left home to join the navy. Hearing it now—that big, stadium rock anthem with the soaring guitar and hard, wounded voice of the singer, angry at the love lost and the damage done—he pictured his mother alone in the apartment and for a moment he imagined what relief it would be if the jeep were to swing too far into the opposite lane, where it might meet a truck with no headlights, seeing in his mind's eye the explosion that would consume them, a blast as instantaneous as a ship's missile striking a plane.

But this was weakness. He would not be weak.

Three years had passed since he'd left Alden without saying a word to his mother about where he was going. And though in the last twenty-four hours, since the incident, he'd been tempted to call her, that would mean having to account for himself, when all he wanted to do was tell someone the story. Someone who hadn't been there.

Yesterday had been like any other morning. Coffee and cereal in the wardroom, and then a walk along the aft deck, before the temperature rose above a hundred degrees and the railings became too hot to touch. Looking out over the stern he'd seen the milky bellies of jellyfish flipped by the ship's wake to face the sun, floating atop the surf along with the garbage tossed from the sides of tankers.

On the passage out, across the Pacific, he'd written the last of his college applications as well as the letters to the banks and brokerages where he hoped to get a job while he studied, behind the counter or in the mail room if that's all they had to offer him. Most of the guys he knew leaving the service were going for jobs with defense contractors—electrical engineering and the like—but he'd known all along he wanted more than that.

Down in the gloom of the Combat Center his shift had started quietly, nothing on his or Siporski's monitors but an Iranian P-3 doing surveillance down the coast and some commercial air flights out of Bandar Abbas, puddle jumping to Doha or Dubai.

Since June, the *Vincennes* had been detailed to Operation Earnest

Will, escorting Kuwaiti tankers through the Strait of Hormuz. Kuwait was Saddam's biggest ally in his war against Iran, and the U.S. Fifth Fleet had been tasked with protecting her ships from Iranian gunboats. America was officially neutral in the Iran-Iraq war, but everyone knew who the enemy was: the ayatollahs, the ones who'd taken the hostages back in '79, who'd bombed the marine barracks in Beirut.

Their gunboats weren't regular navy, but Revolutionary Guard. Basically a bunch of loyalists in speedboats loaded up with mortars and small arms. A helicopter pilot told Doug he'd seen four guys prostrate on the deck of an idling Boston Whaler, their heads bowed west to Mecca, RPGs leaning up against the rails like fishing poles.

As the duty officer in charge that morning, Vrieger took the call from the frigate *Montgomery*. Five or six gunboats had been spotted out of the tiny island of Abu Musa heading toward a German tanker.

When Vrieger called the captain—a man eager for his admiral's stripes and the combat he'd need to get them—he immediately ordered general quarters. Boots began stomping above and below, hatches slamming closed, the ladder steps rattling as men poured into the Combat Center to take their stations. Eighty thousand horsepower started churning so loudly it sounded as if the rear of the ship were detaching. They were doing thirty knots before the skipper got down from his cabin, the command net in Doug's ear already starting to fill with chatter, the signal weakening as half the ship began listening in on the Sony Walkmans they'd figured out could be tuned to follow the action.

And then as quickly as it had arisen, the incident seemed to dissolve. Ocean Lord, the helicopter the captain had ordered up to fly reconnaissance, said the boats appeared to be dispersing already, heading away from the tanker. When command in Bahrain heard this, they ordered the *Vincennes* back to course.

"Is that it, Captain?" Ocean Lord's pilot asked.

"Negative," he replied. "Follow the boats."

On his radar screen, Doug watched the helicopter start to track west, the boats it pursued too low in the water to register a consistent signal on the surface radar.

Less than ten minutes later it began.

"Taking fire!" the pilot shouted into his radio. "Evacuating."

This was all the excuse the captain needed to ignore his command's orders. Soon enough he'd steered the ship to within eight thousand yards of the Iranian boats. There was still no air traffic on Doug's screen except the same P-3 making its way along the coast.

Upstairs, the bridge called twelve miles, meaning the ship had passed into Iranian territorial waters in violation of standing orders. Doug looked back over his shoulder at Vrieger, who shrugged. Vrieger disliked the captain but he wasn't about to be insubordinate. The haze was too thick to get a good visual on the boats; all the bridge could make out were a few glints in the sun. The raiders appeared to be idling, imagining themselves safe.

At seven thousand yards, the captain ordered the starboard five-inch mount to open fire. Doug heard the explosion of the gun but confined at his console he could only picture the blasts disappearing into the hot, sandy vapor. Once it started, it didn't let up. Round after round, the concussions echoed back against the ship's housing.

That's when Siporski first spotted the plane.

"Unidentified out of Bandar Abbas," he said, "bearing two-five-zero."

Vrieger stepped forward from his chair to look at his petty officer's monitor. Doug could see it now on his screen as well.

"Tag it," Vrieger ordered.

They had to assume a hostile aircraft until they got an ID. The plane's transponder sent back a Mode III signal, indicating a civilian flight. Vrieger opened his binder to the commercial air schedule and, squinting to read the print, ran his finger down the columns of the Gulf's four different time zones, trying to match the numbers up, the arc lights flickering overhead with each discharge of the deck gun.

"Why isn't it on the *fucking* schedule?" he kept saying, his finger zipping across the tiny rows.

Someone yelled that the starboard mount had jammed. The captain, pissed and wanting to engage the port gun, ordered the ship hard over and suddenly the whole room lurched sideways, papers, drinks, binders spilling off desks and sliding across the floor. Doug had to grab the side of his console to remain upright, the cruiser's other gun beginning to fire before they'd even come fully about.

"Shit," Siporski said, as they leveled off again. "It's gone Mode I, sir, bearing toward us two-five-zero."

Responding automatically to the signal, the ship's Aegis system popped the symbol for an F-14 onto the big screen. Someone over the command net shouted, "Possible Astro." The Iranians had scrambled F-14s out of Bandar Abbas a few times but it was rare for them to get this close. They were the best planes they had, sold to the shah back in the seventies.

Vrieger immediately challenged with a friend or foe.

"Unidentified aircraft you are approaching a United States naval warship in international waters, request you change course immediately to two-seven-zero or you will be subject to defensive measures, over."

No reply.

"Damn it," Vrieger said, having to shout to be heard over the gunfire. "Thirty-two miles, Skipper. What do we do?"

That's when Siporski called out, "Descending!"

Doug didn't see this on his monitor. His screen showed the plane's altitude rising into the commercial air corridor.

"Descending!" Siporski repeated. "Two-five-zero, descending!"

It was Doug's duty to provide his commanding officer with all information relevant to the ship's air defense. That was his duty. And yet he froze, unable to speak.

A minute later, Vrieger ordered fire control to paint the plane. It had popped on the big screen only two minutes before. Standing orders were to fire at twenty miles. Under ten would be too late. Vrieger challenged the plane again but again got no reply.

"Lieutenant Vrieger!" the captain shouted. "What the fuck is the status of that bogey?"

Doug watched the plane rise steadily on his monitor.

A year ago an Iraqi F-1 had mistaken the USS *Stark* for an Iranian ship and fired two missiles, killing three dozen American sailors and nearly sinking the frigate. Doug had not come here to die.

"Did you hear me!?" the captain yelled. "What is that plane!?"

Vrieger kept staring at Siporski's screen, cursing to himself.

"F-14," Vrieger said at last. "Sir, it breaks as an F-14."

"FANNING."

He opened his eyes to see Vrieger reaching back from the front seat of the jeep to shake his leg. "Here," he said, handing him the envelope of cash. "You're the one who speaks the phrases. This guy looks closed up. You got to get in there quick before he leaves."

They were parked on a narrow street lined with darkened storefronts, posters with once bright photographs of soda cans and soccer stars plastered over one another on the walls between shop doors.

Closed shutters were spaced in no particular pattern across the beige stucco walls of the apartments above, lights visible between the down-turned slats. A bulb still burned in one vendor's room, a metal grate pulled down over the store window.

Doug felt unsteady crossing the street. The acrid smell of rotting fruit filled his nostrils and he thought he might be sick as he reached the curb. Holding on to the grate, he reached through it with his other hand and tapped on the glass, pointing to the shelf of cigarettes.

The man looked up from behind the counter where he stood over a ledger. More unshaven than bearded, wearing a striped shirt with the sleeves rolled up, he could have been anywhere from forty to sixty. His face was long and deeply creased. He adjusted his eyes to see who it was who had disturbed him and then shook his head and returned to his calculations.

"I would like cigarettes," Doug said in mauled Arabic, his voice raised, uttering one of the twenty sentences he'd learned from the phrase book. "I would like cigarettes."

This time, the man lifted his head slowly, and called out in English, "Kloz'd."

Grabbing the wad of greenbacks in his fist, Doug banged on the glass. The man put down his pen and walked from behind the counter to stand on the other side of the door.

"Lots," Doug said. "I need lots. Ten cartons."

Muttering something he couldn't hear through the glass, the storekeeper unlocked the door and raised the grate high enough for Doug to dip his head under and enter.

"Only because my customers did not buy what they should this week," he said. Turning his back, he added, "Otherwise, I would not sell to your kind. Not today."

From behind a bead curtain, the scent of cooking meat drenched the stuffy air.

More than ever, Doug desired to be gone from these wretched foreign places with all their filth and poverty, to be back in America, starting on his real life, the one he'd been planning for so long. But he found he couldn't ignore the dark hair on the man's neck and his small, rounded shoulders and his baggy cotton pants and the sandals strapped over the dusty brown skin of his feet.

Reports on yesterday's incident were still coming in, Vrieger had told him. At the base, command wasn't letting the crew see or hear any news from the outside.

It was Vrieger who had reached his hand up to the ceiling panel and turned the key, illuminating a button on Doug's console he'd only ever seen lit in the dwindling hours of war games: permission to launch.

"Marlboros," he said, leaning his elbows on the counter, trying to put a stop to the spinning motion in his head. "Give me Marlboros. All of those cartons. I need all of them."

The shopkeeper stepped onto the second rung of his ladder and reached up to the shelf, where the red-and-white boxes were stacked. Down to his left, behind the counter, a television sat atop a milk crate, the sound turned off. A mustachioed announcer in a double-breasted suit spoke directly to the viewers. The screen then cut to an overview of the inside of an air hangar filled with rows of boxes, groups of people walking along the aisles between them; then came a cut closer in: a man in uniform opening a long black bag for the camera, which zoomed in to hold the shot of a young woman, twenty-five maybe, though on the grainy screen, her face bloated, who could tell? Her corpse grasped in stiffened arms a child of three or four, his body and little grayed head mashed to his mother's chest. The dead arms gripping tightly the dead boy.

"Eighteen miles," someone—Doug still didn't know who—had shouted into the waning strength of the command net, "possible commercial air."

The wake of an SM-2 missile looked like a miniature version of the space shuttle blasting off from Cape Canaveral, the launch fuel burning a hot white plume. But down in the battle chamber Doug had heard only its deafening roar and, seconds later, as the symbols on the big screen collided, the eruption of cheering.

"So," the shopkeeper said, placing the stack of boxes on the counter and indicating the television with a nod of his head, "you know these murderers, do you?"

"My ship," Doug said, standing up straight, whatever reprieve drunkenness had offered abruptly gone. "My ship."

It had taken a while for the initial reports to be confirmed. "Iranian Airbus. Passengers, two hundred and ninety, over."

The shopkeeper's coal-black eyes widened, his upper lip quivering.

"These Iranians, they are too much, but this—this, shame!" he said, pointing into Doug's face. "You are *butchers*, you and your government are *butchers*."

Doug counted twenty-dollar bills from the wad in his fist, setting them down one by one on the counter.

"I'll need a bag," he said.

"I will not take your money!" the man shouted. "I will not take it!"

Doug counted out another three bills, placing them on top of the rest. Rage welled in the shopkeeper's eyes.

Once he had gathered the cartons of cigarettes into his arms, Doug remained standing there at the counter for a moment. On the television, shawled women keened over a small wooden coffin.

Twenty days of his tour left now. Twenty.

"You should know, sir," he said, "under the conditions, you should know, sir, that we would do it again."

Then he turned and walked out of the shop and across the darkened street, throwing the cigarettes into the backseat of the jeep.

"What's his problem?" the kid asked.

"Just drive, would you?"

As they sped along the road back to Juffair, Doug sat upright, the wind full in his face, figuring in his head how long it would take for the letters he'd mailed in Manila to make their way into the offices of the brokerages and the banks.

Part One

Chapter 1

A plot of land. That's what Doug told his lawyer. Buy me a plot of land, hire a contractor, and build me a casino of a house. If the neighbors have five bedrooms, give me six. A four-car garage, the kitchen of a prize-winning chef, high ceilings, marble bathrooms, everything wired to the teeth. Whatever the architecture magazines say. Make the envying types envious.

"What do you want with a mansion?" Mikey asked. "You barely sleep in your own apartment. You'd get nothing but lost."

Finden, Doug told him. Build it in Finden.

And so on a Sunday morning in January 2001, Mikey had picked Doug up at his place in Back Bay and they had driven west out of Boston in a light snow, the gray concrete of the overpasses along the Mass Pike blending with the gray sky above as they traveled the highway that Doug had traveled so often as a kid. It had been six years now since he'd moved back up to Massachusetts from New York. What had brought him was a job at Union Atlantic, a commercial bank whose chairman and CEO, Jeffrey Holland, had entrusted Doug with the company's expansion. In the years since, his salary and bonuses had accumulated in the various accounts and investments his financial adviser had established, but he'd spent practically nothing.

"You're pathetic," Mikey had said to him once, when he'd come back to Doug's apartment for a beer and seen the college furniture and books still in their boxes. "You need a life."

A solo practitioner, Mikey had gone to Suffolk Law at night, while he worked at a bail-bond office. He lived with his girlfriend in one of the new condos in South Boston, six stories up and two blocks east of the house he'd grown up in, his mother still cooking him dinner on Sunday nights. He liked to call himself a well-rounded lawyer, which in practice meant he did everything but drive his clients to work.

A few miles short of the Alden town line, they turned off at the Finden exit onto a wooded road that opened out into the snow-covered meadows of a golf course, used at this time of year for cross-country skiing. They passed under an old, arched brick railway bridge and soon after reached the first stretch of houses.

The town was much as Doug remembered it from the days when he'd driven his mother to work here: mostly woods, the homes widely spaced, with big yards and long driveways, the larger homes hidden from view by hedges and gates. When they reached the village center, he saw that the old stores had been replaced by newer clothing boutiques and specialty food shops, though their signage, by town ordinance, remained conservative and subdued. The benches on the sidewalks were neatly painted, as were the fire hydrants and the elaborate lampposts and the well-tended wooden planters.

On the far side of this little town center, the houses became sparse again, one large colonial after the next, most of them white clapboard with black trim. They passed a white steepled church with a snow-covered graveyard and a mile or so farther along turned onto a dirt track that led down a gentle incline. A few hundred yards into the woods, Mikey brought the car to a halt and cut the engine.

"This is it," he said. "Five acres. Up ahead you got a river. The other side's all Audubon so they can't touch you there. One other house up the hill to the right, and a couple more on the far side of that. Any other place, they'd put eight houses on a piece this size, but the locals ganged up and zoned it huge."

Stepping out of the car, they walked over the frozen ground farther down the track until they reached the bank of the river. Only four or five yards across and no more than a few feet deep, it flowed over a bed of leaves and mossy rock.

"Amazing," Doug said, "how quiet it is."

"The town's asking for two point eight," Mikey said. "My guy thinks we can get it for two and a half. That is if you're still crazy enough to want it."

"This is good," Doug said, peering across the water into the bare black winter trees. "This is just fine."

THE HOUSE TOOK a year to complete: three months to clear the land, bury the pipes, and dig a foundation, another seven for construction, and two more for interior work and landscaping. For the right sum, Mikey oversaw all of it.

By the time it was done, the real estate market had progressed as Doug had foreseen. After the tech bust in 2000, the Federal Reserve had cut interest rates, making mortgages cheap, and thus opening the door for all that frightened capital to run for safety into houses. The attacks on 9/11 had only sped the trend. These new mortgages were being fed into the banks like cars into a chop shop, stripped for parts by

Union Atlantic and the other big players, and then securitized and sold on to the pension funds and the foreign central banks. Thus were the monthly payments of the young couples in California and Arizona and Florida transformed by the alchemy of finance into a haven for domestic liquidity and the Chinese surplus, a surplus earned by stocking the box stores at which those same couples shopped. With all that money floating around, the price of real estate could only rise. Before Doug ever opened the front door, the value of his new property had risen thirty percent.

The first night he slept in Finden he remembered his dreams as he hadn't in years. In one, his mother wandered back and forth along the far end of a high-school gymnasium, clad in a beige raincoat, her hands in her pockets, her head tilted toward the floor. They were late again for Mass. Doug called to her from beneath the scrub oak in their tiny backyard. Its bark peeled away, he saw veins pumping blood into branches suddenly animate and forlorn. A priest waited in an idling sedan. In the distance, he heard the sound of a ship's cannon firing. Oblivious to all of this, focused only on the floorboards in front of her, his mother kept pacing. As the deck beneath him began to list, Doug rolled to his knees to break his fall.

He woke on his stomach, sweating. The wall was an uncanny distance from the bed, the pale-yellow paint someone had chosen for it beginning to glow dimly in the early-morning light. He rolled onto his back and stared at the stilled ceiling fan, its rounded chrome fixture as spotless as the deck of the *Vincennes* on inspection day.

Here he was, thirty-seven, lying in his mansion.

Reaching for the remote at his side, he switched on the TV.

. . . *Israel denies Arafat request to leave West Bank compound,* the CNN ticker began . . . *Pakistan in discussions with U.S. to hand over chief suspect in murder of Wall Street Journal reporter* . . . *CT residents to pay $50* *more per year for garbage collection after State Trash Authority loss of $200 million on deal with Enron . . .*

His BlackBerry began vibrating on the floor beside his keys; it was his trader in Hong Kong, Paul McTeague, calling.

At Doug's level of bank management, most people relied on underlings to handle recruiting, but that had never been his practice. He insisted on choosing his own people, right down to the traders. McTeague had been one of his. They'd met a few years ago on a flight to London. A Holy Cross grad, McTeague had grown up in Worcester and learned the business with a specialist on the floor of the NYSE. A rabid Bruins fan, his conversation didn't extend much beyond hockey and derivatives. Twenty-eight and itching to make a killing. The human equivalent of a single-purpose vehicle. In short, perfect for the job. Usually Doug would have waited awhile before clueing in a new guy as to how he, in particular, ran the flow of information, i.e. avoiding intermediate supervisors. But he could tell right away that McTeague was his kind, and so he'd told him straight out: If you've got a problem and you're getting hassled, just call.

Two months ago, when the head of the back office at the Hong Kong desk had left, Doug had installed McTeague as the temporary replacement, thus putting him in charge of all paperwork and accounting, and expanding the dominion of an employee with direct loyalty to him. The more raw information Doug could get stovepiped up from the front lines without interference from all the middling professionals, the more direct power over outcomes he wielded.

"You're a genius," McTeague said when Doug answered his phone. "The Nikkei's up another two percent. Our economy's still in the tank but Japanese stocks keep rising. It's a thing of beauty."

A month and a half ago, in early February, he and McTeague had been at a conference in Osaka. After one of the sessions, they had gone to Murphy's, the bar where the Australians pretended to be Irish. They were about to call it a night when Doug saw a senior deputy in the Japanese Ministry of Finance stumble in with a Korean woman half his age. The man shook his head in resignation as his young companion made her way straight for the bar and ordered a bottle of scotch. Interested to see how things would play out, Doug ordered another round and he and McTeague settled in to watch. The argument in the corner grew steadily more heated. The woman was demanding something the man didn't want to give, the Tokyo deputy apparently at wits' end with his mistress. Eventually, after being harangued for half an hour, he stood up, threw cash on the table, and walked out of the bar.

That's when the idea had occurred to Doug: the young woman might know something.

"Do me a favor," he'd said to McTeague. "Comfort the girl."

And a good job of it McTeague had done. At some point after they'd had sex, the deputy's mistress told him that the Ministry of Finance had a plan. They were about to launch another price-stability operation. The Japanese government would buy up a boatload of domestic stocks, sending the Nikkei index higher and thus shoring up the balance sheets of their country's troubled banks. It was a classic command-economy move, using public money to interfere with the market's valuations. In the process, the Japanese government would hand a major loss to the foreign, largely U.S. speculators who had been shorting the value of their stock market for months.

The operation, of course, was secret.

And thus it was that in mid-February, Atlantic Securities, the investment banking firm that Union Atlantic had purchased and renamed two years earlier as part of its expansion, had become the one American firm to go from bearish to bullish on the prospects for the Japanese economy. Under Doug's supervision, McTeague had placed large bets on the Nikkei going higher, using Atlantic Securities' own money. The resulting trading profits had been substantial and were still flowing in. It would be awhile yet before the Ministry of Finance's plan would become public and there was a lot of money to be made in the meantime.

"So," McTeague asked, eager as ever, "how much cash do I get to play with tomorrow?"

"We'll see," Doug replied. "Call me after New York opens."

The chilled marble of the bathroom floor felt particularly solid against the balls of his feet. Two huge sinks in the shape of serving bowls, one for the master and one for his wife, were set beneath mirrored cabinets along the far wall. Beyond were two shower stalls with shiny steel heads that jetted water from the walls and ceiling. Opposite these stood a patio-size cross between a Jacuzzi pool and a bathtub, the whole thing decked in slate.

Walking to the window, Doug looked out across the front of the house. Mikey had done a good job: a stately, circular driveway, an enormous freestanding garage mocked up like a barn, and, surrounding it all, pleasing expanses of lawn. Through a row of bare maples that had been left up the hill to mark the property line, he could see a dilapidated barn and beside it an ancient house with weathered shingles, a listing brick chimney, and a slight dip in the long rear slant of its roof. It was one of those old New England saltboxes that historical preservation societies kept tabs on, although not too closely by the looks of it. Whoever owned it didn't seem to be occupying the place. Weeds had risen in the rutted gravel drive. On the one hand, it was the farthest thing from a Mickey D's and a strip mall you could get, just the sort of nostalgia for which people loved towns like this, casting the dead starlight of American landed gentry, dotted with graveyards full of weathered headstones and the occasional field of decorative sheep. Allowed to decay too far, however, it could cause a decline in the value of Doug's property. If some absentee WASP who'd retreated to his compound in Maine thought he could just let a house rot like this, it would have to be sorted out. He'd put Mikey on it, he thought, as he slipped out of his boxers and stepped into the shower.

Downstairs, he passed through the mansion's empty rooms and, finding the touch-screen keypad by the front door inscrutable, pushed an Off button and saw the screen announce: Fanning Disarmed.

Mikey was good. He was very good.

As he came down the front steps, the late-winter sun was just beginning to strike the side of his garage. Glancing over the roof of his car, he saw a woman in a blue ski jacket coming out the back door of the old house up the hill, which was apparently inhabited after all. Tall and rather thin, she had longish gray hair and a stiff, upright posture. With her were two large dogs, a Doberman and some sort of mastiff. It looked as if the animals were too strong for her, that she might be pulled down by them, but a yank of her arm brought them under control and they led her in orderly fashion along the stone path to the overgrown driveway. At first Doug thought she hadn't noticed him at such a distance. But then, as he was about to get in his car, she glanced in his direction, and Doug waved.

She made no response, as if surveying an empty landscape.

Rude or half blind, he couldn't tell. Driving slowly, he turned onto Winthrop Street and, lowering the passenger-side window, rolled up beside her.

"Good morning. My name's Doug Fanning. The new place here—it's mine."

For a moment, it seemed she hadn't heard a word he said and was perhaps deaf to boot. But then, abruptly, as if the car had only now appeared, she came to a halt. Bringing the dogs to heel, she leaned down to look into the car. The deeply lined skin of her face had the same weathered gray hue as the side of her house. Without a word, as if he weren't even there, she sniffed at the air of the car's interior; the Lexus he'd leased for the new commute was still pine fresh.

"Trees," she said. "Before you came. All of it. Trees."

And with that she stood upright again and kept walking.

Chapter 2

For months now Charlotte Graves had tried to avoid looking at the new place. And yet how could anyone's eyes not snare on the enormity of it? It had been designed to draw attention.

As she and the dogs came down the drive the following morning, it came into view once again: a hulking, white mass of a building, three full stories in the middle, with wings on either side and someone's idea of an orangery or sunroom protruding from the far end. A cupola the size of a small bandstand stood atop the pile, betwixt two fat, brick chimneys. A columned portico framed the enormous front door. Either side of this, along the front of the house, were yew shrubs set in beds of newly delivered wood chips. It looked, more than anything else, like a recently opened country club, and indeed the landscaping of the yard, with its empty flower beds cut from the imported turf like oval incisions on a piece of bright-green construction paper and its perfectly crosscut lawn running to the river's edge without so much as a transitional weed, reminded one of the manicure of a golf course. In line at the drugstore, Charlotte had overheard a real estate agent describing it as a Greek Revival château.

This was what had replaced the woods that Charlotte's grandfather had given to the town for preservation. This steroidal offense.

Over the last year, as it was being built, she had often reminded herself that the house was merely the furthest and most galling advance of the much larger intrusion, the one that had begun decades ago, first at a distance, a sighting here or there, a fancy stroller in the library stacks, a concern for caloric totals voiced over the meat counter. More recently had come the giant cars, the ones that looked as if they should have gun turrets mounted on their roofs, manned by the children glaring from the backseat. For years the news had made so much of bombings in the Middle East, and of course in dear old New York now as well, and of the birds of prey we released in retaliation but they never mentioned the eyes of the wealthy young and the violence simmering numbly there. She had seen it at school, the way her students had grown pointed, turned into swords wielded by their masters. As soon as she began speaking of such things openly the principal had gone to the retirement board and they had got rid of her. Nearly forty years of teaching history to the children of this town and they had hustled her out for speaking the truth.

With the Bennetts on one side of her and the woods on the other, Charlotte had always thought she would be safe from the worst of the intrusion. Her house, the old family place, was a redoubt of sorts. After all this time living in it, its memories were for her neither a comfort nor a haunting. They were simply the traces of beings with whom she shared the place. Time by herself had done that to Charlotte, slowly worn away the hard barrier of the self that had clenched against loneliness for so many years at the beginning but in the end lacked a source of power. Unfed by the barriers of others, social fear tended to wither.

The membrane between herself and the world had begun to breathe. And while this gentle dissipation had put to rest the anxiety she'd endured in the earlier years, when still wed to the story of marriage, it had increasingly opened her to a more profound, if not exactly personal, terror. Say, for instance, not the thought but the unsought intuition of every soul at stake on the planet hour to hour. A thing not to be borne for more than a minute without destroying the integrity of her individual mind. So you let in just a few fates at a time, hoping the blinders would hold. With the dogs, she could just about manage. How comforting it turned out even their ornery presence could be when the dumb quantity of humanity pressed its case.

Before the mansion had been erected, there had been the chainsaws and backhoes, trees dragged like corpses to the road. Then the engines of the diggers, the cement mixers, the nail guns. She had stayed indoors, unable to watch. They removed so much earth, the angle of the land itself had changed. The maples they left along the top of the hill, from where she could now see all the way down to the river, did a poor job of hiding the new site even with the leaves out, and as fall had come round again the naked wood frame of the unfinished house had shown clearly through the bare branches.

As a teacher all these years, seeing for herself the small-mindedness of those who ran the town of Finden, Charlotte should have known it would come, that the town would betray the trust her grandfather had placed in it. Her father might have done something about it. A man with a bedrock faith in the law, he had prosecuted malfeasance to the last. Episcopalian by birth, Presbyterian by temperament, Quaker in abstention, secular to the bone. He would have found a way to stop these cretins. But not her younger brother, Henry. No. After a few brief discussions with the lawyer, Cott Jr., Henry had suggested that if Charlotte found it too much to bear, perhaps the time had come to sell the house and move somewhere, as he put it, more practical.

Thus it had been left to her to wage the battle. Naïvely, she had begun with an attempt to persuade, writing letters to the selectmen and the newspaper. When that produced nothing but a few polite replies, she'd begun gathering signatures outside the supermarket, informing people of the town's plans. Just a few years earlier, most people would have at least stopped and said hello. She had been their teacher, after all, or their children's teacher, or both. But now they looked upon her with pity.

Budgets were budgets, the town said. They regretted deeply the necessity of putting a parcel of land up for auction. But the referendum for school funding had failed at the polls and they had to look to their assets. Never mind the breach of faith. Never mind the lobotomized, negligent short-termism of it all, as if a one-time windfall could ever fund an annual expenditure. What had government become these days but the poorly advertised fire sale of the public interest?

But, oh, how they would rue the day now! Because at last Charlotte had done what she should have years ago: she had fired Cott Jr., the incompetent, collaborationist son of the old family lawyer who'd done little more than play at resisting the town's grab, and she'd gone herself into the records down at the town hall. And there she'd discovered the mendacity of these idiots. Cott Jr. had said she had no legal recourse. But he was wrong. She'd filed her own suit now. She didn't need an attorney to stand up before a judge. She would crush these scoundrels all on her own. And though it was late in the day, the trees already felled, that monstrosity already erected, still how sweet the victory would be when eventually she evicted that little charmer and razed his house to the ground.

Just thinking of it slackened the muscles of her shoulders and chest, as if for these many months she'd been wearing a shirt of chain mail, the bands of which were only now beginning to warm and expand, allowing her to breathe.

Heading up the road past the Bennetts', she came to the low wooden fence that ran along the edge of the golf course. Wilkie and Sam nosed toward the gap that led onto the fairway. Seeing no one on the tee and the green clear, she followed them through onto the rough grass. The sky had brightened to a pale blue.

How insane it had all been. How perverted. This business with the house all of a piece with what had gone on at the school, where they had run her out for describing the world as it was and most everyone had simply gone along with it, so enamored of authority they couldn't imagine disagreeing. For years she'd assigned a photo-essay on lynchings in her unit on the Jazz Age. Then one day the department head told her she would have to stop because the objections from parents had grown vociferous. She had continued nonetheless, distributing the materials at her own expense with a new cover page explaining the topic's contemporary relevance, including quotes from the novels of Tim LaHaye, along with a line from one of the parents' letters, complaining that the assigned reading was too negative.

"Yes. So was Dachau," she'd said to the woman on parents' night.

These people who behaved nowadays as if the world were a menace sent to sicken or debilitate their children. What meagerness of spirit. To treat your own offspring as so inherently weak. They pumped their addled sons full of Ritalin and Adderall and their sullen daughters with whatever the psychopharmacologist recommended, but the unimpeachable facts of history were considered bacteria. She had done nothing more than describe such people to themselves. For that, she had been deemed unfit. Her only contact with students now was the occasional child one of her former colleagues sent to her for tutoring.

Held back by the dogs sniffing at something on the fairway, Charlotte paused, looking down the slope of the first hole to the stream and the footbridge that led across it.

Her father had played this course in the summers. Each Memorial Day weekend he would drive them up here, along the post road through Connecticut and Rhode Island and across to Massachusetts. Her mother in the front seat, her eyes covered in dark sunglasses, her lacquered Nantucket creel on the floor by her feet, hands folded on her lap as she gazed out the window in controlled displeasure at one aspect or another of the arrangements—luggage or dinner plans or how soon on Tuesday their father would have to get a ride to Boston to catch the train back. Until August he would come only on weekends, spending the weeks alone at the house in Rye and commuting into the city. Most of the other families they knew went to Long Island or the Cape, but despite their mother's annual disgruntlement they came here, to this town where their father's family had always lived, to the house he'd grown up in and inherited.

What could Charlotte have known then of how she'd return here by herself? Nothing. At the time, the adventure seemed ever new. Rushing with Henry into the house ahead of their parents to claim their rooms, rolling on the cotton-tufted bedspreads, the air tinged with naphthalene and the richer scent of pitch from all the wood: the dark ceiling beams, the slanted floors, the narrow steep steps back and front. After a day or two, when her mother had aired the place out, the smell of mothballs faded, but the tar-like taste remained all summer, as fixed in the house as the old latch doors and twelve-pane windows. The red Jeep in the barn had a sticker for the lake, and they'd drive there with an ice chest full of lunch, stacks of towels, and an umbrella her mother read under while they swam. Later, running to the back of the field at dusk to pick asparagus among the tall grass; or across the road to Aunt Eleanor's house for sugar or cooking oil, the screen door on the back steps slapping behind her; watching the slow, dying flail of the greeny-black claws of lobsters held between her father's thumb and forefinger just before he dropped them into the boiler; the ridged metal shell-snappers set out with little forks to get at the thin meat in the legs; mosquitoes bouncing against the porch bulb after dinner when her father smoked a cigarette and looked back into the house at them like a man in a darkened theater watching the scene of a play. He'd wink at her and Henry on his way out the door with their mother to some party nearby, as if to say, lucky you, staying here, free to play at what you like, you always have more fun than me—and Charlotte could never tell if he meant it. Waking to the sound of the river, starlings in the crab apple tree by her window, eating cereal with Henry in his pajamas, the weightless late-morning hours before they went to the lake, idling in the backyard, on the mown grass, mountains of white cloud floating in the vast blueness of the summer sky.

A shield. That's what the memories were, the ones that had risen in her with such force of late. A barricade thrown up against the depredations of the present.

Down on the second tee, a golfer arranged himself. Wilkie and Sam took no notice, their snouts still pressed to the ground. Of Charlotte's drifts into reminiscence, the two of them did not approve. She found this hard, given all the love she had shown them over the years. She understood they missed the woods and the chance to run untethered by the river as they used to; they resented being leashed on every walk now.

When she'd first moved to Finden, it had been to rest, the summer after Eric died, for what she thought would be only a few months before returning to New York. There had been no living thing in the house with her, no pets or plants, the garden untended. It had stayed that way all through August because why settle in where you weren't going to stay? Then her landlord in New York, not wanting any trouble after what had happened, had asked that she not renew the lease. Part of her wasn't sure she could face going back in any case. That fall, she took a temporary job teaching history at Finden High while she figured out what to do. At some point, a colleague had come by with a cutting of a jade plant and they had gone together to a nursery to buy geraniums and bulbs.

For most of her time here, there had been only the plants and the garden, which she'd tended with great care. It was just in the last six or seven years that she'd taken in the dogs. Samuel had come from a litter of purebred mastiffs owned by George Jakes, the son of Mr. Jakes, who'd always been their plumber and who looked after the property during the year, when the family was back in Rye. George had brought the puppy over one day when he'd come to fix the tub and asked if Charlotte would mind the company because while his children wanted to keep all seven of them, it wasn't practical.

A small fawn-colored creature with floppy ears, Samuel lay happily in her lap that first day. She hadn't considered how large he would become and might have hesitated if she had, if only because of the strength it required to hold him back once he gained his full stature. All through her adolescence and young adulthood Charlotte had prided herself on her lack of sentimentality, a badge of honor in a household dominated by her father's pragmatism. She considered pets a maudlin affair, lacking the fundamental seriousness that characterized worthwhile emotional life. Despite all this, Sam's dopey comfort with himself peeled at least one layer of reserve from Charlotte, and even as he grew into a larger animal, she continued to let him lie with her on the couch, his head in her lap as she read the paper.

Wilkie, the Doberman, had come from the pound a year or so later. A story in the local newspaper said an unusual number of homeless dogs were being put down so she'd driven over and visited with the keeper, who told her she could have any one she liked. A roar of barking had filled the aisle of wire cages. Amidst all the noise, Wilkie stood silent and intent at the far end, the sinews of his legs and neck visible beneath a gleaming coat.

He slept the first week in the yard and then a month or more in the vestibule before claiming a large wicker basket inside the back door. Once Sam had fought him out of the dining room and Wilkie had claimed the hall, they got along grudgingly and lay beside each other on the warm stones in front of the fireplace. Slowly, her days had formed themselves around their habits: rising before dawn, a long walk before breakfast, a nap in the late afternoon, dinner earlier than she ever used to eat, and another walk before bed.

Naturally, conversation ran in everyone's head, snippets of talk, a moment's complaint dismissed, plans for the week or the hour or the minute debated back and forth. If you lived on your own, of course, the volume tended to rise, filling the silence. Fair enough. She'd had decades of this as a single woman. If you added the everyday fact of people speaking to their pets, and more, of their sensing, sometimes keenly, the wishes, wants, or moods of the animals they lived with, then none of what had begun happening a few months ago should have been thought abnormal. She resented the judgment she knew others would make: dogs don't talk. There's help you could get.

As a young woman living in New York, she had visited certain apartments with Eric, apartments of those who considered themselves radicals, the rent on walk-ups paid by suburban parents while the children decried the system, the main attribute of which was an authority so pervasive the masses couldn't see it. Dime-store Marxism peddled to the disaffected. And then there was the other strand, the young men and women who ate their peyote and read their Huxley and spoke of the subtler tyranny of the ordered senses. Damp is how she remembered them, pale, long hair pasted down the sides of their faces, sweating in overheated apartments eating cake and oranges. Visiting in those rooms, observing, Charlotte found herself standing behind a cordon sanitaire, a line drawn in the invisible but deeply staining ink of class. It's not that her parents would have reproved her for doing such things or taken drastic steps. They would merely have been disappointed, their distaste, like hers, more aesthetic than political.

For years afterward, a criticism had lodged itself in her: that she'd been afraid of experience, a coward, a debutante stuck in the mind of the ball. But what sloppiness and vagary those believers had been delivered into. What bathos of posture and commercialism. All their therapy and their divorces and now their wretched houses built up to her door. And what of their radical perception now? Would they even think to credit Charlotte's mind for a minute?

So a few months ago the conversations in her head had grown a bit in volume, and pushing outward the bicker and debate had circled into her companions, Wilkie and Sam, with whom she'd always communicated in one way or another. So what? They'd taken to conversation in the way she would have predicted from their personalities: Sam the more arrogant of the two, convinced of himself, Wilkie making up for self-doubt with an added righteousness. Were the flower children-cum-yuppies going to cart her off for an imagination gone too florid?

If she were honest with herself, however, Charlotte had to admit the animals themselves had begun to trouble her of late. At first they had merely taken up one side or another of exchanges long conducted internally, most of them quotidian: when to put in the storm windows, when to take them out; whether to read the paper or give oneself a rest from news of death. Helpmates, they were. Companions who cared enough to take a view of the daily dilemmas. But recently their talk had begun to veer from what occupied Charlotte's conscious mind. More and more the topics were their own.

An odd couple they made, she considered, walking behind them now as they moved along the bank of the stream. Sam with his blond coat and oafish head, that openmouthed lumber of a walk, his tongue hanging from his mouth; Wilkie, so dark and slender, so precise in his movements, lithe and graceful and possessed of a mystery absent in Sam's bluster. She hadn't asked the keeper at the pound who his previous owner was or how he had ended up there because she thought it unfair to Wilkie to judge him on his upbringing. His good demeanor had spoken for him that day.

The two of them led her over the footbridge, past the green, and back onto the road again. The turning of the earth had brought the light of the sun into the tops of the trees now, and it cast long shadows across the pavement and the fronts of the houses whose east-facing windows shone with the white-and-orange flood. Another few minutes and they were back by the stone wall that ran between the road and Charlotte's front yard.

As they turned into the drive, Fanning's great, gaudy pretense came into view again.

Planks of the tree fort she and Henry used to play in had still been rotting up in the old sycamore by the river when they cut it down, a tree from whose branches her father had hung a swing that swung you out over the footpath high enough at times it seemed you could fly right into the water.

When she'd seen that intruder coming down the steps yesterday morning, the first thing she'd noticed was his suit, too slick by half. It fit him more like a diving outfit than a proper set of clothes. But then why should one expect anything discreet from such a person? That was not the logic of his kind. Theirs was the reign of endless display.

"The new place is mine," he'd said, shoving his car up beside her.

They would see about that.

In the breezeway, the dogs sat on their haunches, waiting. As she reached for the latch, Charlotte glanced down into Sam's face: the loose, moist folds of his jowls, the curtains of his ears, his eyes a dark vacuum.

Your town walls are fallen down, he said. *But such is the descent of the devil at this day upon ourselves, that I may truly tell you, the walls of the whole world are broken down, such a gap made in them, that the very devils are broke in upon us. And what use ought we to make of so tremendous a dispensation? What use?*

Chapter 3

Stuck behind a Volvo moving in slow motion through the center of Finden, Doug examined the suburban scorecard stacked up its rear window. According to the stickers, the driver or various members of her family had attended Andover, Stanford, Cornell, and Yale Medical School. When the woman came to a complete halt in front of the coffee shop and began chatting with a friend on the sidewalk, Doug leaned on his horn, wishing sorely it were the trigger of a cannon. The two women glared back at him in disdain.

For you I served, he thought. For you we killed. For *this*.

As he often did to calm his nerves at such moments, he dialed Mikey.

"So what's with the neighbor?" he asked him.

"I love you, Doug, but I have no idea what you're talking about."

"The place next door. Up on the hill. Turns out some old hag lives in there. She didn't exactly roll out the welcome mat."

"You mean Miss Charlotte Graves? Yeah. I've been meaning to call you about her. She's a problem."

"The way she's keeping that place, she must be violating some kind of ordinance, right? Some Keep Finden Beautiful shit? You should be able to find something to get her on."

"Trouble is—"

"She's just the type, isn't she? Trees, she said. And then walked off. Like I'm the first person ever to cut down woods to build a house in this town? Like her fucking ancestors didn't clear cut it three hundred years ago. I'll tell you something, Mikey, some days I wish I was a Russian gangster with twenty cousins and a stretch Hummer. Just to piss people like her off."

"I think you got that covered, my friend. But listen. When I say she's a problem I'm not kidding. She's filed a lawsuit against the town—saying she owns your land."

"What the hell are you talking about?"

"My guy on the board of selectmen told me. She wrote the complaint herself. He says it reads like something out of the Old Testament. But she's *pro se*, so some judge'll have to give her a hearing and try to piece her shit together on the taxpayer's dime. And I'll have to show up to make sure he tosses it out. It's a nuisance suit—she's crazy."

"Get rid of it, Mikey. You hear me? I don't need that shit. Not now."

"Don't worry about it. I'll take care of it."

Up ahead, a third woman, in a Burberry jacket and duck boots, this one steering a stroller, joined the nattering pair obstructing the roadway.

"I got a situation here," Doug said, tossing his phone aside and stepping from the car.

"Where do you think you are?" the pearled young matron demanded, as he approached the Volvo. "Los Angeles? Are you planning to fly into some kind of rage?" She turned back to the driver. "All right, then, Ginny. We'll see you Tuesday."

"Okay! Bye!" the woman behind the wheel called out in her bright, chipper voice. And with that, she stepped on her accelerator, leaving Doug standing by himself in the middle of the street as the cars behind him began to honk.

THAT MORNING he'd slept through his alarm, which he never did, caught up in dreams again, the remnants of which stuck with him as he cleared the town traffic and made it onto the Pike, still moving at a frustrating pace along the crowded inbound lanes. He'd dreamt of his cousin Michael and it had reminded him of when Michael had told him the story of Doug's father. His mother had met him when she had gone to help serve his family's Thanksgiving dinner. This would have been 1964 and she would have been seventeen. When the dinner was through and the dishes washed, the son had driven her home, all the way from the North Shore, an hour at least. This part Michael could say for sure because he'd heard it from his own father's mouth. That, and the fact they'd been on dates. Two or three and it had ended by Christmas; or maybe it was five or six and had run on into January; he was in college in Western Mass or he'd just graduated or was working for his father before going. His father was rich, that much was clear, because Doug's uncle John had got a break as a young electrician with a contract to service all the companies the man owned. It was Uncle John who'd recommended his little sister for that day, thinking she might get a regular job out of it. Michael had been told never to speak of it, especially not to Doug. But they were sixteen and they were drunk in

Uncle John's basement while everyone else finished up the Labor Day barbecue in the yard and Michael had told him.

So that was his father. The nameless son of a nameless family who at one time had lived about an hour's drive away.

What Doug had already known—what everyone knew—was that by February 1965, his mother was pregnant and without a boyfriend, let alone a husband. She stayed with her parents that year and for a year or two after, while Doug was a toddler. Her parents were religious people who never renounced their obligation to love their daughter or their obligation to be ashamed. They continued to share a pew with her at St. Mary's, though now the family sat at the back of the church. She had many different jobs but by the time they moved into the apartment on the top floor of the blue triple-decker on Eames Street, she mostly cleaned houses and cooked. They had a small backyard that ran down to a creek, and through the trees on the far side of it you could hear the cars moving along the state route. Back then there had been nothing along that highway but a few warehouses and a depot for the Alden town trucks. But when Doug had turned six an auto-parts store had gone in. Soon after that came a mattress discounter, then a gas station, and six months later a Burger King. They cleared land for the first mall, an oval of white concrete with an open-air courtyard and fountain, surrounded by the largest parking lot anyone had ever seen, which backed right up to their creek. Once the cineplex went in with its own vast parking lot, lit by even brighter lights, Doug's bedroom never got fully dark anymore, the glare of the strip strong enough to color his shade a pale yellow into the small hours of the morning.

On Saturday evenings Doug and his mother went to Mass and again on Wednesdays, and though he hated it from an early age, mostly for the pity shown him by the adults and the pity shown his mother, before he even knew why, he followed obediently along until thirteen or so when he told his mother he didn't believe in God or the Church and didn't care what she thought about it. She'd lost most of her bargaining power to the drink by then and didn't much resist. Daytime was a raw period for her, a time to be endured, after which the relief of the first glass of wine came, a routine that left little margin for argument or delay. He was taller than her well before he reached high school and there weren't many places in the apartment for her to hide her bottles. Early on he'd learned he could cut her off more or less at will, and after that he never needed to; the threat alone sufficed to win whatever concession he needed from her.

Never a talkative woman, she said even less when she'd drunk three or four glasses.

After the first bottle, her silence deepened into something more profound, her daily withholding of words buoyed up into a principle of sorts, an almost enjoyable one it seemed, a queenly disregard for the commonplace of chatter or conversation, as if he were a man in whose presence she was determined to remain permanently coy. Conspicuous in her withdrawal. She had her television and her magazines, and as long as he was there to watch her getting along without him then indeed she could. And when she fell asleep on the couch at the end of the night Doug would carry her to her bed and turn out the light.

Once he'd gotten his license he had taken control of the car and begun to drive her to work. Heading down the state route you always knew exactly where Alden stopped and Finden began because the strip ended. After the muffler shop and the liquor store strategically placed on the town line to serve the residents of the dry community next door, you came to a traffic light. Beyond that it was as if time had stood still. Just the fluted gray railing running up the side of the highway and behind it, on either side, woods. It continued like that all the way east, seven miles or more toward Boston, until you reached the next town, where another liquor store stood just over the line and the malls and burger chains and car dealerships started up again.

All his mother's work was in Finden. Over the years, she cleaned for different families in the mornings but as long as he could remember, she'd always worked afternoons at the Gammonds', where he would come to pick her up in the afternoons. They lived at the end of a white gravel drive in a large brick house with green shutters and flowers in the window boxes.

In spring and fall, Mrs. Gammond would often be working in the garden. She had white hair and fine mottled skin and Doug had always remembered her necklace of jade with its large stones of sea green and imperial purple, separated by rings of silver, resting across her chest like the jewels of some northern queen.

She would ask him how school was going and which subjects interested him and comment on the weather as they waited for his mother to emerge from the house.

"Such a handsome son you have," he could remember her saying.

People had always liked him for his looks. As a child, he'd got lost in the supermarket and all the other mothers had crowded around, saying how adorable he was. As a teenager, he'd begun jacking off naked in front of the mirror on the back of his closet door, goading himself on, his looks beginning to handle like his first real weapon, his first experience of control.

"She says I'm the best cleaning lady she's ever employed," his mother said once on the ride back to Alden, a wry smile on her face, as she smoked her first cigarette in hours, asking Doug to conspire with her for just a little while, to take her slender joke, to be with her for a few moments, on her side. "Maybe one day she'll give me a medal. A shiny medal."

The only man who ever visited their apartment was Father Griffin, in his horn-rimmed glasses and black raincoat. His narrow bird face was gaunt with sympathy. Knowing how to time his calls, he would arrive just before supper, when Doug's mother had drunk only a glass or two and was still sociable. He'd share parish news—of the sick and the dead and the newly born—and stand up to leave as soon as Doug took supper out of the microwave.

What the navy recruiter had to offer was a way out of that apartment and the sight of his mother drowning. Doug had signed the papers the day after his eighteenth birthday. For a week he tried coming up with the words to tell his mother he was leaving but they never came and so he decided he'd call her instead, once he reached the base. He took a bus to the Naval Station Great Lakes, and after three days there ended up phoning his cousin Michael instead to let the family know where he'd gone.

Most of the other recruits struck him as innocents without a plan: patriotic boys itching to stick it to the Evil Empire, kids with eyes set wide apart who looked as if they'd arrived through some damp, half-witted dream into a bunk and a bench in the galley, washed off the prairie like shallow soil. Right away he knew he'd do the minimum and get out. He kept figuring he would write his mother a letter or a postcard, but then again she knew where he was and she hadn't written or called.

He met sailors who no longer knew where their folks lived and didn't seem much to care. At first, he thought he'd begin to forget like that, that his memory would wipe itself clean. But it didn't. It wasn't at the low times that he thought of his mother but when things were going well, when accomplishment and momentum felt real, at the end of a well-executed maneuver or when he got his first promotion. Then, just as he grabbed on to a bit of excitement, to the sense that things might work out, he'd picture her spending the night on the couch, waking with a headache at dawn, shuffling to her bed for a few more hours of sleep, and like a kill switch, the image would cut dead the power surging within him. Noticing how the memory of her held him back, he decided he would no longer permit himself guilt. It was a priestly game, after all, a game of sin and forgiveness, one that could eat a life whole.

As HE ROUNDED the exit for South Station, Doug could see the eastern face of the Union Atlantic tower shimmering in the morning sun. It was taller than 60 State Street and framed in crisp white lines, its glass much brighter than the dark reflective obelisk of the John Hancock. Jeffrey Holland had built it against all kinds of opposition, striking the deal when prices were low because no one wanted to put up with the Big Dig on their front doorstep, despite the fact that it would eventually be a park leading to the water. The tallest building in the city, it now dominated the financial district and had become the centerpiece of skyline night shots during Red Sox broadcasts and the network legal procedurals set in town, the Union Atlantic logo—the outline of a cresting wave—lit in bright blue along the south-facing superstructure, the whole gleaming edifice a bold announcement of intent, its scale impressing clients and competitors alike. Holland understood well the logic of images creating impressions which became facts. Insider chatter about overreaching had been no match for the persuasion of size and ambition. The foreigners in particular loved it, the Koreans and the Chinese, whose business they were getting hand over fist now. At Doug's encouragement they'd entered into talks with the Four Seasons about a hotel next door. Union Atlantic alone could fill two-thirds of it with clients.

"Good morning, Mr. Fanning," the new receptionist on the senior management floor said as Doug stepped off the elevator. He was a twenty-something metrosexual in Banana Republic gear whose smiling deference was so total it almost begged a crude response. "I've sent a few packages down to Sabrina for you."

Doug had gone through three secretaries before he found Sabrina Svetz. She was an aspiring writer looking for a day job. A brunette with the angular features of her Slavic ancestors, her looks were peaking now in her late twenties, the severity of the bone structure no longer hidden by youthful chubbiness, but still on the glamorous side of gaunt. He liked that she fundamentally resented her job and had other ambitions. It clarified their relations. She was a shameless flirt and ill-suited to working in a bank, always nosing around for odd bits of detail about people's personal lives. He'd waited three weeks before taking her out for a drink and sleeping with her, a perfunctory exercise they'd engaged in two or three times since and which gave Doug what he needed from her: an understanding between the two of them as individual actors, bound by the bargain they had struck, not some bullshit out of a company handbook about what got reported and to whom. He'd made it perfectly clear before they took their clothes off what the sex would and wouldn't mean. Being a somewhat hardened woman, for reasons he didn't care to know, she understood right away and consented. She'd often eat her lunch in Doug's office with the door closed, telling him about her dating life and discussing who was hot and who wasn't among the staff.

She was writing a novel set during the Spanish Civil War and had a thing for Iberian men, particularly those whose grandparents were old Fascists willing to talk.

"Our Leader awaits you," she said, not bothering to look up from her screen as he approached her desk. The downside of such close relations was that she felt comfortable indulging a degree of sullenness that would otherwise have been considered unprofessional. The gain, however, was worth it. She did exactly as instructed even if it meant telling the chief of administration to screw off. She had no loyalty to the organization but plenty to Doug.

This was important. When Holland had hired Doug, Union Atlantic had been a regional, commercial bank. It took in deposits, offered checking accounts to the public, and made loans to businesses and real estate developers. It had the conservative balance sheet of the highly regulated institution that it was. But Holland's plan for the company was much larger. Through acquisition, he wanted it to grow into a financial-services conglomerate with an investment banking arm, an insurance division, and a private wealth management business.

Holland had given Doug two jobs, one as head of foreign operations and the other as the man in charge of the newly created Department of Special Plans. The purpose of the latter was to formulate long-term strategy for how Union Atlantic should navigate the new, deregulated environment, in which Congress was slowly repealing all the old, New Deal reforms that had prevented banks from owning the insurers and investment houses Holland wanted to buy. Doug had done a ferociously good job. On his advice, the bank had brazenly commenced acquisitions that were strictly speaking still illegal but that Doug foresaw would be approved by the time the deals were finalized, in part because of Union Atlantic's own lobbying but also because their competitors, as soon as they caught on, would follow suit adding their own legislative pressure to scrap the old protections. Leading the pack, Holland, Doug, and the management team had been able to cherry-pick the most profitable companies to acquire. In less than six years, while several of the older behemoths had stumbled, Union Atlantic had grown from a stand-alone commercial bank into Union Atlantic Group, a global player and one of the four largest financial companies in the country. Holland had capped it off with the new tower. Soon thereafter he'd appeared on the cover of *Fortune* and *BusinessWeek*. The leading industry analyst, a prick named Koppler, pronounced Union Atlantic Group the herald of a new paradigm for multi-platform financial services and its stock rose six percent in a day.

All that was before the fall of 2001. The 9/11 attacks had cut nearly seven hundred points off the Dow. Then, less than two months later, Enron had collapsed. Like many banks, Union Atlantic had provided the Houston energy trader and its off-balance-sheet partnerships with considerable amounts of financing. Meanwhile, Atlantic Securities, the investment banking arm, had sold Enron's bonds to investors and had purchased many of them with its own money. Still, that wasn't the worst of it. In December, Argentina had defaulted on its sovereign debt.

For years, Argentina had been a poster child for the International Monetary Fund, obediently implementing the Washington Consensus on structural adjustment, privatizing state-owned industries and public-sector utilities, mostly by selling them to foreign investors, and it had brought inflation under control by pegging the peso to the dollar. In the process, the bonds that the Argentinean government sold to finance its spending had become hugely popular with Western banks. They paid a higher rate of interest than the bonds of first-world countries, and given the IMF's ongoing support of the Argentinean economy, they seemed a safe bet, even after a deep recession in the late nineties.

Countries as economically mature and as connected to the global system as Argentina didn't walk away from their sovereign debt; it simply wasn't done. Or at least never had been until December 2001, when the new government, ushered in after riots in Buenos Aires, defaulted on $81 billion owed to creditors around the world.

Up to this point, the American financial press had been happy to more or less ignore the cash that Union Atlantic itself had burned through in its recent spree of acquisitions. Now, however, given their exposure to the Argentinean crisis, the breathless coverage gave way to jitters, and with those came a sharply falling stock price.

And so once again Holland, seeing his grand plan imperiled and impatient with his doubters, had turned to Doug and the Department of Special Plans and said: Fix it.

To do this the company had to beat the market's expectations for its earnings for at least two quarters in a row. The quickest way to accomplish that was to pump up the revenues at Atlantic Securities, especially in its futures and derivatives business. Attracting more clients, and thus earning more commissions from handling their trades, wouldn't be enough; they would have to trade with the firm's own money—proprietary trading as it was called—in order to enjoy the larger profit margins that came with such direct risk.

But there was a major obstacle to this strategy. In order to place such large, proprietary trades in the futures markets, Atlantic Securities had to post margins with the various exchanges it traded on. Enough cash, in fact, to cover any potential losses. This put a strain on Atlantic Securities' cash flow. Too much of its capital was being tied up in margin accounts.

The obvious solution was for Union Atlantic, the regular commercial bank with a strong capital base of customer deposits, to lend Atlantic Securities the money it needed. The two entities were, after all, owned by the same holding company. But federal regulations limited this "lending across the house." And the company's own internal policies set strict limits on the practice. Divisions within the group were supposed to negotiate with one another at arm's length. This was all well and fine when you had time on your hands. All very punctilious. One of those procedural safeguards in-house counsel derived such satisfaction from enforcing, never having generated a dime of profit in their lives. But a few more quarters of bad earnings reports, and a strategic plan years in the making could begin to crumble.

And so Doug had done what he'd been hired to do: he'd exercised his impatience. To get around the regulation, he had created a new corporation he dubbed Finden Holdings. Its sole purpose was to borrow cash from Union Atlantic and lend it to Atlantic Securities. This wasn't illegal, strictly speaking, but the lawyers and auditors knew enough to keep the details in the footnotes. With this invention, the big money had begun to flow into the accounts of Doug's foreign traders. Soon enough, profits were up.

In the first quarter of 2002, Union Atlantic Group exceeded Wall Street's earnings forecast by more than any other company in the sector. Once again, they had proven themselves agile and determined. And this satisfied Doug. It satisfied him a great deal. Not because of the likely size of his bonus or the further expansion of his informal dominion. The execution was what gratified him. The focus and precision and directedness of his will. At such times, his churning mind turned lucid and through it power flowed as frictionless as money down a fiber-optic line, the resistance of the physical world reduced to the vanishing point. He felt then like the living wonder of the most advanced machine, as if he'd been freed of all organic hindrance to glide on the plain of pure efficiency. A place of relief, even peace.

Having Sabrina around to fend off the nitpickers and cover for him when he let his lesser, administrative tasks slide had been a great help.

"We have an office in Madrid, right?" she asked now, sidling into Doug's office to hand him a manila folder.

He nodded.

"I need you to take me there on a business trip. For a week or so."

Now and again Sabrina employed this sort of presumption, a compensatory fantasy, he imagined, for the inherent powerlessness of a person with an advanced degree in short fiction. It was as though she'd bargained on receiving a certain cultural cachet that had yet to materialize and in the meantime needed a bridge loan of prestige paid out in the quasi-glamour of international travel. Her parents were doctors who'd covered everything through graduate school but had drawn the line at outright patronage.

The paper she had just handed him was McTeague's latest request for cash to post as margin on the futures exchange in Singapore. The amount was enormous. In addition to money to cover Atlantic Securities' own trades, he was asking for large sums to cover the trading of his growing list of clients out in Hong Kong, mostly hedge funds who'd been attracted to McTeague's high profits and wanted in on the action.

"We're the victims of our success," he said to Doug, once Sabrina had got him on the line. "Half of Greenwich wants to give me their money. If we don't lend them the margin, someone else will."

He sounded jacked up, teetering on nervous, which was just where Doug wanted him, on that vigilant edge, pumped about what he had in hand but wanting more. When news of what the Japanese Ministry of Finance was doing to prop up the Nikkei became public, he could turn McTeague off. But at present he was working perfectly.

"Three hundred and twenty million. That's a lot of money," Doug said. "Keep me close, you understand? I want to see the daily numbers."

"Of course," McTeague replied.

"You know Holland's waiting for you, right?" Sabrina said, ignoring the fact that he was on the phone as she sat sprawled on the couch, leafing through a magazine. "He called down here himself."

THE ARCHITECTS of the Union Atlantic tower had understood well who their client was. Not a corporation, not a board of directors, and certainly not a twelve-member building committee, but one man, the head of all three: Jeffrey Holland. The new headquarters had been his project from the outset and no major decision regarding it had been made without his approval. In the chairman's suite, a brocade upholstered sofa fit for an English country manor sat beneath a painting of a river valley and snowcapped mountains, the canvas framed in faded gold leaf. The sofa afforded a view, through floor-to-ceiling windows, onto a flagstone terrace beyond the railing of which was visible only sky. This office—really its own structure sitting atop the tower—had everything an acquisitive soul might want of architecture without the distraction of postmodernism or the discomfiture of real innovation. The gesture toward minimalism in its frame and fenestration was sufficient to give it the patina of restraint, while in every significant detail, from the fluted columns of the dark-wood bookcases to the enormous Oriental carpets, it retained all the pleasures of empire. It was a big, bright compliment of a room.

Which, of course, fit well its function. When you wanted a French media-and-defense conglomerate to do its banking with you rather than with Chase, this was a fine place to chat with their chairman about his country house, his daughter's art-school plans, and the benefits of proximity to Harvard before the lesser suits took him downstairs to explain the offer. You didn't do PowerPoint in a room like this; you put people at ease.

"He's on the phone," Holland's secretary, Martha, said, as Doug approached. "Not that that will stop you."

He continued up the hall to the open door of the sun-flooded office. The man himself stood by the far window with his back to Doug looking north over the Fleet Center to the webbed white cables of the new Zakim bridge that spanned the mouth of the Charles. He spoke to the view, his hands in his pockets, the silver dagger of an earpiece extending an inch down his cheek.

". . . . which is why those aren't the only provisions we want in the bill. Everyone has an interest in transparency: us, the consumer, the courts. Who doesn't want bankruptcies sped up? Who doesn't want them rationalized? And I don't think anyone's been better at communicating that than you, Senator."

He shook his head back and forth in disagreement with whatever he was hearing on the other end. When he turned and spotted Doug, he gestured with a nod for him to sit.

"Of course, Senator, I understand that, and believe me the last thing I want is my own lobbyist getting in the way of . . . I understand that."

Holland was a tall man, six-three at least, broad shouldered and bulky in the chest without quite being overweight. He'd never been an athlete in college, yet he had an athlete's bodily ease, his big shoulders rolled back, his girth part of the motion of his walk as he approached you, more an element of persuasion than anything to be embarrassed by. That same animal confidence was part of the motion of his face with its wide, agile mouth, full cheeks and thick nose, and the soft blue eyes, such an intimate part of the larger seduction. Photographs captured only the bluntness and gave little hint of the effect his physical presence had on others. Doug had seen it a hundred times, the way he rolled in on a mark—client or politician or friend—leveling their defenses at the outset with the big handshake, the big knowing smile, the slightly colder stare pushing the last barrier aside, so that by the time he opened his mouth his target was already nodding in agreement.

"Well," Holland said with a chuckle, "if Bob Rubin can call himself a Democrat, I guess I can too. And believe me, we're talking to your colleagues. No reason this should be a party-line matter. The public needs to hear about the safeguards, see how it would make credit cheaper for everyone in the end. We're ready to roll all that out. It's just a matter of timing, which is why I wanted to get your sense of where things stand . . . Of course, of course, we'll be in touch."

He removed his earpiece, took a seat, and swung his feet up onto the desk.

"Grassley's an asshole."

"He's still with us, right?"

"Sure he is. The bankruptcy bill's been his for years. Trouble is, if it ever gets passed he'll need a whole new fund-raising strategy." He joined his hands behind his head and stretched out to full length. "But that's not my main concern right now. Have you looked at your cash position lately? You've got us lending to your traders hand over fist. Don't get me wrong—your profits are impressive. But you're tying up a lot of capital."

He stood, thrust his hands in his pockets, and began pacing behind his desk.

"We're attracting clients," Doug said. "And we're lending them the money to play the market with. It's not our risk, it's theirs. That's the bigger point. The business is growing."

I understand the position you're in. That's what Doug had told

Holland during his final interview for the job. The board wants results. They want them quickly. What didn't need to be said, what Doug's tone of absolute confidence had said for itself: There will be times when it would be better if you didn't know everything. I understand that too.

Holland had no idea how he and McTeague had discovered the plans of the Japanese government nor had he briefed him on the finer details of the Finden Holdings arrangement.

Coming up in the industry, Doug had met a lot of guys like Holland, men in their fifties and sixties who had never been in the military. Like the rest of them, Holland loved that Doug had run air defense on the most advanced ship in the navy and that he'd seen action in the Persian Gulf. He derived pleasure from it, the same satisfaction, it struck Doug, as the pleasure he himself used to get inspecting missiles down in their bays, running his hand over the shiny white warhead of an SM-2, feeling through the tips of his fingers all that locked-down, riveted potential. That's what he was for a man like Holland: an attractive weapon. Doug worked best with the men who understood implicitly the balance of excitement, ignorance, and reward he offered. And no one had understood it better than Holland. He knew his aggression had to be channeled through others. He needed tentacles up into the board, laterally into the senior management with eyes on his job, and down into the bowels of the operation, where the consequences of loyalty were more concrete. Like a ship's captain, who in principle relied on the chain of command but in practice drew close those he trusted, Holland surrounded himself with people who owed their jobs to him, and it was through these officers, of whatever rank, that he worked his will. He loved that all the secretaries had crushes on Doug, and that the rest of the department heads loathed him. Deep into the bullshit of management science, Holland had consultants threaded everywhere, hard at work rubber-stamping his plans, providing cover for whenever an initiative failed. But at base such caution bored him, and if he were honest with himself he would have to admit that it embarrassed him too. To all such mealymouthed, process nonsense, Doug was the perfect antidote: a means to direct action. Yet, as with any secret weapon, the pleasure and protection lay in the having of it, not in the use.

"What about our own trades?" Holland asked. "Where do we stand?"

For all his bluster about cash flow, this was why he had asked Doug to his office: to hear news of profit.

"Hong Kong netted thirty-five million last week. Next week, it'll be forty."

Holland glanced up, raised his eyebrows, and smiled. Then he strolled to the opposite side of the office to gaze from the window. Beneath a cloudless sky, the water of the harbor shimmered, a white ferry churned slowly from the pier, planes in the distance glided onto the peninsula of runways at Logan, the whole brilliant vista softened by the tint of the glass.

"That guy from *Time* called again," he said. "He's coming next week. They've decided to go ahead with the profile after all."

"Congratulations," Doug said.

"Thanks. So what's the news with you? Are we neighbors yet? Have you moved out to Finden?"

"Yeah. Which reminds me. You know a woman named Charlotte Graves?"

"Never heard of her. What the hell are you going to do with all that space, anyway?"

"I don't know," Doug said. "Make a killing maybe?"

Holland laughed. "My wife loathes people like you," he said. "Probably because she used to be one."

Chapter 4

From inside the blooming lilac, Charlotte whispers, *Come. You're missing it. Come and see.* The pleasure, somehow, always hers. Mother and father with their drinks on the veranda in wicker chairs watching; traffic whirring in the distance on the post road. *You're missing it,* his sister whispers. The air is soft in the first spring heat. Henry tries to walk toward his sister but his legs are fixed to the ground. Her whispers fill his ears from behind those coned purple flowers, the sunlight on the arced branches a brilliant diffusion. *Here, what you've been looking for, here it is,* she says, as the siren begins to sound.

Swallowing dryly, turning his head on the pillow, Henry half opened his eyes. The room was pitch-dark, only one edge of it discernible from a strip of light under the door. A hotel, certainly: the familiar hush of conditioned air falling into the padded gloom of rug and curtains and armchair, the tiny red signals of the television and the motion detector. But where? What city? For a moment, the yearning for a world saturated with meaning pulled him back toward sleep, but he caught himself and reached for the bleating phone, the grid of the present regaining administration of his mind, leveling in an instant the fading kingdom of dreams.

He was in a suite on the Atlantic coast of Florida and it was one fifteen in the morning.

"Mr. Graves? Is this Mr. Henry Graves?"

"Yes. Who is this?"

"Sir, my name is Vincent Cannistro. I'm vice president of market operations at Taconic Bank."

"Hold on a moment."

He reached up to switch on the light.

"This better be serious," he said. "In which case, why am I talking to you?"

"That's a perfectly fair question, sir. Fred Premley, our CEO, is currently in Idaho and we have been trying to reach him by cell phone for a number of hours now. I have a car headed to his location at this time and we expect to be in contact with him shortly."

"And your chairman?"

"Our chairman, sir, he's in that same location."

Henry sat upright and reached for his glasses, bringing the room into focus. Briefing books for the conference were piled on the desk opposite.

"So you're in a bind and your management's gone fishing. Have I got it right so far?"

"Sir, I would have to say that is more or less correct, yes."

"All right, then, Mr. Cannistro. What's your situation?"

There was a pause on the line. Even in his groggy state, Henry could sense the fellow's unease. He'd heard men's voices like this before, taut as a drum, overly formal, restraining with effort the profanity they'd been hurling at their subordinates for hours or even days. This man was making a call well above his pay grade. If things didn't turn out right, he could lose his job.

"We've got a liquidity problem," he said.

"Well, you don't call at this hour if you're unhappy with the examiners. What's your position?"

"We're on the short end of an interest-rate swap. We owe a hundred and seventy million. Payment was due nine hours ago."

"A hundred and seventy? Whose rates were you betting?"

"Venezuelan to rise."

"Jesus. That was stupid. I assume you hedged it. You covered it with something, right?"

"Sir, that's the problem. The model had us covering the position with oil futures. They were supposed to drop if Chávez trimmed his rates. They didn't drop."

Henry rested his head back against the wall. For a moment he'd thought maybe his caller had jumped the gun and done nothing more than further damage his bank's reputation with the Federal Reserve, in which case he could go back to sleep. Pulling the covers aside, he rose, took a pad of paper and pen from the coffee table, and settled himself into an armchair.

"Mr. Graves, are you there?"

"I'm here. That's the most inane hedge I've ever heard of. And you're telling me you can't raise the money for the payment?"

"As of this hour, no."

"I see," Henry said, nodding to himself. Under normal circumstances even a small retail operation like Taconic would have credit enough with the market to cover such incompetent trading. But they had been carrying a lot of bad tech loans for a year or more now and their retail base was being squeezed on one end by Chase and on the other by the national discounters. In the last few weeks they'd begun borrowing heavily to cover their own trading positions.

As president of the Federal Reserve Bank of New York, Henry Graves had oversight responsibility for all the banks in his district, including Taconic. He also regulated the large bank holding companies that had come to dominate the industry. But the New York Fed, unlike the other regional Federal Reserve banks, was more than simply a supervisory institution. It was the operational hub of the whole Fed System. It acted as the Treasury's agent in the market, buying and selling T-bills. Nearly every country in the world held some portion of their sovereign assets in accounts at the New York Fed. The wire service the bank ran cleared a trillion dollars in transactions each day. Simply put, Henry Graves was in charge of the biggest pumping station in the plumbing of global finance. His most vital function was to keep money moving. To do it quickly. And, above all, to do it quietly.

Which meant making sure a situation didn't become a crisis. Taconic's problems, small as they were in the scheme of things, couldn't be allowed to spread. The bank's ultimate failure, if that's what it came to, would pose little systemic risk. In receivership, it would be broken up and sold. But in the short run, a nonpayment of this size could cause trouble for Taconic's creditors. A resolution, however temporary, was needed before the morning bell.

"Who do you owe the money to? Who's your counterparty?"

"Union Atlantic."

Henry's thought was one of relief. At least they were dealing with a known quantity, and a bank under his supervision. Union Atlantic meant Jeffrey Holland. A bit glib, a bit of a showman. In it for the sport of the deal. Not Henry's favorite banker, but he could be reasoned with. He and his wife, Glenda, had showed up at the same hotel in

Bermuda where Henry had taken Betsy just after she'd gotten sick. The four of them had eaten dinner together out on the terrace one evening. They'd sent a huge arrangement of flowers to the funeral.

The other line started to ring and he told Cannistro to hold.

"Did that jackass get a hold of you yet? What an idiot, huh? An upstate strip-mall bank betting on Chávez! Did you get a load of that? What a goddamn mess."

Sid Brenner, head of payment systems. The master plumber, as they called him, the man with his fingers on the dials. You could count on two hands the number of people capable of programming the network that wired that trillion a day through the market. Most of them worked at IBM. Sid had been with the Fed thirty-five years, starting just a few months before Henry. Born in Crown Heights, he lived there still—three kids, one an officer in the Israeli army, the other two professors. Any day of the week he could have walked down the Street and made five times what the Fed paid him, but he never had.

"We've got time," Henry said, a half-truth they would let pass between them. "I'll get on the phone. We'll work it through."

"None of my business, but if you give these jerks a free ride, I'll wring your neck. They should be lucky to get a loan at eight percent."

"I'll talk to Holland. Did everything else settle?"

"Yeah, just a gaping hole in Taconic's reserve account."

"What's your sense of who else knows at this point?"

"About the swap in particular? Not so many. That they've been scrambling for money for eight hours? Not exactly a secret."

Henry woke his secretary, Helen, at home and asked her to set up the calls with Holland and Taconic's management, as soon as the car reached them.

As they were about to hang up, she asked, "Are you all right?"

He crossed the room and pulled the curtains aside. Through the glass he could see down to the beach, where the lights from the hotel reached the tranquil water's edge. He slid the door open and stepped onto the balcony, the night air heavy with moisture.

Like Sid, Helen had been at the Fed for decades, starting out as Henry's assistant in the counsel's office and moving with him to the presidency. When they were together, priorities sorted themselves in the space between them with little more than a glance or nod. She could interpret the nuance of a bank officer's evasions as readily as the nervous chatter of some freshman analyst. He disliked involving her in personal matters but ever since Betsy had died four years ago, he'd found it impossible to meet his own standard of segregating entirely work and private life.

"Did my sister call?"

"No. There's been no word."

He rested his forearms on the railing, feeling in the thickness of his head the pitched forward slowness of jet lag. The flight from Frankfurt had been ten hours, the drive up from Miami all stop-and-go traffic owing to a jackknifed truck that had torn the roof off one of those Volkswagen bugs, the whole scene bright as day under halogen floods.

A few weeks ago, after listening to one of Charlotte's tirades about the house next door, he'd raised the question of whether it might be time for her to move. She'd practically hung up on him and had replied to none of his phone calls since.

"I'm sorry you've had to deal with this," he said to Helen. "It's unprofessional of me."

"Don't be silly," she replied. "Do you need anything else? It could take awhile to get Holland at this hour."

"No. Just the account positions. And I suppose you better call down to D.C. and find out where the chairman is, just in case. I don't think we'll need him."

"By the way," she said. "Did you speak to the plumber about the leak at the house?" He had happened upon it the other evening in the back hall, a rust-colored sagging in the wallpaper over the side table. "It's not the kind of thing you can just forget about. You could get a burst pipe."

In which case, what? he thought. Water in the living room? A lake beneath the piano? He barely used the downstairs anymore, getting home after ten most nights and heading straight to bed. Even upstairs he'd withdrawn into one of the guest rooms, where he found it easier to sleep surrounded by fewer of Betsy's things. His wife's death had hit him with startling force for a month or two, during which his body ached from the moment he woke to the moment he went to sleep. But his job's demands didn't cease. And soon there were days when he thought of her less often; half a year later there were days he didn't think of her at all. This seemed wrong, inhuman even, that forty years of marriage could fade so easily through a slip in time. Did it mean he was a callous person? Unfeeling? Who was to judge? As for his private life now, the person he thought of, whom in a sense he'd always thought of, was his older sister, Charlotte. A woman Betsy had done little more than tolerate.

"If you give me the plumber's number," Helen said, "I'll call him myself."

"No," Henry replied. "It's all right. I'll see to it when I get back."

DOWNSTAIRS, THE COCKTAIL lounge was deserted save for an elderly Latino man in a vest and bow tie reading a newspaper behind the bar. Basketball from the West Coast played in silence on the television mounted above his head. Henry ordered a ginger ale and walked out onto the terrace, taking a seat at a table by the steps to the lawn.

Between the hotel and the ocean stood a row of shaded palms lit from beneath, their fronds perfectly still. Waves barely lapped at the shore. The big investment houses had made a killing on resorts like this, consolidating the industry, securitizing the mortgages, first in line to get paid when a chain went bankrupt, first in line to finance the entity when it reemerged.

The ginger ale had too much sweetener and not enough fizz. Another penny for Archer Daniels Midland and the corn-syrup giants.

Stop, he thought to himself. Enough.

He could never tell if exhaustion bred the automatic thought of production and consequence or whether the habit itself did the tiring. Either way, it had become incessant. As an undergraduate, studying philosophy, his first challenge had been skepticism, how the mind could know with certainty that objects existed. By the time he went to law school, he'd settled happily on a social, pragmatic answer: that to believe otherwise led to absurd results. These days much of the world seemed drained of presence to him, not by his doubt of anything's existence but because objects, even people sometimes, seemed to dissipate into their causes, their own being crowded out by what had made them so.

Over the gentle surf, he heard the hum from the air-conditioning vents high on the roof of the hotel, and his brain, once more, ran the stimulus to ground: the steel smelted from ore mined on some island of the Indonesian archipelago; forged into sheets on the hydraulic presses of a foundry outside Seoul; shipped across the Pacific to sit in a warehouse in Long Beach where it showed up in the Commerce Department's numbers on inventory; ordered, packaged, trucked over the plains to an Atlanta wholesaler; bought by a contractor in Miami, who stood with a foreman directing workers riveting the vents together, operating the crane that raised into place the engine, itself assembled with parts from ten countries or more at a Maytag plant out in Iowa or perhaps Mexico, calibrated to the precise wattage required to pump cooled air into the hundreds of sleeping chambers, where its faintly medicinal scent blanketed the slumbering travelers. And allowing each step from the miner's lowly wage to the construction buy: loans, lines of credit, borrowed money—the vast creationary incentive of compound interest, blind artificer of the modern world.

He wondered how it would be if the humming were just that to him: a sound.

Leaving his glass on the table, he wandered out onto the lawn. He wouldn't be able to sleep before he'd resolved Taconic's troubles but until their CEO and Holland were on the phone there was nothing more he could do.

On the far side of the pool area a footbridge led over the sand and the shallow water to a jetty that formed the outer edge of the marina. He crossed it and walked alongside the yachts and cigarette boats attached to their moorings with chains that glittered dimly beneath the dock lights.

In the summers, he and Betsy had always gone up to Maine, to Port Clyde. A night in the mainland cottage, a day getting the boat out of storage, two weeks on the island. The same every year. Just as he rode the same train to work that his father had ridden. His father who'd worked for Roosevelt's SEC, back in its early days, who had been a scourge to penny-stock fraudsters and pyramid schemers, arriving home each night with a briefcase full of pleadings and depositions, rarely back in time for dinner. He'd believed with fervor in the rules he'd enforced, in the idea of the government as the good leveler of the field. In 1944, he'd driven a Sherman tank through the streets of Paris to cheers. Back in the States, he'd spent his whole career going after securities fraud as if it were an insult to the country. How dare anyone think they were above the democratic rule of law that he had fought to defend. Fair procedure meant everything to him. He'd been delighted when Henry chose to go to law school, though he would never have argued for or against it. Of the Federal Reserve, however, he'd always been a bit suspicious, given how badly it had failed in the Depression. And then it wasn't exactly democratic either, with men from the private sector controlling the regional banks, appointing officers like Henry. An essential public function—the conduct of all monetary policy—handled beyond the public eye, by unelected officials. Of that his father had been wary.

"You have to remember," Henry could recall his mother saying, sipping her gin and tonic at the dinner table across from their father's empty chair, "your father is a man of *principle*."

Henry had followed his father's lead in never interfering with his sister's life, even after the disaster of her affair with Eric. The old man had always hewed to his line about being proud of his daughter's independence. The principled position. But then he wasn't around anymore.

Tires were lashed to the thick wooden posts at the end of the dock, where the dark water sloshed up against them. How was it that after all these decades his sister could still draw him back in? He'd thought once that having his own family would be a barrier of sorts, and for a while it had been, when his daughter, Linda, was a child. But it hadn't lasted long. In her way, Betsy had always resented his sister, and he couldn't entirely blame her. It wasn't that they saw so much of her in any given year. It was something else. Something about the nature of her claim on Henry.

"Your marriage should be donated to the Smithsonian," Charlotte had said to him once.

He should have been insulted, but he'd always enjoyed her wit.

As he turned back up the jetty toward his room, his cell phone began to vibrate.

WHATEVER SUSPICIONS he'd harbored about Taconic's management were quickly confirmed by his conversation with Fred Premley. It turned out the bank had been hemorrhaging cash on the swap for nearly a month. Clearly news had leaked into the overnight market. Which meant the problem was already worse than its notional value. If he'd been doing his job, Premley would have approached Henry's staff two weeks ago and borrowed from the Discount Window. But he was trying to attract a buyer for his company, so he'd avoided that public sign of distress. Instead, he'd just held on, hoping circumstance would save him. They had never met, but from the orotund tone of his voice, Henry could just picture the double chin. This was the kind of Business Roundtable chump who spent his lunchtime decrying government intrusion and now found himself on a cell phone in the middle of the night pleading with the government to save him. In the morning, there would be teams of examiners at the doors of his office, but right now they had to patch something together. After listening to his prevarications for a few minutes, Henry made it clear a specific request would be required.

"Well, then," Premley said, "I guess I'm asking if the Discount Window would loan us the one seventy."

Henry glanced at the fax Helen had sent through. Taconic had forty million in its reserve account.

"You might have got that, Mr. Premley, if you'd approached us in a timely fashion. But you've left it a bit late, wouldn't you say?"

There was a pause on the line.

"You'll get thirty," Henry said, "and that's generous."

"You're serious."

He said nothing.

"What about the rest?" Premley asked.

Henry had reached the limit of his official, public authority. From here on, they entered the informal realm. "The rest will need to be restructured," he said. "Tonight."

"I don't disagree, but my VP he tells me Union Atlantic's been holding out for hours. They don't want to refinance."

"That's hardly surprising under the circumstances."

He let the silence that followed hang there on the line between them. He needed to soften Premley up with fear so that he would accept the harsh terms Union Atlantic would offer once Henry placed his call to Holland. He said nothing for another moment or two, time enough, he figured, for the man to begin wondering about his own liability once the shareholder litigation began.

"Tell Cannistro to set up the transfer for the thirty million and keep this line open, all right, Mr. Premley? We'll see what we can do."

Turning on the television back in his room Henry saw that Frankfurt and Paris were down in early-hours trading. He pressed the Mute button and closed his eyes for a minute. The back offices in London were starting their day now and would begin to notice that Union Atlantic's payments were being held up. A call or two out to the trading desks where the young jocks sipped their coffee, stroking the fantasy of the one-day killing, and the lines would start to hum, bank stocks getting ready to head lower at the bell. He could see the sheen on the hard black plastic of the phones that would start to ring, the five-screen stations at Roth Brothers feeding Reuters and Bloomberg, the digital glide of ticker tape high along the wall, servers linked, nested, and cooled on the floor below, batching for export the first of the day's reports to the redundant facilities in Norfolk or Hampshire, windowless steel barns surrounded by fence and barbed wire.

"Remarkable how total the distraction can become, no?" Charlotte had said a few months ago in one of their loopy conversations. "Just don't forget yourself in the midst of it all."

Lifting his eyelids, he gazed at the figures running along the bottom of the silent screen. On his BlackBerry, he found the number for Mark Darby, his counterpart at the Bank of England, and left him a voice mail telling him there had been a glitch, that Union Atlantic's accounts would settle before the start of business in New York. Darby would get the word out and if all went well, in the next hour London might still open smoothly.

"Isn't there some regulation against men our age being up at this hour?" Jeffrey Holland asked in that warm, charming voice of his, after Helen finally patched him through. He knew perfectly well that Henry had at least ten years on him, and thus, true to form, the question doubled as a compliment. Henry figured it was the poor compensation that had kept Holland out of politics.

"Not to my knowledge, but I'm sure Senator Grassley would introduce a bill if you put a word in his ear."

Holland chuckled. He'd helped nix a reporting provision the Fed had wanted in the latest markup of the finance bill.

"I should mention it to him. No phone calls after nine o'clock."

"So did you have any warning on this Taconic business?" Henry said.

"None at all. I heard about it today. They must have moved around between lenders. They certainly didn't come to us."

Henry found this difficult to believe but chose to let it pass.

"Do you know this fellow Premley?"

"I've dealt with him once or twice. They brought him in to fix the place up and sell it. Not such a good bet, apparently."

"Between us, the Discount Window just extended them thirty of what they owe you."

"And you think we should roll over the rest?"

"Well, you've got an uncovered position yourself. It's two thirty in the morning."

He could hear what sounded like ice being put in a glass. Holland swallowed and cleared his throat. He wouldn't resist now. In the worst case, Union Atlantic would end up writing off the loss for whatever they couldn't recoup. Alerted to its weakness, Holland might even try to buy Taconic, once its stock price fell into the basement. A flap with the shareholders three months hence measured little against his bank being technically illiquid when the markets opened. They both knew this. Besides, Henry regulated Union Atlantic Group. Holland would offer terms now. The call itself was all that had been necessary.

"It must be an odd job," Holland said. "To have to keep imagining the real disaster. The whole leveraged shooting match falling to pieces."

Henry had wandered again onto the balcony, where the breeze had picked up off the water, the waves a bit larger now, boats bobbing against their posts, the fronds of the shaded palms swaying. How could anyone not imagine it these days? After the currency scares, 9/11, the Argentinean default, each of them managed one way or another. The system, in the public eye, still strong, people's faith in the value of the money in their pocket such a basic fact of life they couldn't imagine it otherwise. And yet if you'd been on the calls with the Ministers of Finance or with Treasury on the twelfth and the thirteenth—Henry from Basel, his senior staff some of the only people left in lower Manhattan other than the fire and rescue crews—you knew it could have gone differently. One more piece of bad news and the invisible architecture of confidence might have buckled.

About this Holland was right. Henry was paid to worry so the average citizen didn't have to.

"We do our best," he said.

"I'll have my people talk to Premley."

"I appreciate that," Henry said. "And of course, the less press about this the better. For everyone's sake."

"Naturally."

"Well, I'll let you get back to sleep, then."

"Look after yourself, Henry. The country needs you." And with that he clicked off the line.

Henry gazed down into the pool lit by wasted power, its surface ruffled by the new motion in the air, which had begun to raise the surf along the beach. Once more he heard the humming of the machine on the roof, the engine of the air conditioner whirring away. He thought of the speech he had to give in a few hours downstairs in the ballroom; the plane ride to LaGuardia; the car ride back up to Rye. And soon enough, the trip he'd have to make to Massachusetts, to sort out this business with his sister, to find somewhere for her to go.

His given family, once and again.

Chapter 5

Finden High, a brick pile with arched windows and a squat clock tower, had been erected in 1937 as part of a public works project. Like many such buildings, its bluntness was only partially offset by its few art-deco flourishes, such as the stainless steel that framed the front doors and the zigzag lines carved beneath the modernist clockface. To the grim utility of a factory, its designers had added just a whiff of style. It stood across Wentworth Street from an expanse of playing fields that extended all the way to the river. Not far from the varsity soccer pitch was the spot, commemorated with a plaque and a bench, where the Town Historical Society had decided that the first white families had alighted from their riverboats after traveling the short distance from Boston late in the 1630s. According to records, these settlers had wanted to name the then sparsely populated Algonquin hunting ground "Contentment," but taking a more practical view the Massachusetts General Court had overridden their decision, imposing upon them instead the solid English name of Finden, considered a better fit with the recently established towns of Roxbury, Gloucester, and the like.

As the students were told each fall in the assembly on local history, which served as a pep talk-cum-guilt trip, one of the settlers' first acts was the founding of a public school, which the community had maintained throughout its uneventful history of development from a trading post to a farming town to a twentieth-century suburb. Lately, the assembly had featured more on the Native American contributions to local custom but it still concluded with the principal sounding a note of pride about the percentage of seniors going on to four-year colleges, a fact the students were somehow meant to connect through the mists of time to that centuries-old journey down the river by the pious and the brave.

That spring of 2002, however, one particular student, Nate Fuller, was in danger of depressing this statistic. He had failed to fill out his applications to colleges back in the fall and failed again in the spring to apply to those with rolling admissions. His guidance counselor had called him in several times, requesting updates on his progress but he had none to report. Nor did he have a plan of how he might spend a year off to better his chances of getting in the following autumn. His teachers described him as adrift.

Most days this milky-skinned seventeen-year-old could be seen walking the halls dressed in frayed chinos and a blue hoodie, his brown hair grown over his ears and his eyes puffy with sleep. His father had died back in September, and he had been out of school for three weeks. He'd never caught up on the work he'd missed, let alone visited college campuses or written essays on his motivation to learn. Nonetheless, despite his general air of fatigue, he still possessed the changeable quality of the young, his affect shifting quickly from moroseness to affability and back. And though he cared little for his classes, he'd recently promised his mother to meet with the tutor that his American history teacher said he needed if he hoped to pass the AP exam.

On a cloudy day in the middle of April, after his latest dud of an appointment with the guidance counselor, he headed out the back of the school building and through the courtyard onto Pratt Road, where the yards were still wet with the morning's rain. Friday afternoons were usually the sweetest time of the week, replete with the promise of escape, but today he had the chore of meeting the tutor. He could blow the appointment off if he wanted and simply tell his mother he'd gone. But such deception would require its own energy and the visit would only take an hour.

Between his mother's new job at the library and his effort to be out of the house in the evenings, he and his mother didn't see much of each other these days. During the meals they did share, Nate didn't begrudge his mother her remoteness: how she didn't seem to hear what he said, how she responded in non sequiturs—bits of news about old friends or relatives, or recollections of trips they had once taken. Time together was tolerable that way. The two of them absent like that.

The difficulty arose when, on occasion, she would come to him with some fact in hand—a grade or health form—something she felt the sudden, fitful need to measure up to as a parent. Then they couldn't avoid each other, and all her straining in the last year to keep their lives together, to keep them in the house and to pay the bills, would pour into her panicked voice and no matter how small the subject she'd raised it would seem suddenly to be a matter of life and death. That was when he couldn't bear it and would agree to whatever she asked so they could both turn away again.

A year ago his father had been flying high, pulling Nate out of school in the middle of the day to eat lunch at the Four Seasons or driving him in an old Rolls-Royce out to the tip of Cape Cod late on a weekday night to watch the reflection of the moon on the dark waters of the Atlantic. Knowing that his mother was sitting at home stricken with worry about where they might be made it hard for Nate to simply enjoy such moments, however much his father did. He had lost his last consulting job a year and a half earlier and Nate knew they were running out of money. The rush of ideas about the next business he planned to start came at Nate so hard the words took on physical force, like a wind blowing fine shards of glass. The descriptions of projects and investors, elaborated down to the last digit and address, were painful in their detail.

This relentless drive of his had lasted six months. Then, in the middle of June, his father had come home and gone to bed, where he had stayed for most of the summer, making only occasional forays into the garage or basement to escape the heat. He ate little and barely spoke, while Nate's mother did her best to make it appear as if all were as usual.

Eventually, regaining energy, he'd begun to leave the house again, taking long walks on the trails over by the Audubon. He would depart before dawn and return around lunchtime. When he didn't come back one afternoon, Nate's mother called him at the supermarket where he worked after school and asked if he would go looking for him.

A quarter of a mile into the woods, Nate had come to the aqueduct that spanned the marsh, its concrete surface spotted with graffiti left by the kids who drank there on weekends. He and his father had crossed this bridge together countless times before, just meandering on a weekend afternoon, scouting out parts of the river they might row down if they had a boat. Until recently, Nate had thought nothing of their idyll of a companionship; it had simply always been there.

He crossed the bridge and continued along the path that followed the ridgeline into the forest. The Audubon preserve was a mile or so farther along, accessed from a road on the far side. Not many people walked up through this area so he wasn't surprised not to meet anyone on the trail. But he only went so far. He didn't walk all the way to the far end of the path that led down to the water's edge; and he didn't explore under the arches of the bridge on his way back or search up along the riverbank as he could have, as he might have. Rather, he stood at the aqueduct's black, wrought-iron railing looking out over the turning leaves, wishing his father wouldn't keep making his mother worry so.

The next morning, the police sergeant said only, "Up by the aqueduct," when Nate's mother asked where his father had hanged himself. The officer didn't mention when his father had done it. And so Nate had no idea if he'd still been alive as he'd searched for him, too self-conscious to even call to him aloud.

About the months that had followed, Nate didn't remember much. Luckily, his closest friends treated him with kid gloves for only a week or two before starting to give him the same shit they always did, returning his life to at least a semblance of what it had been.

He thought of them now, Emily and Jason and Hal, tempted once more to ditch this tutoring nonsense and call them to see if they'd started hanging out yet.

As he walked farther toward Winthrop Street, the houses grew sparser, this being the oldest, wealthiest part of town, made up mostly of estates.

Charlotte Graves, 34 Winthrop, along with a phone number. That's all Ms. Cartwright had written on the note card. When he had called the woman to set up the appointment, she had been curt to the point of rudeness and offered no directions.

The mailbox bearing that number stood between two driveways, leaving it unclear which house it belonged to. The driveway to the left led down to a white-columned mansion stretched out along the riverbank, recent by the looks of it but built in a neoclassical style that invited you to forget the fact. Its thick cornices and stately windows and the perfect lawns that surrounded it were somehow resplendent even in the light of an overcast day. The other drive was a weedy track heading up to a barn and a shingled little box of a house, which looked as if it had been built centuries ago and not much cared for since.

A tutor of history, Nate thought. What were the odds?

He knew which his father would have picked. Which house he would have talked his way into, putting everyone at ease, charming them with his glittering words. For all Nate knew, his father already had. For all he knew, the mansion's owners were among those in Finden whom his father had convinced to lend him boats or vintage cars, a habit he'd got into during that last spring of adventure.

Slowly, he headed down the hill to the mansion, where he climbed the steps to press the brass bell. The first ring produced no response. Glancing through a window, he didn't see much of anything inside. He leaned over and, pressing his hand to the glass to block the reflection, saw that the entire front room was empty, not a stick of furniture in it. No rugs on the floor, nothing on the walls. On the other side of the door it was the same—a vast high-ceilinged room, a fireplace at one end, and nothing else but bare boards and plaster. One of the big new houses built on spec, he figured, waiting for an owner. He rang a second time, just in case.

Curious, he stepped along the front of the house and peered through another window into another bare room. The emptiness of the place intrigued him. All that finished space marked by nothing. Without content or association. A perfect blank.

But not quite, it seemed. Through the next window, he saw a flat-screen TV set up on a crate facing an old cloth couch. There were no chairs or tables here, no lights or fixtures, just the television and the couch and an empty beer bottle beside it. The real estate agent? he wondered; but then how could he or she show the place? It was an odd, slightly forlorn sight.

Giving up, he headed back across the circular drive, past a fountain with a cherub in the middle, and headed up the hillside to the neighboring house. This one looked as if it were sinking slowly into the earth. Hydrangeas had grown up to the lower panes of the downstairs windows and the peeling gutters overflowed with leaves. At one end, a drainpipe had broken off and leaned now against the side of the house. Up on the roof, the faded aluminum rods of an old television antenna had come loose from the chimney and tilted precariously toward the street.

There weren't many places like this left in Finden. Ever since Nate had been a kid, they'd been building new houses everywhere they could, dividing up lots, turning fields and woods into new developments, the traffic worse every year.

He wondered if Ms. Cartwright had given him the wrong address, if perhaps this place was uninhabited. In fact, he hoped that it would be. But as soon as he tapped on the back door, he heard barking and the scuffle of paws on linoleum. From somewhere in the house a voice called out words he couldn't discern. And then he heard footsteps approaching. A harsh whisper followed.

"Don't be silly," the voice said. "Since when does the devil knock?"

Then, more loudly, "Who is it?"

"It's Nate Fuller. Are you Charlotte Graves?"

The door came open just a crack, and the snouts of two dogs pressed into the gap, followed a moment later by the deeply lined face of a gray-haired woman.

"Of course I am," she said. "Who else would I be? Are you some sort of Mormon? They usually come in twos."

"No," he said, raising his voice to be heard over the barking. "I'm here for the tutoring. I called last week? We spoke on the phone?"

"Did we?"

She considered him for a moment and then reluctantly pushed the dogs' heads back into the house.

"Yes, I suppose we did," she said. "I guess you'll have to come in."

She pulled the door open and stood aside. As soon as Nate entered, the Doberman leapt up, planting his front paws on Nate's chest and pinning him to the wall. He bared his teeth and began barking. A big, slobbering mastiff stood behind him growling.

"Stop being so paranoid, Wilkie!" the woman yelled. "He's got nothing to do with Elijah Muhammad. Now just come away!" she scolded, swatting the dog's head with a dish towel. The attacker pressed against Nate for a moment longer, the whites of his eyes bright in the dark pointed head. Reluctantly, he stepped off, joining the other one, the two of them standing either side of their owner like henchmen guarding passage to the rest of the house.

The kitchen looked like a set from *The Grapes of Wrath*, the wooden countertops warped and stained, the sink streaked with rust, the claw-foot stove losing its white enamel. The refrigerator appeared to be the only modern appliance, and even it was a pretty busted piece of merchandise. Yet this wasn't poverty. That didn't describe it. It was something else. Something Nate couldn't place.

"Is this a bad time?" he asked, hopefully. "I could come back another day?"

"No," she said. "It's as good a time as any. I remember your call now. You're the one trying to make up for lost time."

"Yeah. AP history."

Something seemed to catch her eye on the red-and-white speckle of the linoleum floor; her hands came to rest in the stretched pockets of her cardigan. For a moment there was complete silence.

"I don't do this much anymore," she said in a reflective tone, as if the commotion with the dogs had never happened and she were alone in the room, making an observation aloud to herself. "Tutoring, I mean."

Nate didn't know what to say. It seemed a private moment. Already, despite her surliness, he feared she'd be disappointed if he left.

"Ms. Cartwright—she mentioned you used to teach at the high school?"

The woman nodded, emerging from her inward turn.

As he picked up his backpack and moved toward the center of the room, the Doberman began growling again.

"Would you like some water?" she asked. "Or perhaps an Orangina?"

"Water's fine."

She moved to the sink, filled a pewter tankard, and handed it to him. It looked like something a knight might drink from.

"Well," she said, "I suppose we ought to get started."

He'd imagined a few preliminary questions. About what they had covered in class and what he had missed. But there was none of that. She had been reading about the law of property recently, she said, and this led her to the subject of taxation.

Perched on the edge of the couch, she folded her hands on her lap and stared fixedly into the ashes of the fireplace. After a moment of silence, she coughed slightly and said, "It's customary for students to take notes."

"Right," he said, reaching into his bag for pen and paper, "sure."

"The Sixteenth Amendment is generally neglected," she began. "But not in this household."

With this she commenced an uninterrupted half hour on the adoption of the federal income tax, and the long road to the passage of this general levy on corporations and the wealthy, an idea championed by the Populists and the Socialists and the Democrats under Bryan, shot down by the Supreme Court, agitated for in one campaign after the next, until finally the Republican progressives took it up as the answer to deficits and the tariff mess. Taft, a president who'd failed even to register on Nate's syllabus, was savaged by Ms. Graves as a generally ponderous and ineffectual man.

"But it should not be forgot," she said, "that it was he, who in 1909, stood before Congress and proposed an amendment to the Constitution allowing the government to collect the money."

From an ancient wingback chair losing feathers through the frayed fabric of its cushion, Nate took in the remarkable state of the room. Every surface from the side tables to the mantelpiece and a good portion of the floor was covered in paper: journals, newspapers, magazines, manila folders overflowing with yellowed documents, the piles adorned with everything from coffee mugs to used plates to stray articles of clothing—red wool gloves, a knitted scarf. And everywhere he looked, books: hardbacks, paperbacks, reference volumes, ancient leather-bound spines with peeling gold lettering, atlases, books of art and photography, biographies, novels, histories, some splayed open, others shut over smaller volumes, the overstuffed bookcases themselves standing against the walls like sagging monuments to some bygone age of order, entirely insufficient now to contain this sea of printed matter.

" 'An excise tax on the privilege of doing business as an artificial entity.' That's what Taft called the corporation tax." She quoted from a tome open on the coffee table in front of her. "It took another four years before enough states ratified the measure and a bill from Congress could be sent to Wilson. But there it was, the principle established: for the privilege of earning money in this, the people's system, you, the wealthy, will pay.

"Now," she said, warming to her point, "move forward half a century. It's 1964. The Republicans are in disarray, a party in the wilderness, without the White House, Congress, or the Court. The Civil Rights Act has just been passed. And along comes a man named Barry Goldwater. And he's got an idea: make government the enemy."

Almost as remarkable as the sheer quantity of stuff was how completely oblivious to it Ms. Graves appeared to be. She'd made no comment about the condition of the place as she'd led Nate in, letting him clear his own space to sit. It seemed that as far as she was concerned nothing was amiss. And yet, for all the mess she lived in and all her rambling, she didn't strike him as incoherent. In fact, Nate had never heard anyone speak with such conviction, except perhaps his father. Certainly none of his teachers. This was history, after all. And yet she spoke as if she were waging a rhetorical insurgency against the enemies of civilization.

"And look at us now," she continued. "Look at how ingeniously they have coded our politics. Using the same line of attack on our own sovereign authority to suit all their other ends. Of course, over time one begins to imagine connections between the darker forces. But then you say to yourself, No, Charlotte. You're dramatizing, you're giving in to conspiracy. You're satisfying some desire to moralize because, let's be honest, you're nothing but a stack of Eastern prejudices. But then you pick up this"—she scanned the books at her feet, spotted the one she wanted, and opened to an earmarked page—"and you think, well maybe so. But just listen to how *they* put it. Here's Lee Atwater—you've probably never heard of him—explaining how it worked. 'You start out,' he says, 'in 1954 by saying, "Nigger, nigger, nigger!" By 1968 you can't say "nigger"—that hurts you. Backfires. So you say stuff like forced busing, states' rights, and all that stuff. You're getting so abstract now that you're talking about *cutting taxes*, and all these things you're talking about are totally economic things and a by-product of them is that blacks get hurt worse than whites.'

"That's what *he* says," she insisted, clapping the book shut. "And so then you think, I'm not mad. Not at all. Taxes *are* about race. Like everything else. As if sometime in the sixties the public square in our mind changed colors. From imaginary white to imaginary black. And we've been running from it ever since. As if anything you couldn't fence in or nail to your house were the equivalent of the public pool menaced by the dark and the poor. But the public pool's not in *your* backyard, you say. It's nowhere close. True. But it's in my country. Am I not allowed a patriotism of ideals? Is that what we've come to?"

She paused to breathe.

"You see, then, what I mean?" she asked.

"I guess so."

"Not that *you* would agree with any of this, would you?" she said, leaning down to address the mastiff. "He's become such a reactionary lately. Haven't you, Sam? All your religious blather. Do you have dogs?"

"No. We used to have a rabbit."

"Don't be *ridiculous*."

"Sorry, I—"

"No, no, I wasn't talking to you. Sam here's just a bigot. Thinks you're a Catholic. Rabbits you say. My grandfather was fond of shooting them. They'd pop up in the yard and he'd rest his gun on the sill right there and open fire. Drove my grandmother to distraction. You'd think they'd have come back in strength by now but I never see them. He, of course, was a mugwump. Have you covered the 1880s? Republican, of the very old stripe. Bolted the party in '84. Small-town lawyer, edited the *Finden Gazette*. Didn't like machine politics. Laissez-faire, of course, but it was another time. He railed against the trusts as much as the city bosses, and there he was prescient. You look at the World Trade Organization today and it's all rather familiar. The way those conglomerates are making up the rules so they can run roughshod over the locals. Nothing the railroads didn't do to the state legislatures," she concluded, examining a patch of the mastiff's back for ticks or lice.

"I'm afraid the bullies here need their walking," she said. "I'm sorry if I've run on a bit. But there's a lot to cover." She looked up at him then, meeting his eyes directly for the first time. "You will come back, won't you? Next week?"

These last many months the intuition of others' needs had become Nate's second nature, as if his father's going had cut him a pair of new, lidless eyes that couldn't help but see into a person such as this: marooned and specter-driven. What choice did he have?

As soon as he got out of the house, he phoned Emily.

"Give us your location," she said. "We're in transit."

Fifteen minutes later, Jason's Jetta pulled up behind the Congregational Church in the center of town and Emily rolled down the passenger-side window.

"All right, the medevac's here."

In the backseat, Hal lay slumped against the far door with his eyes closed, a cigarette dangling from between his lips. A lanky, effete, mildly gothic boy, he prided himself on his superior intellect and perpetual indolence. To the alarm of his parents, he'd clicked through on some Internet ad and got himself admitted to a university in Tunis. From there he planned to spend the fall traveling the Maghrib.

"The Valp's holding," Jason said, speeding onto a side street. "But if we don't get there soon he'll smoke it all himself." They avoided the streets still heavy with commuter traffic until they had crossed all the way to the other side of Finden and pulled up in front of a white stucco house with three Japanese maples in the front yard surrounding a giant vertical boulder that looked as if it had been airlifted out of Stonehenge.

"What's with the rock?" Emily asked.

"I don't know. His mother's got a witch thing going on," Jason said, stepping out of the car. "She runs some kind of regional coven."

"I hung out with this Valp guy once," Emily said. "All he talked about was North Korea. Those rallies they have with the colored cards, you know? Like at the Olympics, where everyone in the crowd holds one up to make an image. Apparently they're very good at it over there."

She sounded bored, as usual, wearied by this petty world of high school. Emily had lived in London with her parents sophomore year and returned with a coolness unimpeachable by anyone except the three of them, who mocked her attempts to exempt herself from the indignities of Finden High.

Up on the lawn, from beside the obelisk, Jason was waving for them to come inside. "Christ, can't he just score the shit and get out of there?" Emily grumbled, leading the other two up the driveway.

Arthur Valparaiso had a slightly intimidating presence at two hundred and twenty pounds with a shaved head and clad this evening in an orange judo outfit. They had apparently interrupted some kind of deep-focus session, in which Arthur assumed a single lunging pose for up to an hour, a feat his girth rendered implausible. But now that he'd been disturbed, he was inclined toward a bit of company before completing the sale. As Nate's father had once said of God, the worst thing about drugs was the other people who believed in them.

The bong was produced, the music turned on, and the usual desultory conversation commenced. Knowing that the goal was an early exit, the four of them went light on the smoke, letting Arthur suck down most of the bowl, which had no discernible effect on him. Despite the smallness of his hit, Nate felt a tingling starting up at the back of his head, and slowly his thoughts began to wander as he stared at the walls of the basement rec room, which were covered with pictures of crowds: black-and-white aerial photographs of rallies in squares and piazzas, newspaper clippings of marches on the National Mall, stadiums full of rock fans shot from above.

"Have you read much Guy Debord?" Hal asked their host in a voice made all the more languid by the pot.

"Who the fuck is he?"

"French. He shared your interest in the masses. He writes about spectacle, how all this ginned-up collectivity contributes to our alienation."

"Crowds are where it's at, dude," the Valp said. "They're the future. Individualism is, like, a relic. Burning Man—that's the future."

Nate had discovered a vinyl beanbag in the corner. From there he watched Jason attempt to effect a game of pool, but it came to nothing. Eventually, a plea was made to Arthur and the transaction completed. Back in the car, a joint was rolled in the front seat and passed around as they sped down the state route toward the Alden strip, managing eventually to land themselves in the front row of a movie theater, at the foot of a huge screen that dashed their brains with the blood and pillage of some beast war of Middle Earth created, it seemed clear, by other, older drug-takers. They emerged into the parking lot more than two hours later, weakened and lethargic, having no sense of what to do or where to go.

For a while they drove, entranced by the clutter of lights and the bass tones of the car speakers, managing at one point to navigate a drive-through at a Dunkin' Donuts, and coming down as they munched their crullers and cinnamon buns in silence, gliding back into Finden.

A faint numbness behind the eyes was all that remained of Nate's high by the time they dropped him home.

He stood awhile in the front yard once they'd gone, staring at the darkened façade, only the porch light and the light up in his mother's bedroom on. It wasn't as decrepit a house as Ms. Graves's nor was it new or by any means empty. He needed to cut the grass soon. The shutters needed paint. Inside, nothing had changed for a long time.

They had arrived for the first time at this house in a rainstorm, he and his brother and sister standing in the front hall listening to their mother shout at their father about how dark it was, how cramped the kitchen and ugly the cabinets and ugly the wallpaper, how the boxes hadn't arrived and there were no blankets upstairs, and what would they do? How would they manage? As if he had led them all into disaster.

That was ten years ago and the wallpaper was still there, and the cabinets, and the mirror at the top of the stairs which his mother had never liked.

Climbing onto the porch, he closed the front door quietly behind him and switched off the porch light.

Once, when their mother had taken their father off to New York to see a specialist, his sister had thrown a party at the house and a girl had been sick on the front staircase, and though she'd tried her best to clean it, the detergent his sister had used had left a paling stain, which Nate passed over now as he headed up the stairs.

Anywhere people lived memory collected like sediment on the bed of a river, dropping from the flow of time to become fixed in the places time ran over. But in this house, since his father had died, it seemed sediment was all that was left: the banister, the hall mirror, the bathroom's black-and-white tile, the ticking on the runner carpet that led to the foot of his mother's door—all of it heavy with his absence.

This was the trouble with staying away with friends and getting high. He felt wrong for forgetting his family even for a few hours, as if to keep faith with his father required an unceasing grief.

Knocking gently on his mother's door, he turned the handle open. She was reading in bed, the covers pulled up to her waist. She glanced up over her reading glasses, her oval face gaunt, as it had been for months. She'd lost considerable weight in the last year and still ate very little.

"Was that Emily dropping you off?"

"Yeah," he said. "We saw a movie." He paused for a moment, feeling the obligation to offer her something more.

"I went to that lady for tutoring."

"That's right, I'd forgotten. How was it?"

"She's a little strange. But it was okay."

It never stopped being terrible, how alone his mother looked. He couldn't make it go away, even by being here, even if he were never to leave.

"Sleep well," she said, looking at him with a tender, somewhat distant expression, as if she hadn't seen him in a very long time.

Chapter 6

By Nate's third visit, Ms. Graves had stopped discussing American history altogether and thus any topic that might appear on his exam. Jumping off from Wilson at Versailles, she had waded into the diplomatic correspondence that detailed Britain's haphazard Middle East strategy following the Armistice.

"It came down to a lack of troops. Their army was fading away, you see. Someone had to maintain law and order. And so the British did what empires always do—they installed puppets. The Hashemites! Losers to the Sauds in the battle for the Arabian Peninsula! Why not give them Jordan! Of course it was only supposed to be a temporary fix, six months of police work until the mandate could be rearranged, a gentlemen's agreement, but look what we got! What should obviously have been the Palestinian state run for eighty years by an imported monarchy. Cancer number one. But why stop there? Ms. Gertrude Bell is a very fine and knowledgeable woman but not quite fit to rule Mesopotamia and given that the French had chucked brother

Faisal out of Syria, he was in need of a job, so why not give him Baghdad—another Hashemite installed to rule an incoherent people in an incoherent country! Truck in the Sunni elites! Throw in the Kurds! Can't you just picture it?" she asked, tossing her arms in the air. "Little Mr. Whatsit in his Whitehall office carefully drawing his map. If it weren't so lethal it could be read as farce."

When Nate ventured that the units he'd missed in class were on the Revolutionary War, Ms. Graves closed her eyes, held her palm out like a guard at a crosswalk instructing him to halt, and said, "I can't do George Washington. I simply can't. Triumphalist or otherwise. You'll have to go elsewhere for that."

Slouched again in the wingback chair, Nate let go of whatever responsibility he'd felt to prepare for the test. What did an AP credit matter when he hadn't even applied to college? It didn't compel. Not like the woman in front of him, who was so clearly driven by her own imaginings. It reminded him of the time his father had borrowed someone's yacht and sailed Nate out to Block Island to visit a businessman he had met on an airplane, a man who owned a paper company and might want to make a deal, only the businessman wasn't home when they arrived at his waterfront house; the maid said he'd gone to Brazil. And so they sat together on the empty beach sipping the gin his father had brought in a thermos, the liquid warm now and rather bitter.

Thus, while it surprised Nate when Ms. Graves asked at the end of the session if he would like to continue their work over dinner, it seemed to make an odd kind of sense, and he didn't hesitate to say yes.

At five thirty on a Friday afternoon they were the only customers at Finden Szechwan. A sunken-eyed waiter greeted them and the two dogs with a resigned nod of the head, directing them toward a banquette in the corner.

"At least their prices don't seem to have changed," Ms. Graves said, studying the menu through her reading glasses. "But you shouldn't worry about that. I'll take care of this. I'm celebrating, you see. I got a letter today about this suit I've filed. There's going to be a hearing soon and it turns out that the case has been assigned to the perfect judge. You noticed, I'm sure, that enormous house next to mine."

"Yeah. It's pretty impressive."

Her head recoiled, as if he'd tossed a rat onto the table.

"Of course," she said, slowly gaining hold of herself, "there's no reason you should understand. I forget so easily—the ignorance of the young. How would you know these things? No one's taught you." She put down her menu and leant across the table toward him. "In which case, allow me. That house," she said, her voice dropping, "that house is an *abomination*!"

"It was just an opinion," he said.

"No!" she cried. "That's precisely what it isn't! That's precisely what's become so endemic. That cheap, mindless relativism. You're all awash in it. Of course it's a pluralist society. So we're modest. In the big things: religion, metaphysics. We're non-absolutists. That's secularism. That's maturity. That's what the zealots can't abide. But this business of opinions. As if the world had no discernible qualities. As if there were no history. It's a disaster. It's an abandonment of the Enlightenment. All in the name of individualism. And they expect people to just stand by and watch. I was run out of my job on this sort of hogwash. The whole four-hundred-year effort sacrificed on the altar of the inoffensive. It's unspeakable."

"Right," Nate said, afraid of the woman for the first time.

"But that's just it!" she exclaimed, thrusting her hands out to her side, knocking Sam in the face. "You're agreeing with me because you think that's what I want. That's the problem. Do you think *I* was the one who brought *The Autobiography of Malcolm X* into the classroom?

No. That's what they forget. It was *students*, black students God forbid, bused out from the city, who told me they'd stop coming to class if I didn't assign it as a counterpoint to King and the nonviolent wing of the movement. And more power to them. They were right. But by the time the authorities got rid of me those children were swallowing that book down like just one more palliative drop of minor guilt and minor catharsis, one more petty event in their two-bit little moral Olympiad, where everyone always wins gold. The young limbs of the body politic cleansing themselves for future efficiency. I played them the tapes of his speeches, and even met them halfway by showing the damn movie. But it was all just one big entertainment to them."

The waiter had come over to take their order but in her enthusiasm Ms. Graves failed to notice him.

"However, I digress. The point is, that house, you mark my words, it'll be gone. This town, those selectmen—they broke the law."

Nate glanced at the idling waiter, trying to clue his tutor to his presence.

"Oh, hello there," she said, reaching into the pocket of her cardigan, from where she produced a faded newspaper coupon advertising a two-for-one entrée special. "We were wondering," she said, handing it to the waiter, "which of your dishes qualify?"

The man's already sagging countenance drooped. He took the worn clipping from her and turned it back and forth a few times, as if delay might save him from this final indignity.

"This is no good," he said. "It expired. Three years ago."

"Well that's rather silly. It certainly succeeded in luring us in here. Are you saying you have no special offers at all?"

"Oh, no. We got specials. We introduced pad thai. It's right up there on the board. Special. Seven ninety-nine."

"But this is a Chinese restaurant."

"Not next week it won't be," he said. "We're closing."

The Doberman had spotted a cat on a windowsill across the room and begun to snarl.

"I agree, Wilkie," Ms. Graves said, "this is ridiculous. We came in here with the perfectly reasonable expectation of a discount. But never mind. On we go."

When the moo shu arrived, she barely touched it, pouring herself a cup of tea instead.

"So. Tell me. Why is the world a problem for you?"

"How do you mean?" Nate asked.

"Well, for some people the world is a more or less obvious place. It's transparent to them. It isn't, in itself, a conundrum to be overcome. Which means their interests are simply tastes or preferences. But if the world's a problem to you, your interests are different. You're conscripted by them. You know what conscription means, don't you?"

"I think I'm registered for it."

"You understand my question. What interests you involuntarily?"

Smearing plum sauce over his third pancake, Nate tried to surmise what exactly she was after.

"You mean, like, what makes me unhappy?"

Wincing slightly, Ms. Graves said, "I suppose that will do, but you understand I'm not asking about the trivial here. Failing to win some prize, or that sort of thing. I ask because you listen to me in a rather particular way—and believe me, I spent years being listened to by people your age—and it suggests to me the world's not obvious to you. I simply want to know why."

When he asked if it would be okay if he finished the lo mein, she fluttered her hand dismissively, never removing her eyes from his face.

Seeing no reason not to, Nate mentioned his father.

"Yes. I imagined it was something along those lines. Where did he do it? In your house?"

"No, in the woods."

She considered this for a moment.

"Inverting for you, I would imagine, the standard inquiry, Why kill yourself? to the less often asked, Why not? A sophomoric question, but then there are times in life when that makes it no easier to avoid."

Nate nodded slowly. It was weird to be talking about this to Ms. Graves but she wasn't wrong and she wasn't pretending. In fact, it was a relief to tell someone about it and not receive in return awkward condolence. To just say it and have it heard.

"Mostly it's just lonely," he said.

"You'll get used to that. Maybe you'll meet someone one day. Which may or may not ameliorate the feeling. When did you say this happened?"

"Last September."

"Ah," she said. "You're in the early stages. When you get to my age, the borders open up a bit. The barriers between times aren't so strictly enforced, which is a problem that you might say I'm conscripted by. This way in which we're not just dying animals. Do we have souls strapped to our bodies? That division seems too neat to me, but that's an intellectual matter. It lacks force in the end. But decay—rot—that's more complicated. It has a purpose, after all. It leads to new things. To other life."

A few minutes later the waiter approached to ask if they would like dessert. Ms. Graves shook her head and the waiter went to fetch the bill. The remains of their food had quickly congealed. She placed a few dishes on the floor for the dogs and for a while their lapping tongues were the only sound in the dining room.

By the middle of May, the AP exam had come and gone. But still, each Friday afternoon, Nate went to the old woman's house. He had stopped giving her checks but she didn't appear to notice. Her lectures, if you could call them that, grew more disjointed as the weeks passed. Comments on Henry II's abrogation of jurisdiction from the ecclesiastical courts of twelfth-century England led into a discussion of precursors to the English Revolution four hundred years later, which apparently had something to do with the poetry she read aloud describing Adam's conversation with God: " 'In solitude / What happiness, who can enjoy alone / Or all enjoying, what contentment find?' Can you hear that?" she asked. "He's asking God how a person can be content alone."

With her voice veering from angry to elegiac, she sounded as if she were narrating stories brought to mind by family photographs, the actors all intimates, their deeds still full of consequence and culpability. At the end of an hour or sometimes two, as Nate sat at her kitchen table drinking tea or stood in the doorway to go, rather than offering him some blandishment or goodbye, she would announce without transition what she saw in his expression.

Once, she said, "Boredom is easy. Which is why sadness hides there so readily. But don't be fooled for long. Dying of boredom. There's reason behind that idiom. It'll kill you sure enough."

Her peculiar affect freed him to ask things he otherwise wouldn't.

"What if I don't meet someone?"

"Then you won't. And that will be the condition under which you'll live. But remember: people won't save you."

Each time, on his way to and from her house, Nate would pause at the top of the hill to see if there were any signs of life down at the big house along the river, a car in the driveway or a light on inside. No FOR SALE sign had appeared in the yard and yet there was still no evidence anyone lived there. Since that first day, he hadn't been able to get the place out of his mind.

Finally, on the last Friday in May, after Ms. Graves had rattled on till nearly six and Nate had left more tired than usual by her river of words, he decided there would be nothing wrong with having another look. And so he headed down the slope in the rich light of the spring evening, the grass beneath him freshly cut. Mounted on the corner of the garage, he noticed a surveillance camera and wondered if it fed its images to a screen in the house or to some security firm's office hundreds of miles away.

He passed out of its range, walking around the far end of the mansion which consisted of a glassed-in sunroom, unfurnished, with an open-air deck above. At the rear, a brick terrace extended onto the lawn, which ran forty yards or so down to the riverbank. Nate looked through one of the smaller rear windows into a pantry lined with bare white shelves. Next to that was a room whose perfectly polished wood floors glinted in the sun. He came to a set of French doors off the kitchen, which was a huge space with a slate counter island, two stoves, two sinks, and a double-wide fridge. In the corner stood a small wooden table with one chair, dwarfed by the room they had been placed in.

There were no cameras that he could see along this stretch of the house. He tried the door handle. To his surprise, it moved smoothly downward, the door coming open a few inches. He shut it again immediately, terrified of setting off an alarm.

A minute or two passed and he heard nothing.

What harm could it do, he thought. No one was here and he

wasn't going to steal anything. He cracked the door just wide enough to listen. No sound but the hum of the fridge.

As soon as he stepped into the kitchen and closed the door behind him, he could feel blood rushing to his head from the excitement. He walked to the counter and paused there to listen again. The room smelled of wood wax and cleaning fluid. Moving farther into the house, he crossed the marble floor of the front hall and proceeded into a room nearly as large as the downstairs of his entire house. The outsize fireplace had no grate in it and its mantel was bare. Beyond this was the room with the couch placed at an angle facing the giant TV in the corner. The beer bottle he'd seen on that first day that he'd peered through the windows was gone and there was a stack of files on the floor.

He had never trespassed before. He had no idea it could be so exhilarating, all his senses alive with anticipation. The fear of being caught was close to exquisite. And who was it that lived like this? What kind of life did it imply?

Entering the back wing of the house, he stood at the foot of a staircase, stopping once more, trying to detect the slightest sound.

Upstairs, he walked down a central hallway, passing more unfurnished rooms on either side. The scent of pine freshener and just a hint of paint hung in the motionless air. While the thrill of transgression still filled him, he was beginning to find the emptiness of the place almost soothing. A house so unmarked, so unstained by memory or disappointment. It didn't even feel like Finden anymore.

At the fourth door along the hall, he glanced through what seemed to be the entryway to a suite of some kind. Entering it, he came up short at the sight of a king-size bed, recently slept in, the sheets ruffled, the pillow still bearing the wrinkled impression of a head. On the floor, a cordless phone rested facedown, and next to that stood a water glass. The only other objects in the room were a television and a standing lamp.

For several minutes he stood motionless, staring at the bed.

Along the opposite wall was a walk-in closet. Ten or twelve suits, blue, black, and dark gray, hung in a row on one side while dozens of freshly laundered shirts still in their plastic were lined up along the other. At the back stood a dresser, a pile of laundry heaped against its bottom drawer. Dress shoes arranged beneath the suits gave off the scent of newly polished leather. Cautiously, his hand beginning to tremble, Nate reached out to feel the arm of one of the suit jackets, marveling at how smoothly the fine wool moved between his fingers. That's when he heard the sound of a car door slamming shut.

Chapter 7

Doug didn't usually return to the house at such an early hour. But that afternoon he'd received a call out of the blue from Vrieger, his old commanding officer. It turned out he was living south of Boston and had heard through friends that Doug worked in the city. He'd phoned around noon from a restaurant not far from the office and asked if they could meet for lunch. Doug's first inclination was to say of course he couldn't, that he scheduled appointments weeks in advance, and that they would have to set a later date. But to tell Vrieger that seemed ridiculous and he found himself saying, yes, it was fine, that he would be there in an hour.

Walking beneath what remained of the Central Artery, he crossed into the narrow streets of the North End, glad to be out of the office for a little while at least.

The last week had been hectic. The Japanese Ministry of Finance's intervention to prop up the country's stock market had finally been made public, causing the Nikkei index to start dropping. Doug had phoned McTeague straightaway, instructing him to trim back Atlantic Securities' positions, limiting their exposure. McTeague had seemed reluctant at first, arguing that it was only a blip, that they would be getting out of the market too soon if they sold now. Eventually, Doug had been forced to make it clear to him that the choice wasn't his to make. The firm's bets, built up over the course of months, were huge by now and would take time to unwind. Done right, however, they could get out with nearly all their profit intact and the whole Finden Holdings operation would still count as a major success. If McTeague's clients wanted to keep going, pouring more money into the strategy, that was their business and their risk.

Making his way up Prince Street, Doug entered the restaurant and found Vrieger at the bar sipping a glass of bourbon, a nearly full ashtray at his side. In the decade and a half since Doug had last seen him, he had put on a bit of weight, but on the whole he looked remarkably unchanged with his ramrod posture and hair still clipped regulation short. He wore a version of his same square metal glasses, as unfashionable now as they had been back in the eighties.

"Christ," he said, when he spotted Doug. "The least you could have done was get a bit uglier."

"Lieutenant Commander, a pleasure to see you."

"So you're a corporate guy, huh? A suit. You always said that's what you wanted to do."

"Did I? To tell you the truth, I don't remember talking about it."

Doug ordered a beer and the bartender produced a few sandwich menus. Before the two of them had last parted in San Diego, Vrieger had told Doug that he planned to sign up for another tour. As he began describing it to Doug now, that third stint of his had taken him back to the Persian Gulf during Desert Storm. Later, in the mid-nineties, he'd run clandestine interdiction off the coast of North Korea as part of a loose nukes operation. The way he told it, he'd pissed off too many captains along the way to expect further promotion. "Truth is," he said, "after *Vincennes* I didn't really care. I just wanted to keep going." When the navy assigned him desk duty back in Norfolk, Virginia, he'd decided to quit. "That was four years ago," he said. "I thought I'd get a job out at Raytheon. Test battle systems. Something like that. I lasted through about two interviews." Since then he'd been living with his father in Quincy, working at a liquor warehouse.

He reported all this in an affectless tone, his eyes fixed on the television over the bar, where cable news was spooling a loop of satellite images of building complexes in the Iraqi desert, as a commentator detailed the suspicious movement of trucks.

"So what about you? You seem to have done okay for yourself."

Doug told him about getting his first job in New York, and how he'd spent his time learning the business, listening to the geeks and the quants, the pale men in ill-fitting suits who could tell you the yield curve on a Brazilian pipeline bond without looking up from their sandwich. And how when it came time to charm the Ivy League VPs, he'd just opened with a compliment and let them do the rest of the talking. And later, when he fired some of them, how disdainful the look in their eyes had been, as if all along they'd known he was a hustler and that they should never have let him into the club they were so fond of saying no longer existed, believing with fervor that all of finance was a meritocracy now.

"You'd recognize it," Doug said. "Bullshit hierarchies and a bunch of rules you got to get around to get anything done."

"You married?" Vrieger asked.

"No. You?"

"Are you kidding? Nine months is my record. And she was a

drinker. But you? I mean, come on. You're a pretty boy. You must have to fight 'em off."

Doug couldn't remember the last time he'd been asked such questions by anyone. He and Mikey never talked about personal stuff and no matter how often Sabrina Svetz tried, he'd never given her much detail either. The one woman he'd stayed with for more than a few weeks was Jessica Tenger and he hadn't thought about her in ages.

They had met at a party in SoHo. Vrieger was right that Doug had grown used to girls requiring nothing more than a few minutes of easy flattery before they made it clear they were willing to be led. The thing about Jessica had been how directly she played the game. Her second question was where he lived, and her third when he planned on leaving the party. Back at his apartment they had ordered food and already finished having sex by the time it arrived. She hadn't slept over that night or any other.

They hadn't asked each other questions about work or discussed current events or how their days had been. In fact, they said very little to each other at all.

As he described her to Vrieger, her narrow hips and pageboy haircut, he remembered how he'd kept the lights on during sex and how she preferred keeping her eyes closed, allowing him to look at her without being watched. She could give herself over to whatever waking dream occupied her mind, the particulars of which he didn't need to know. Raised over her in a push-up position, he would watch himself: the pleasing proportions of his biceps; his gleaming chest; the flat shield of muscle running across his abdomen into his groin; and the splendid view of himself disappearing inside her like the fluke of an anchor grabbing the seabed. The tightness and precision of his body felt alive then, and he would come to the sight of it in motion.

They might have continued on indefinitely. But one evening, after leaving work early, Doug had phoned her and she'd said to come by her apartment, which he'd never seen, over by the Hudson on Washington Street. The place was a semi-converted warehouse space with rough wood floors, iron columns, and windows high up the walls. It turned out she was some kind of sculptor. A series of worktables occupying one side of the apartment were covered in small bins of everything from copper wire to sand. On one of them, a few pale white heads, human size and made of wax by the look of them, lay on their sides. She poured wine, and as soon as they'd sat down on her couch Doug had realized that whatever they'd had was over. It had nothing to do with her being an artist or living in that apartment. She could have been a lawyer or an actress or a grad student. It was the specificity of the circumstance that broke the circuit. The particularity of her life, as he could see it now. Like all particularity, it had a terminal air about it. At work, which was to say in his life, his mind glided over the present, headed always into possibility. But that apartment—that announcement of all those specific, irrevocable choices—it demanded that he stop. That he remain still.

"I don't have a lot of time these days," he said to Vrieger. "To tell you the truth, I don't think about relationships much."

In the pause that followed, Doug began to wonder why he had agreed to come here. Was it out of obedience to his old commanding officer? This made no sense; he wouldn't have so much as taken a call from the captain. Vrieger's pull came from somewhere else. As Doug watched him order his third bourbon of the afternoon, it struck him that the thing about Vrieger, which he'd sensed ever since that summer in the Gulf, was how the events they had been through had acted on him like a trance, as if no matter where he might be, no matter what might be going on around him, he was still fixed back in that one place: the Combat Center of the *Vincennes*, July 3, '88, his finger on the launch button. The years hadn't changed that. Doug saw it in the constancy of his gaze at the television: that permanent alert habitual in the survivors of emergency.

"We're going back in, you know," Vrieger said. "You understand that, right? We're going all the way to Baghdad. They're polishing the missiles as we speak. Fifth Fleet's already scheduled the hardware for the Gulf."

Doug hailed the bartender and ordered another beer.

"Cat got your tongue?" Vrieger asked, a note of aggression creeping into his voice. "I don't know about you," he went on, "but the ones I remember are the women. The ones in those black sack dresses with their heads covered, just the slits for the eyes. The wailing that came out of them. You remember that? It's strange, isn't it? Down on the ground like that by the coffins, being held back by their families, like they can't control it. You wonder: Why don't we do that? Grieve like that, I mean. Give in to it. Grief's like an illness here. A disease."

The TV camera panned across a column of Israeli tanks filing through clouds of dust into the West Bank.

When his drink arrived, Doug asked the bartender if he minded changing the channel. The guy reached up and hit the Plus button once, leaving them with a close-up of a rotating diamond ring set in a velvet case above another ticker, this one running with product detail and a number to call.

"Is it that easy for you?" Vrieger said.

"What?"

"To turn it off. To forget."

"Who said I was forgetting anything?"

Placing his empty tumbler upside down on the bar, Vrieger tilted his head to examine the cut of the glass. "Well, tell me then. I'm interested. How do you hold it? What we did."

This was why Vrieger had called. And maybe why Doug had come.

That summer of '88, a few days after they had shot down the airliner, a crew member from the USS *Sides* had told a reporter for some newspaper that he had seen bodies falling from the sky. On their return to San Diego, the entire crew of the *Vincennes* had been awarded combat action ribbons for their engagement of the Iranian gunboats. Vrieger had won the navy's commendation medal for heroic achievement. He'd had to carry that around, too, all these years.

Doug took a cigarette from Vrieger's box and lit it. "You know what the Iranians did?" he said. "After they signed the cease-fire with Iraq? They went into their gulags and rounded up all the political prisoners—leftists, mujahideen, whoever they thought might take advantage of the armistice. And they murdered them all. Either you repented and started praying or they murdered you. Tired old guy rotting in some cell for years? Pop. Sixteen-year-old kids? Pop. Girls? They raped them first and then popped them. Wives brought in to see their husbands hanged. That's what they do to their own people. I'm not even talking our guys—Beirut, Khobar Towers—none of that."

Vrieger's next bourbon arrived. Without the cable news to soak up his watchfulness, he gazed into the amber liquid with a kind of dejected fervor, as if staring into the dark mouth of a tunnel, listening for the roar. "Interesting," he said.

"What's that supposed to mean?"

"You're still bound to the wheel of fire."

"Here's where I lose you."

"Yeah," Vrieger said, "that's right." With a slightly trembling hand, he raised his glass to his lips and drained it. "That's King Lear being woken by his daughter at the end of the play. When his world has gone all the way to shit. You do me wrong to take me out of the grave, he tells her. Thou art a soul in bliss, but I am bound upon a wheel of fire, that mine own tears do scald like molten lead." He paused, his mouth in a slight wince, as if he were physically pained by the words. "You're still in hell. That's what I'm saying. You're still in the hell of revenge."

According to the clock above the cash register, Doug had been at the restaurant nearly an hour. In a little while, McTeague would be arriving at the office in Hong Kong, getting ready to withdraw a bit more of Atlantic Securities' money from the market. Doug needed to get back, to look the numbers over once more, to make sure they were reducing their exposure at a quick enough pace.

"Do your folks still live around here?" Vrieger asked, breaking the silence between them.

"Who told you that?"

"You did. When I first met you."

"Alden," Doug said. "And it's just my mother."

"Wasn't my business then and it isn't now."

He scooped up a handful of nuts and, removing the cigarette from between his lips, leaned his head back and poured them into his mouth. "I don't mean to get at you. You got out, like you wanted to. You built a life. You've got something. I guess it's just a question of what you bring out with you. Me? I didn't bring much. Fact is, I'm going back."

"Back where?"

"The Gulf."

"What the fuck are you talking about?"

"I know a guy down in Virginia. He started one of these security outfits. Lots of ex-military. It's still pretty small but he says if I get through the training, he'll give me a job. I'm telling you, everybody's ramping up. Logistics. Force protection. They don't know where they're going yet, where they'll be needed. But it's going to be a shit-storm."

"You're kidding me. Why the hell would you do that?"

"Why not?" Vrieger said. "I've got nothing here. Nothing to go the distance with. At least there I'll be back inside. It's got nothing to do with making up for what we did. Or winning or being forgiven or any of that. I guess you could say it's sad or fucked up or I'm traumatized or whatever. But I don't really care about any of that anymore. I'm not looking to be cured."

WALKING BACK UNDER the rusted struts of the Central Artery, the roar of jackhammers filling his ears, Doug felt light-headed. By the time he reached the cool of the tower's lobby, the dizziness had given way to exhaustion. His legs would barely move one in front of the other. Unsure if he would make it to the elevator, he took a seat on one of the chrome benches running along the glass wall of the atrium. He watched employees come and go: the senior secretaries paddling by with their shoulder bags full of crosswords and knitting, junior analysts in serious suits, building security in purple sport coats returning with their takeout. A young woman coming off the elevator glanced in Doug's direction and, recognizing him, appeared confused at the sight of him on his own with no papers or briefcase or BlackBerry in hand.

Finally, he managed to get his phone out and dial Sabrina.

"Call the garage for me, would you?" he said. "Have them bring up my car."

By the time it appeared in front of the building, he felt lucid enough to take the wheel. He headed for Storrow Drive thinking maybe he would walk along the river to clear his head, but the mere thought of it tired him further and so he kept driving, exiting onto the Pike, where the lanes were clogged with traffic. It took him twenty minutes longer than usual to reach the house. Tossing his keys on the kitchen counter, he headed up the stairs to his room and flopped down on the bed, not even bothering to remove his shoes.

On the verge of sleep, he heard a sound behind him, coming from the bathroom.

He opened his eyes and remained perfectly still. Listening intently, he discerned two cautious footsteps. The house contained nothing worth stealing but the televisions; they were still here. Whoever it was had been waiting. Slowly, very slowly, he moved his hand to the floor. Reaching under the bed, he fingered the steel crosshatching on the butt of his pistol and coaxed it into his grip. Between the next footstep and the one that followed, he counted five seconds. The sound was just a few yards from his shoulder now. When he heard it again, he grabbed the gun up off the floor, cocked it, and swiveled upright, shouting, "Back it up!" just in time to see the young man's knees buckle as he fainted, falling into the room with a thud.

Coming up off the bed, Doug strode to the door, checked the hallway, and then crossed the room again to the window to see if there was anyone in the driveway or yard. Finding them clear, he turned back to the boy slumped in the bathroom doorway. He had disheveled brown hair and was dressed in frayed jeans and a sweatshirt. Doug nudged him with his foot but he was out cold.

Squatting down, he reached one arm under the kid's knees and the other beneath the middle of his back. He was heavier than Doug had anticipated, his head lolling backward, his waist sagging between Doug's arms. An odd sensation—that warm, unconscious body pressed up against his chest. Crossing the room, he set him down on the rumpled sheets. He looked peaceful lying there. Unsure what to do, Doug stood over him awhile, experiencing something peculiar, a feeling of sorts. A passing sorrow as he watched the boy breathe.

Chapter 8

Above Nate, a fan spun noiselessly. Pain stretched up his right side from his waist to his shoulder, and his head ached. Looking to his left, he saw a man with his back to him standing at the window dressed in suit pants and shirt. Instantly, his stomach clutched tight, the constriction spreading into his chest and throat, making his heart thud.

He tried sitting up, but dizzy, lay back onto the pillow again.

"So. You mind telling me what you're doing in my house?" the man asked, without turning to face him. His hands jangled keys or change in the pockets of his trousers.

"I . . . I was just cutting across the yard—"

"And you wound up in my bedroom?"

"I shouldn't have, it's just—"

"Cutting across the lawn from where?"

"Next door."

He turned back into the room now and looked directly at Nate. "From that woman's house? You were in there?"

He had shiny black hair cropped short, a wide jaw, and a dimpled chin. He was six-one at least. The muscles of his chest and shoulders, evident beneath the fitted shirt, torqued his upper body forward slightly, like a boxer leaning in to his opponent.

Online, there were plenty of men whose pictures made Nate go dreamy and hard, in a melancholy sort of way. But they were other-worldly.

"I asked you a question," the man said.

"Ms. Graves. She's my tutor."

His eyes narrowed, his lashes bunched at the tips as if wetted, as if he'd just stepped from the shower.

"She sent you over here, didn't she?"

"No. I swear. I was just curious. That's all."

"You do this often? You just wander into people's houses?"

"No."

"You could have been killed. You realize that?"

Nate nodded, holding his breath.

"Are you hurt?"

"I don't think so."

"All right, then. Let's go."

He led Nate along the hallway and down the curved front stairs, which brought them into the hall Nate had passed through less than an hour before. This was it, he figured; he would be told to leave now. But rather than heading for the door, the man kept going into the giant kitchen. From the fridge, he took a bottle of vodka and poured himself a glass. Leaning against the counter, his legs slightly spread, he swirled the clear liquid with a tight little motion of his hand. To each of his gestures there was a precision, a kind of surface tension to the way his body moved. He had a cocksuredness about him that the jocks at school could only hope to emulate. A cool, level stare that announced straightaway he needed nothing.

"I guess I should call the police now," he said.

"You're kidding, right?"

"You live in Finden?"

"Yeah."

"You think this town's just a playground for you? You can just do whatever you want because it's all safe and cozy in the end? You were trespassing. You were breaking the law." The cuff of his shirt sleeve slid back from his wrist as he raised his glass to his mouth.

"I didn't take anything," Nate pleaded.

For a minute or more the man made no reply, all the while staring directly at Nate. There was a perversity in his silence, a gaming of discomfort. Nate could sense it in the air between them. And yet there was something else too, something tantalizing: being looked at this hard, with that edge of threat. Part of Nate wanted to shut his eyes and let himself be watched, but he didn't dare.

"That tutor of yours, she's out of her mind. She thinks she owns this place."

"Yeah. She mentioned that."

"And you say you were just curious. About what?"

"That it was so grand, I guess. And empty. I didn't think anyone lived here."

The man glanced across the room, as if noticing its bareness for the first time. In profile, he was even more gorgeous, with his five-o'clock shadow and his perfectly shaped nose and his full, slightly parted lips. Entering the house had woken Nate's senses but what he experienced now was of a different order, as if the whole physical world had been made exact, sharpened by the knife of desire.

"I suppose I could use some furniture," he said, finishing his drink and setting it down on the counter.

"I think it's kind of cool the way it is."

"Yeah? Why's that?"

"I don't know. It feels open, I guess. Like you could do anything you wanted to."

"What's your name?"

"Nate."

"What are you, a high-school student?"

"I'm a senior. I graduate in a few weeks."

"Well, Nate, I've got stuff to do, so I think it's time for you to leave."

Pointing the way out, he followed Nate from the kitchen.

"You're not going to call the police?"

"Frankly, I don't have the time."

As the man held the front door open, Nate could see the electric orange of the streetlamps flickering on up along on the road. If he left now, like this, with nothing more said, how would he ever get back here?

He hesitated on the threshold a moment. Then he blurted out, "I could help you."

"What do you mean?"

"If you needed to know stuff. About Ms. Graves. About her lawsuit."

The man's lips parted, and he smiled for the first time, a look of conjecture playing across his face.

"Interesting," he said. "And why would you do that?"

For all his effort, Nate couldn't stop the blood from filling his cheeks now.

"I don't know," he said. "Just because."

For another long moment, the man was silent.

"Sure," he said, finally. "Why not? I'm usually home about ten thirty. Try knocking next time."

NATE JOGGED the half mile to Jason's house and arrived in a sweat.

"Where the hell have you been?" Emily shouted over the sound of the voice booming from the stereo in Jason's room. She lay on the unmade bed, leafing through a copy of *Harper's*.

"Sorry. I got held up."

The evening here was still getting under way. Jason sat at his desk, parceling out whitish-brown stalks and heads into small glass bowls. In the corner, Hal, who'd apparently taken the liberty of showering, sat lounging in Jason's blue terry-cloth bathrobe, an unlit cigarette in one hand, an empty pack of matches in the other.

"You know," Hal said, "I was thinking—"

"Quiet!" Jason insisted. "It's almost over."

Obediently, they all listened to the voice on the speakers as it swerved back and forth between reasoned calm and a kind of prophetic verve. A professor, it sounded like, a researcher on some very extended leave.

"So you see," the voice continued, "the entirety of human history has been acted out in the light of the traumatic severing of our connection into the mother goddess, the planetary matrix of organic wholeness that was the centerpiece of the psychedelic experience back in the high Paleolithic. In other words, the world of hallucination and vision that psilocybin carries you into is not your private unconscious or the architecture of your neural programming, but it is in fact a kind of *intellecti*, a king of being, a kind of Gaian mind. Once you sever from this matrix of meaning, what James Joyce called 'the mama matrix most mysterious,' once you sever yourself from this, all you have is rationalism, ego, male dominance to guide you, and that's what's led us into the nightmarish labyrinth of technical civilization, all the ills of modernity. We must import into straight society almost as a Trojan horse the idea that these psychedelic compounds and plants are not aberrational, they are not pathological, they are not some minor subset of the human possibility that only freaks and weirdos get involved with but rather the catalyst that called forth humanness from animal nature. That's the call I'm making."

The audience applauded as the volume of the recording faded out.

"Where the fuck do you get this stuff?" Emily asked.

"Interesting," Hal allowed. "If nothing else, it's a good highbrow excuse to get wasted."

"That's not the point. We're not 'getting wasted.' This isn't a party."

"Sure," Hal said. "We're widening the lens."

"Exactly," Jason said, rising from the desk to pass them each their dish. "We're taking what he calls the 'heroic dose.' The dose where you can't be scared anymore because there's no ego left to be frightened."

The shrooms had a stringy, dirt-like texture that made Nate gag. The Brita was passed around and it took them a glass of water each to swallow down the bitter mush. Ingestion complete, Jason slipped on some panic-retarding French pop, all mild falsetto and ethereal synth. The night's opening gesture made, they recommenced their lounging. Half an hour or so passed as the disco scrim luffed in the air about them.

"One day," Hal said idly to Jason, "I think you'll run a cult. Not in a bad way, at least not at first. We'll read about you on an island with lots of women and children, all of you awaiting some astral bus. My career will be over by then, at twenty-eight or -nine, and I'll wonder if I should join you."

"Listen," Jason said, "here's a public service announcement, okay? The free-association thing—it can be a problem. I mean, 'astral bus'? That's the kind of thing someone could just catch on, and before you know it, we're lost. Think of it like meditation. The thought comes and the thought goes. You're not the thought."

"I'm just saying I think you'll run a cult."

"Okay," Jason replied, "okay."

Heavy liquid began to pool at the back of Nate's skull. He lay down beside Emily and closed his eyes, the afterimage of the ceiling lamp burning like an eclipsed sun on the backs of his lids.

"Shit," Emily said to no one in particular.

The music came in waves now, cresting in the middle of the room, sloshing against the walls, and dripping onto the floor before rising once more above their heads.

"Dinner's almost ready, guys."

Seeing Mrs. Holland standing in the doorway, the four of them came to shocked attention. "Why don't you clean this place up, Jason? Your friends don't have to put up with your laundry, do they?"

She wore a white rayon dress belted with snakeskin and sipped a clear liquid from a tumbler held firmly in both hands.

From across the room, her son glared at her.

Smiling vaguely at the other three, she laughed, as if to say, Isn't he a card? and then turned away, leaving the door open behind her.

"Now *that*," Hal said, "is the mama matrix most mysterious."

"Save it," Jason snapped, rising to close the door. With his back to it, he made as if to address them, though as he parted his lips to speak, something on the carpet hauled his attention off, and like a general trying not to evidence distress before his troops he had to master himself anew before speaking "We've got a situation," he announced. "There's less time than I thought. We need to get down there and we need to consume some of that food in an orderly fashion. You understand? It's early going. We can handle it. We just need to act quickly."

Hal stood, tightened the belt of his bathrobe, and shouted, "I'm ready."

"This is a very bad idea," Emily said.

But Jason was already out the door and they were following him down the curving staircase.

THE HOLLANDS' KITCHEN appeared roughly the size of a tennis court. Seeking a base of operations amidst this vastness, they made for a distressed farmhouse table on the far side of the room. When they got high in the car, Nate could let sensation spill over with no interference from the world. Not so now. Circumstance had forced him to his own personal battle stations, where he waged a desperate campaign against the inner flood.

"I'm on this wacky Listserv," Mrs. Holland called out from the range, "with these old friends of mine, and who knows who else for that matter—anyone, I suppose, everyone—the terrorists!" She cackled. "Anyway, someone sent out this crazy thing *professing* to be a Sumerian cookbook. Can you imagine? Julia Child running around Mesopotamia four thousand years ago. Lunatic really. But I thought I'd give one of these cold dishes a try. Lucky for you Whole Foods didn't have yak. I used venison. With this river grass they're all enthused about. None of you are on a silly diet thing. Emily, you're not doing one of those, are you?"

"No," Emily said, her hands clutching the edge of the table. "I'm on a regular-food diet."

"Well, consider it part of your multicultural education," Mrs. Holland said, pouring herself another drink. "You know Jason's father is all in favor of that sort of thing. *Such* a progressive man."

"She's headed for a meltdown," Emily whispered to Nate. "I've seen it happen."

Nate glanced at the other two, trying to gauge their coordination, affect, and overall cogency. He watched, stunned, as Jason, eyeing a fly that had settled on Hal's face, said, "Hold on," and then took a walnut from a bowl on the table and whipped it at Hal's forehead, missing the insect by three or four inches.

"Oh fuck," Hal said, unresponsive to the nut, but smiling broadly now. "We're out of time."

Slowly, Jason's eyes fluttered shut. Their boat's only rudder was coming loose.

Suddenly, Mrs. Holland placed a bowl of some dark, vaguely living substance on the table in front of Nate. He stared up into her blazing eyes and heard her say, "You guys look like you just ran a marathon. Should I turn up the air conditioning?"

Atop the mush in his bowl, Nate saw a mucus beginning to form, suggesting the larval stage of some dreaded prehistoric creature. What rough beast, he wondered, had come round at last, unborn since these ingredients had last mingled in some glade of the ancient world?

"Keep it together over there!" Jason whispered harshly, bringing Nate into sudden awareness that only an inch separated his face from the gestation unfolding before him. He sat quickly upright, trying not to cry with fear.

"You all go ahead and start," Mrs. Holland said, miles away again. "I have to get this grain paste sorted out."

Emily's neck stiffened. "Something," she said, "something has to be done."

Nodding vigorously, Hal reached under his robe into his trouser pocket and somehow managed to make his cell phone ring, a call that he promptly answered.

"Oh my *god*," he said, loud out of all proportion. "You're *kidding*? Our family kitten? Out there on the *highway*? Right now? Oh, Mom. What can I do? You want me to come right *now*?"

He glanced at Jason, who turned quickly to his approaching mother and, looking somewhere over her shoulder, said, "Gee. I guess, well, so Hal—it looks like he's got this . . . situation. I mean, this pet. This family pet cat. It looks as if it needs help."

Forgetting the premise of the ruse, Hal placed his phone down on the table.

For a moment the only sound was the crackle of insects being burned to death by the caged blue light on the porch.

"And what about your dinner, *mister*?" Mrs. Holland said.

At that moment, Nate realized he had been drafted into a kind of psychic air traffic control, minus training or any chance of success. Mrs. Holland's final, bitter word had dropped from beneath the clouds like an undetected passenger jet sailing straight for the terminal.

"Come on, Mom. This stuff looks like shit."

Her groggy eyes narrowed.

"Is that so? I'm glad you've learned to be so honest, Jason. It's a great quality in a man. I suppose you've told your friends that you've failed too many classes to graduate. Have you told them that?"

"Fuck you," he said, rising from the table. "Come on, guys, we're leaving."

He crossed the room and walked out the back door, the screen slapping behind him. Sheepishly, Emily followed.

"You know, Mrs. Holland," Hal began, spotting a box of matches by the salt and pepper and finally lighting the cigarette he'd been holding between his fingers all evening, "I appreciated the Sumerian angle. It's always interesting to consider the origin of things. Particularly in these times. That sounds like a really wonderful Listserv you have there." He inhaled, blew the smoke up toward the ceiling, and then, pushing his chair back, exited in the opposite direction from the others, back into the front hall.

Alone with her now, Nate watched as the viscosity in the air, which he had prayed was just a passing warp of his eye, began to leak openly into the world, the ceiling above Mrs. Holland becoming a slick, throbbing ooze, the lights in the room starting to pulse, bleeding along the edges of her rigid mother body, and then within her as well, her whole form glowing a dim orangey-red, the ember of some slowly dying need.

"I'm sorry," he said, standing up from the table. "I'm really sorry."

He hurried across the yard trying to catch up with the others, relieved by the lack of brightness on this darkened stage of willows weeping branches into pools of lamplight, the air about him soft and damp. He could hear Jason up ahead, and then he saw them as he rounded the turn and came up alongside them, no one taking any notice. They walked for what seemed a long while down Chandler Drive and onto the college campus. Making their way into the woods, they followed the path to the round stone terrace and stepping onto it saw the expanse of the lake stretched out before them, black and smooth under a dome of stars.

At the railing of the terrace the four of them stood, passengers on the prow of a stilled ship.

Jason slipped his sneakers and shirt off and walked down the steps, wading into the water up to his chest. He turned to the three of them, reached his arms into the air and lay back, falling into the bed of water, his head and body disappearing beneath the dark surface long enough for the vibe to reach uneasily toward after-school specials in which wasted kids drowned and the town held a candlelight vigil, their night on the verge of becoming one of those earnest, tragic affairs covered by local news, involving ribbons and flowers, yearbook snapshots, hope snuffed, etcetera, actual life and grief cheated and frozen by the arrogance of sentiment, and then his head and shoulders appeared again a few feet farther out and Emily laughed.

Stepping out of her sandals, she climbed down to join him.

"This," Jason said, floating on his back, "*this* is the matrix most mysterious. And you know what? It doesn't give a damn about us. It could care less if we even existed."

He began a slow backstroke away from the shore.

Nate remained at the railing, the visible world trailing out behind itself and stretching forward, the glow at the tip of Hal's cigarette and Emily's bobbing head becoming the blurred average of the still-discernible past and the imminent future, the sky likewise a series of white lines sketching themselves back and forth across hundreds of bright centers. Making him wonder if a feeling could have such a pattern: want crossing over fear crossing back over longing crossing menace, the bright center of it all being the awful urge he'd felt standing before the man in the front hallway of the mansion just a few hours ago, wishing the man would just put him out of his misery and touch him.

How did people bear it? Needing to be saved so appallingly.

"The professor's right," Emily shouted. "Kill the ego! Let the world in!"

"Come on," Jason called, "swim!"

Shedding his bathrobe and draping it on the rail, Hal leaned down to remove his shoes and trousers. His bare back was pale and narrow. A boy's body, Nate thought, gangly, uncertain, a protector of nothing.

"You coming?" Hal said.

Nate stripped to his briefs and from the bottom step made a shallow dive, his thin form slipping into the water, the day, the drug, all of it, washed for an instant from his mind by the cold rush, gills opening in his chest as he let it all go. Rising again to the surface, his head was encompassed once more by the warm night air as he turned onto his back, a blazing zigzag of starlight pouring into his eyes.

They swam a few feet apart out toward the formal garden, Jason reaching the white balustrade first and lifting himself up to sit on its wide top. Behind him, on a steeply raked hillside, stood the fancifully clipped trees and hedges, topiary in the shapes of cones and boxes, a few cypress intermixed, all of it seen as much from memory as through the layers of shadow covering it now. He helped each of them up in turn and they crossed the path onto the lawn. On a terraced stretch of grass halfway up the rise, they sat, still dripping, beneath the large pyramid of an evergreen, looking back across the lake to the campus and beyond it to the lights of Finden.

"It keeps coming," Emily said, resting her head on the ground.

"Let it come," Jason replied. "Just let it come."

Many hours later, after the drug had at last worn off and he'd snuck silently back into his house, Nate undressed in his room and put on an old pair of boxers before brushing his teeth. In the mirror over the sink, he looked scrawny, his arms thin like Hal's, barely any muscle on his chest and hollows in his shoulders above the collarbone. Nothing, he thought, like the body of the man he'd met that day. None of his thick presence. Lying in bed with the lights off, Nate pictured the man upstairs in that huge house of his, taking off his tie, his pinstripe pants and pressed white shirt, a perfect strength exuded into the perfect dark behind Nate's eyes, squeezed shut by this waking dream, as he moved his fist up and down on himself, trying hard to fill over the dry silence of the house with the flood of that other, imagined place, shorn of everything but a pleasure so keen it might just have the power to obliterate him. Then, for two or three ecstatic seconds, the obliteration came, its flood receding too quickly, leaving behind the wrecked old world of things as they actually were.

He lay still now. Along the bottom edge of the shade, he could see the faint, bluish tinge of the streetlight. A pile of clothing was dimly visible on the chair in the corner, the spine of a textbook sticking out over the edge of his desk. He closed his eyes again but the fantasy was gone and he was wide awake.

Chapter 9

A quarter past nine, the clock on the mantel read. Too early for bed, if Charlotte didn't want to wake in the dead of night. She took a seat by the open window in the living room, where warm evening air floated across the sill onto her lap and onto the heads of the dogs lying at her feet. She'd run on too long this afternoon with young Nate, carried away on the Works Progress Administration, but she hadn't been able to help herself.

He had caught her unawares that first day he'd appeared and it had been all she could do to muster an hour's lesson. As he'd scribbled the occasional note, a familiar pall of uncomprehending boredom had settled over his face like custard. How many times had she seen the like while pacing her classroom, Lincoln's doleful eyes gazing over the fruit of his more perfect union? Over the years, most students had been baffled by her importuning, her insistence that they see the conditions of their own lives in historical terms. Amidst the general, bovine indifference there had always been a few willing to entertain the notion that the world might consist of more than their uses for it. She hadn't pegged Nate as one at first.

But now she saw things differently. He attended to her words as if it weren't only the content that mattered. Toward the end of her years at the school, even her better students had become mere harvesters of fact, unwilling to be transformed by what they might learn. They were closed to that higher ambiguity that came only from observing at close range a person compelled by knowledge, someone who might show by example how one's first self, illiberally imposed, could be given up in favor of the chosen course. But not this young man. It wasn't that his few questions had been all that penetrating, and indeed his being impressed by the intruder's mansion had struck her nearly dumb. But he considered her arguments; he followed the rhythm of her words.

A generosity of attention. That was the heart of it.

You expect us to believe that? Wilkie said, rising to press his nose to the screen, ears perked up like the wings of a bat. *Come on now, be honest with yourself.*

The boy's skin, pale like butter; his large brown eyes; the way his hair fell in a wave over his forehead. She'd seen the resemblance early on, but pushed the thought aside. But sitting across from him at the Chinese the other week it made no sense to deny how like a younger Eric he looked.

Oh, here we go, Sam said.

How could she ever think, ever get things clear in her head with the two of them nattering like this?

That afternoon, tutoring Nate, just as an idea was about to take form and escape the eddies of modification and caveat, some tiny fact—ash on the carpet, a strand of ticking loose on the sofa's arm—had pulsed up bright in front of her, arresting all her forward motion, and she'd floated there, lost, catching the dark sparkle of Sam's or Wilkie's eyes, who called out to her, *There is no place other than this: welcome,* leaving her terrified but determined to resist, to find the current again before it ceased, and so haul from her stalled mind a coherent thought.

But even now as she tried to concentrate, to keep her mind here in the present, memory, like a troubled friend whispering through the screen, brought the image of her old apartment on West Eleventh Street, those two little ground-floor rooms with the paved square of garden at the back, and the two of them bringing in the firewood Eric had found somewhere the day he moved in with her, his father's old car parked in the rain, the two of them running logs down the steps and into the house, piling them on a blue tarpaulin spread on the living-room floor, the wood dust and strands of bark matted to their coats.

Most of Charlotte's college friends had met their husbands before graduation or secured them soon after. Boys from Amherst and Williams arriving four or five to a car for the dances at Smith, long evenings of the smallest talk imaginable, the young gentlemen speaking like bad pantomimes of their fathers, all summer holidays and the names of banks, little lords of the financial manor. She'd watched women she'd heard speak eloquently in class of Shakespeare or Rome nod their heads and smile, listening patiently to one blandishment after the next, while the boys glanced about to see what else was available, and it made her feel ashamed for her classmates and for herself. It may have been that the boys didn't approach her because she didn't catch their eye, being a bit too tall, neither blond nor pretty in a conventional way, but the defiant expression she wore couldn't have encouraged them either. If one did strike up conversation, she thought it best to compensate for her classmates' hiding of their education; she usually started in on an analysis of whatever she was reading that week. A battlement her pride had been, high and safe.

As a single woman out in the world, it had only seemed the more necessary. At her seat at work behind the reference desk of the New York Public Library, middle-aged men would wink at her. On the subway they'd try worse.

"A bit lonesome, isn't it?" she remembered her mother asking at the table at Thanksgiving the fall she started graduate school at Columbia. "All those hours cooped up studying?"

"As opposed to the ones you spend cooped up in this house?" she replied, which brought silence and a withering stare.

Her father understood; he'd encouraged her from the beginning.

"I'm just being practical," her mother suggested, defending her worries for Charlotte's future. Henry, five years younger, had already graduated from law school, started with a firm, and, to perfect the narrative, married Betsy, whom he'd met one summer on a trip to the Cape. The wedding had been given by Betsy's parents in Hyannis, all white tents and high Episcopal good form, from the Bloody Marys to the starched collars to the understated, almost humble self-satisfaction of the father's toast and the look in Charlotte's mother's eye as Henry took his bride by the arm and led her onto the parquet for the first dance. Or the last dance, as Charlotte thought of it. After all the cotillions and proms and coming-out balls, the dance that fixed you in place. For Henry, it was a dress-up lark dreamed by women into existence for which he was happy to play his role for the day, because what would it ever cost him, and it made his mother so happy (decades later, imitations of the clothes they'd worn on weekends like that would show up in all those catalogues, Ralph Lauren and the others, the smugness of that faded time resurrected as commercial fantasy). At the reception, Charlotte had been seated next to the bride's brother, a Cadillac dealer who'd clearly never read *Appointment in Samarra*. Henry, to his credit, didn't join in the cloying asides about her being next.

She'd spent three years studying: taking seminars, attending extra lectures, working in the library, and reading in the evenings. Her friends were other people in the history department along with the two or three women from college who hadn't moved out of the city. In school, being single didn't register the way it did at home with her parents. Time had purpose without a companion. Still, the solitude got to her now and again. Despite her best effort, she couldn't rid herself of the tug of "Saturday Night" and the need to have something to do. On the weeks she failed to plan ahead and found herself alone, the doubt which concentration otherwise kept at bay entered her, and she heard her mother's voice. The words in the books and journals spread on her kitchen table seemed lifeless then, dead as the time they described. But the feeling always passed; a paper would demand more reading, more research; the vistas would open up again inside her, lending the world that sense of integration, as she discerned more and more of the structure of the present in the society and politics of Europe three centuries before, as though she were glimpsing the hidden order of things. Try explaining that over gin and tonics at the beach club to one of the sons of her mother's friends. Why no, Chuck, I don't get to play much squash. You see, I'm a secular mystic, transported in private hours by the grandeur of human knowledge. You don't say? Well, actually, I do.

Of the men she met in the city, most were married or seemed put off by her lack of deference.

It was at a winter party, given by one of her professors at Columbia, that she met Eric. She knew most of the people there, other graduate students, junior professors she'd taken classes with or heard speak. She noticed him first with his back to the room, examining the bookshelf, his head craned to read the spines. When he turned, he accidentally met Charlotte's gaze and smiled, shyly, before looking into his drink. Something about the curly brown hair that hung over his brow and the creamy skin and the wide, slightly unshaven jaw had caused her to stare. That afternoon, sitting at her desk at the back of her apartment as the light faded in the courtyard, she'd finished writing what she considered her best work yet, a paper on Milton's tenure in Cromwell's government, the result of a year's research. She remained full of the satisfaction of being done, a pleasure so long and scrupulously deferred. Eric looked a bit younger than she was, in his mid-twenties perhaps. Keeping an eye out, she spotted him a few minutes later on the far side of the room and went over to introduce herself. It was the kind of egalitarian gesture she believed in and for once she'd drunk enough to bring it off.

They spoke for two hours that evening, sitting on the bench in the bay window, the Hudson visible through the bare trees. After an awkward few moments, he had started in, dispensing with the pleasantries of asking who she was or where she fit in the party, right away wanting to know what she'd read recently, "the best things," he said, "the stuff that could change you," and he didn't want to hear only about history but about novels, journalism, poetry. And then through and past that, to her thoughts, assuming without question that her ideas possessed the same integrity and significance of any of the books that helped shape them. His need to hear all this seemed almost animal-like, as though by elaborating her thoughts she were feeding him. At first, she spoke haltingly. She was used to the prescribed discussions of seminars; she'd never been asked to offer such comprehensive views. Answering his questions, she felt ideas, long inchoate, come into focus. The plainness of early Protestant worship explained something about why she'd been transfixed in Amsterdam the summer before by Vermeer's painting of an everyday exterior—the brick fronts of the merchant's house, the gray cloud, the women doing their daily work. And this connected in ways she could only guess at to idealism in politics, the insistence on equality, the plainness of it, and thus too, somehow, to the power of the spectacle of troops in Little Rock escorting a black girl to the ordinary activity of school. She understood then, and even more later, that others, the beautiful perhaps, would laugh if she were to confess it, but sitting fully clothed on that window seat, never having touched a hair on Eric's body, she felt more sexually alive than ever in her life. She would have walked into a bedroom of that apartment, closed the door on the party, and made love to him at once if he'd asked.

As it happened, they made love on her couch the next night after dinner, the heat of his chest on hers and the smell of his flesh a blessing she'd thought she might never receive. Before they even climbed in the bath together, before he even raised himself from her and stood, naked and wet, looking down at her in surprise, she already feared the power of her wanting. She was twenty-nine and a fierce social independent, a position that had cost her a sense of future safety. They'd said nothing about anything between them, how could they? And yet even that first night, every time he touched her, there in the soapy water, lathering her hair, cupping her breast in his hand, it felt to her like a promise.

Had God foreseen the subtlety of your modern devils, Sam began, raising his blunt face from the carpet, *he might have added a Commandment: Thou Shalt not Pity thy Self. In the case of Sorrow for a Dead Friend: Suppose, I were Dead; would I have my Friend mourn for me, with an Excessive, Oppressive, Destructive Sorrow? No, sure. Why then let my Sorrow for my Friend be moderated. You dwell in Memory like some Perversity of the Flesh. A sin against the gift of Creation it is to harp so on the dead while the living still suffer.*

She wouldn't be chastised like this. Not in her own house. Not by Sam. Lying there with his fine pale coat and superior manner. It was no great mystery who he had come to fancy himself as. All that pure breeding and King James diction. As though each day she walked Cotton Mather over the golf course on a leash. Did he really expect her to believe that was the case?

Across the room, the television stood mute, its glass a dull, greeny gray. The reception had grown steadily worse over the years, though she'd changed nothing, until finally the static had grown so thick it was hardly worth it, Jim Lehrer's voice muffled beneath the hiss. She'd preferred MacNeil, in any case.

In the kitchen, the refrigerator shuddered off and the quiet of the house was once again absolute.

Eric's place had been much like hers, a studio apartment over by the water on Bethune Street. A mess of books and papers, barely any shelves to put them on, a small wooden table, one chair. The previous fall, he'd enrolled to study philosophy at the New School and had been overwhelmed by the amount of work. He was late wherever they went, unkempt, often tired-looking. Charlotte loved him for it and even more for their hours of conversation and for his letting her kiss him whenever she felt the urge, Eric being happy to let her lead the way, telling him when they would study and when they would stop, when they would sleep and eat. Those first few months he'd get up early and go to his apartment a few hours each morning to get ready for his seminars, he said, and she'd usually find him back at her place napping when she returned in the late afternoon. She'd sometimes sit watching him as he slept, his legs curled up toward his chest, his mouth slightly open against the pillow. Her first guess at his age had been right. He was only twenty-five. The youngest of seven. His mother's choice for the priesthood. Yet the only one of his siblings who hadn't ended up living within a quick drive of the house back in the working-class section of Philadelphia where he'd grown up. Charlotte had been surrounded most of her life by people who'd sauntered to their place in the world, coming to it as if by right. This hadn't been the case for her because she hadn't chosen the course offered. Watching Eric sleep like that, an entire evening in the apartment together still ahead of them, she felt delivered not just from the usual loneliness—so well hidden by the manner she kept up with family and colleagues—but from the years of it she'd already been through, the tiring work of living on one's own, of being such an odd bird, a single woman of her age back then, 1962, getting a PhD, no marriage in the offing. An awkward fit in the world. It was as if Eric gave her those years back by accompanying her now.

He made her young. He let her be silly. She'd never been able to afford silliness. Like fooling around in Henry's apartment, where she'd taken Eric for dinner, fooling around in the bathroom after dessert, their drinks perched on the sink. Stuffy Henry and stuffy Betsy in their appropriate little apartment on the Upper East Side, the settee from the back hall in Rye primped up in the living room, carpets their mother had unearthed from the attic covering the floor, the wedding silver polished to the nines, and the two of them already on the lookout for a house, the closer to Mommy and Daddy the better. Charlotte could barely keep herself from laughing when they sat down again, so punch-drunk and pleased she was.

When Eric's stipend ran down he asked if he could move in. She'd been taken aback at first, that it should happen so quickly, so informally, but then it seemed of a piece with how it had all begun. He'd practically been living with her in any case. They slept together most nights and his clothing had started to accumulate in her drawers. It might have bothered other women, women like Betsy who would have wanted to clarify the issue of his intentions. But Charlotte had given up so much of that racket—the hunt for the possession of the man—

and instead marveled at how effortlessly Eric had slipped into her heart, as if he hadn't even noticed the rigidity she feared had been the cost of exempting herself from all that.

She'd never been able to explain that to anyone afterward. How thankful she'd been to him for loving her just as he found her. There were too many steps to it, too much to account for. And by then they'd assembled their views, Henry and her mother: that she'd been taken in by a bad character. If there had been feeling there, well my goodness it had been misplaced. For heaven's sake. Would you have us think otherwise? That you could still love and admire such a person? None of which, of course, ever had to be stated aloud, their taut lips and averted eyes all too eloquent.

"But I lived with him," she wanted to say. "Shouldn't you ask first what it was like? He loved me. I felt that to be so. He hated having to put me through it."

In these basic facts, she had never lost her faith. Because while it was true, looking back, that he may have been under the influence around the time they met—those first few months when he'd go back to his apartment during the day—and so perhaps true also that his lack of money stemmed from that, once he moved in, he stopped. He had to have stopped, because it was summer, neither of them were in classes and they spent all their waking hours together. She would have known. And those were the best months they had together. The happiest of her life. Waking midmorning, the drowsy, shut-eyed kissing and fondling, his head in her hands between her legs. Morning after wonderful morning like that. Caught up in him. And then wandering out to a coffee shop where they'd eat and read and talk. And then films, what seemed like every night, though it couldn't have been, and cooking soup or scrambled eggs and bacon on the electric stove and eating wherever they could clear a seat amidst the cram of his papers and hers.

He'd taken a seminar in the spring with a student of Karl Jaspers and that summer was working his way through Heidegger. "How's your serious young man?" Henry would ask when they spoke, and of course there was some of that to Eric, the long discussions about authenticity and being, a cascade of words propelled by the need to believe there existed some world, however abstruse, other than mere things and our accommodation to them. But was that so laughable? Not to Charlotte. She and Henry had grown up in the most unexacting faith imaginable, a drawling, self-satisfied Episcopalianism marked by the minister's wife in her mink coat and pleasant enough hymns at Christmas. They would no more have discussed their religion at the dinner table than fry filet mignon. Eric had been raised strict Catholic. When he left the Church, his mother called him apostate and refused to speak to him for a year. There may have been a pose now and again as he tried on the philosophy he was studying, a slight callowness to the high-handed way he dismissed books or people who hadn't grasped the urgency of existential thought, but at the base of it lay an honest hunger. And a sadness.

Oh, come on sister, Wilkie said. *Paint your picture if you want to, but a dope fiend is a dope fiend, and I should know. Your white boy might have been able to keep it under wraps longer than your uptown Negro because he didn't have to score on the street. But the disease is the disease. There comes a day you're going to get desperate, and it's going to get ugly. A woman, if you've still got one by then, she's just another route to a score.*

It had taken awhile, but recently Charlotte had come to recognize Wilkie's pretension as well. That oracular tone of his, the voice of Malcolm X streaming from his black head.

It hadn't been as Henry and her mother imagined. Eric never stole anything. He never put her in harm's way. They didn't stop loving each other. The whole thing was so far outside her experience, at first she didn't know what to do. She asked him if he would please stop, and he said that he'd try. Which he did for a time, though it might have only been weeks. She remembered coming back from the library one late afternoon and finding him asleep on the couch, his sleeve rolled up, a dot of red where he'd punctured the skin. With a cotton ball dipped in rubbing alcohol she daubed at the pinprick and covered it with a Band-Aid, then tidied the house and sat at her desk to type up her reading notes, because what else was she supposed to do, still wanting him as she did? When he woke, he rolled down his sleeve without saying anything, walked around behind her as she worked, and hugged her back to his chest. She heated up fish cakes and a can of baked beans, just as her mother used to on Fridays when the cook was off, and they sat at the little table by the back window and she cried a bit, but he told her it was only to help him get through the next while, the pressure of the work.

"You're the only one I don't feel lonely around," he said, holding her hand.

"Can't that be enough?"

"It will be."

She knew nothing about the course of such things. Why should she? When he asked for money, she gave him what she could. He's got the flu, she said to her mother in the kitchen at Christmas back in Rye, where at the dining-room table beside Henry and Betsy and her cousins it was suddenly obvious how sickly he appeared—her mother, who ever since Charlotte had met Eric had been torn between her desire for a wedding and her wish that Eric had come from a slightly better family, or at least a Protestant one. And of course the age difference ran in the wrong direction. She had married Charlotte's father at twenty-one in the church on Copley Square and following her own mother's example treated her husband as a kind of necessary appendage to the larger body of her household, the grand purpose of which was the flawless production of her children. A purpose Charlotte had years ago begun to thwart, failing to hide her disdain for that whole rigid, sequestered, matriarchal prerogative. If there were anyone in the family she could have confided in about Eric, it would have been her father, who'd admired the way she'd gone off on her own, but still it would have meant the end of things, his comforting her but still intervening to protect his daughter.

In January, Eric stopped going to his classes, stopped reading much at all, and only left the house toward dusk, coming back an hour or so later to spend a little while in the bathroom before napping. In bed, she'd hold him close, her hands reaching up to pat his damp hair. Usually by then, at midnight or one, he returned to a kind of equilibrium, and with the lights out and the building quiet, they talked as they had at the beginning, Charlotte recounting a novel she'd read or thinking aloud about the line of argument in whatever paper she was writing at the time, Eric asking her questions and listening, assuring her that, yes, he wanted to know. She remembered now the night she got up her courage to ask him what it was like to have that liquid in his veins. He said it felt like being able to live inside a memory of a childhood he was certain he'd never had, as if all the world around you had become the setting of a rich, nostalgic dream, some invincible summer. She could tell he was partly in love with the romance of it, the affective correlative it gave to the intellectual conviction about our lost experience of being, as if he were the living experiment for the things he studied and would one day turn it off and write it all down. Naïve, no doubt. But being with him made Charlotte realize how on her own she'd grown grimly practical, a student of what was required for praise and advancement. The pleasure he gave made her forget all that. Yes, he was deluding himself, mistaking a simple thing like taking drugs for the complexity of figuring out how to live, but the very youthfulness of the error opened something in her, a nostalgia of her own for romances she'd never had.

"He didn't use me, Wilkie," she said. "You're wrong about that. I did what I thought was best."

At the beginning of spring, Eric told her he'd been to a doctor and was tapering off. This was why he felt so sick, he said. Some days he barely left the bed. She ran baths and washed him just as he had washed her those first weeks after they made love. It was on a Friday afternoon that whatever supply he'd managed to build up ran out. To go off too quickly was dangerous, he said.

She hesitated at first. They could stay together there in the apartment and see it through, call the doctor if necessary. But he looked awful, his skin green, his eyes sunken. It was just a short walk through Washington Square Park to a building down on MacDougal Street. Four flights up past the old Italian ladies chatting on the landings. Seven or eight kids, in their twenties most of them, crowded into a little apartment, the shades pulled over open windows, everyone smoking, shouts from the street and the sound of motor engines bouncing off the building opposite into the dank, carpetless living room. The boys wore wing tips like her father's. Wing tips and turtlenecks, the girls in corduroy pants and oversize sweaters. They stared at her as she imagined they would at their mothers. Someone was writing up a flyer. There were meetings she should attend. "In the kitchen," someone told her, guessing her purpose for being there. A man with a lazy eye, who spoke with a slight Canadian accent, was the one she gave the money to and received in return a small envelope. Walking back up lower Fifth Avenue, Charlotte noticed the couples hand in hand, emerging from the brightly lit lobbies of the fancy buildings, headed out to dinner, the

Henrys and Betsys, who when they glanced at her saw one of their own, her anxious mind calculating the efficacy of her disguise, wondering if they could ever guess her errand.

To her surprise, Eric had made the bed while she was gone, and tidied the kitchen as well. He'd cleared his books off the table and stacked them by the door.

"You'll take less?" she asked, and he nodded.

Despite the sickness, he looked younger than when she'd met him, his features somehow more open, no longer organized by inquisitive zeal. Again, she offered to phone the doctor. He had never been to one, of course, so there wouldn't have been a number to call. Instead, she put the envelope down on the counter and went into the front room. One thing she couldn't do was watch him at it. Still in her coat, she sat by the window, looking through the bars of the windows at the passersby.

Once the summer came, she thought, they would go up to Massachusetts and use the Finden house for a few weeks when her parents weren't there. They'd take the Jeep to the lake and on the way back buy corn and fruit at the farm stand. Come fall, Eric would get back to his classes, she would finish her thesis. They might get married in a year. She would meet his brothers and sisters. His parents would come around, eventually.

The Day was a public Thanksgiving for the Mercies of Heaven in the Year that is past, Sam intoned. *I laid aside the subject I intended and in the Morning I composed a sermon on the line in 1 Samuel. She wept, and she did not eat. A sermon on the Thanks offering, prosecuting that Observation, that a sense of Affliction was oftentimes a Hindrance to the work of Thanksgiving, but that it ought not to be so. My son died about Noon. My sermon in the Afternoon proved very acceptable, and reasonable, and serviceable.*

Why you? Charlotte thought. Of all I've read and forgotten, why a pompous old preacher? Why not Whitman's singing or blind Milton to keep an aging isolate company?

He rubbed his ear to her foot to relieve an itch. Sensing something was being given out that he was not a part of, Wilkie's head came down off the sill and he pressed his snout into Charlotte's lap.

They followed her into the front bedroom, settling on their blankets as she took off her cardigan and began to undress. It had been so much harder living here, all those years ago, at the beginning. Such tense awareness of being alone in the house, the day's routines acts that she observed herself completing: her dress returned to its hanger, her shoes put back in their sleeve pockets hanging inside the closet door, the watch on the bedside table, cold cream on her face, the bedroom door shut. To forget a bit, the past and herself, that's all she'd wanted then. To move unsurveilled through time's ceaseless unfolding. The critical eye closed, the narrative intelligence laid to rest. Repetition's welcome victory over event. Up at the sound of the bedside alarm, the school day a prevention of other thoughts, along with the work she carried home. And when, inevitably, retrospect intervened nonetheless, she knew, then as now, that others would consider her precious or sad or both, prey to a romanticism gone morbid. So her mother had thought until she died. So Henry still imagined. And who was she to catalogue the varieties in which love and comfort came in order to tell them they were wrong? She could only know what she had felt, say, on the afternoon during that long summer of theirs when they'd stood together in the Metropolitan Museum looking at a small picture by Daubigny, a painting of a village along a river's edge at dusk seen from across the water, light and peacefulness so miraculously captured it produced in her elation. Before she uttered a word of praise, Eric took her hand and said that from whatever he read or studied, all he wanted was the power to describe how a human being could arrive at the lucid sympathy this man must have felt for what he saw. A lucid sympathy. Those were his words. As if he'd reached into her, discerned an emotional thought still unformed, and allowed it definite shape. Difficult not to think you could live a lifetime with another person and never be as richly acknowledged. To then lie with this man in the grass of the park, make love to him before dinner, to keep discussing painting after the food was cold and the time to catch a film had passed. What did they know of that?

Best she move on after that sort of thing. That's what the landlord had told Henry when Charlotte asked him to phone and find out why the man hadn't sent her a renewal on her lease or returned her calls. There had been the ambulance, after all, and the neighbors standing in the hall watching.

Half an hour, it had been, that she'd remained sitting there by the front window. She heard the bathroom door close and after a few minutes open once more, then Eric's steps to the couch. Such a small apartment it was, just the two rooms. There couldn't have been more than fifteen or twenty feet between them. At first glance, he just looked paler than usual, his body in an odd position, back arched, one arm reaching out to the side, his chin turned down to his chest. At the feel of his hand, she shook him, lightly at first, insisting he open his eyes. Annihilating minutes spent waiting for the medics to arrive, clutching his head in her lap. She had never spoken to his parents. They had been living in sin, after all. His father sounded as if he were choking and had to suck hard for breath. From upstairs, Mrs. Ruskemeyer brought a plate of cucumber sandwiches, white bread with the crusts removed, in perfect English style. Charlotte offered one to the policeman, who smelled it before returning it to the plate.

"You the wife?" he asked.

"No."

At the sink in her nightgown, Charlotte stood before her mirror now and applied the thick Nivea cream to the tissue-soft wrinkles beneath her eyes, struck with familiar wonder at how deeply grooved in a mind one cut of time could become. No school tomorrow to fill the day, as it had filled her life. And so the window opened, the bars came off, the passersby began to drift into the room where she still sat with Eric as he died, some of them quiet like generations past, others hot with the temper of dogs' eyes. The membrane porous, the order shuffled. How arrogant, how wrong, for man to believe his animal senses caught the spectrum whole. An adventure time was, if you calmed yourself to its receipt.

Part Two

Chapter 10

On the last morning of leave from her job at Atlantic Securities, Evelyn Jones sat looking out across Lincoln Avenue from the window of her mother's apartment and saw cars beginning to fill the spaces alongside the Second Baptist Church. A gray Cadillac, rented for the occasion, came to a halt at the curb and Evelyn's aunt Verna stepped onto the sidewalk, her gloved hand floating up to make sure of her hat and veil. In her early sixties, she still had a slender, elegant figure, defiantly elegant in fact, a body she was supremely aware of and which she deployed in the world as a kind of standing rebuke to all those who had let themselves go. With her flat chest, almost concave stomach, and rounded upper back, she had the torso of a wasp, curved and rigid.

"Your sister's here," Evelyn said, turning back into the dimness of the apartment. Her mother sat on the couch in the old, black taffeta dress that she had worn on formal occasions as long as Evelyn could remember, its slight V-neck revealing the wrinkled flesh above her breasts. Her makeup had done an adequate job of concealing the bags under her eyes.

"You plan on being late to your son's funeral?" Evelyn asked.

Her mother's eyes scrunched closed and her head tilted up toward the ceiling. "You have no mercy," she said.

Evelyn crossed to the closet and gathered their coats.

"Are we going or not?"

As they walked up the avenue, her mother took Evelyn's arm and held it all the way to the doors of the church and then inside, down the aisle to the front pew, where Aunt Verna awaited them. The minister stepped around from the side of the casket to guide them to their place. When everyone had taken their seats again, he moved in front of the altar and welcomed everyone to the service.

As the slow, heavy rhythm of his opening prayer settled over them, Evelyn gazed at the enlarged photograph of her brother propped on the easel beside the shiny white coffin in a garland of iris and lily of the valley: Carson in his red cape and mortarboard set against the standard sky-blue background of the high-school graduation portrait, his slender face nearly lost amidst the utter conventionality of the image, the generic promise of a bright future for the picture's captive. It was all Evelyn had been able to find in the shambles of her mother's place. Ten years old at the least. She regretted now that she had bothered. It seemed dishonest, this picture. Her brother hadn't died in some media-friendly accident—a bus of young people headed to a sporting event or a man trying to save a neighbor in a flood. He'd been shot in the middle of the afternoon in an apartment entryway and left to die.

The minister, who had known Carson but slightly, offered a brief eulogy employing the biographical facts with which Evelyn had furnished him. And then, as arranged, it was Aunt Verna who rose to speak.

"My nephew Carson Jones is dead," she began, her hands held together at her chest, as though she were lecturing to a group of Sunday-school children. "Some wretched sinner killed him. People always say a part of you dies along with a loved one. They are wrong about that. Part of you doesn't die. That would be easy. Remove the limb and go on your way. But that isn't how love is. When a person you love dies they haunt you—no offense to the rites of burial and I'm sure Carson's soul is up there with the angels—but the fact is their death haunts you, the waste and idiocy of it, the loving soul of that boy, the love he bore his family . . . that love surely does haunt you. As well it should if you're going to walk the streets of this world with your God-given eyes open. I know I'm supposed to be up here saying something uplifting, but let's not deceive ourselves. The world is a hungry place and it swallowed my nephew without a thought. The fact is, he was shot for money. For paper bills. That's what he died for. It's not what lived in the better parts of his soul, but it's what killed him. I'm sorry to say all this, I really am, because Carson was a beautiful young man and his heart was in the right place most of the time, but for those of us who are planning to go on, and I'll tell you ladies and gentlemen, *I am one of them*, we can't pretend and I don't think the Lord would want us to.

"The other thing I guess people always say is that a person is up in Heaven and that they're in a better place now, and I suppose that much I agree with. Carson is in heaven, and it's surely better than what we have down here. God bless his mother and his sister and may he rest in peace." Unclasping her hands, she stepped off the stage and Evelyn lifted her mother's bent form high enough to let her aunt pass back along the row to her seat.

The minister, taken aback by the tone and brevity of the family remarks, assumed his place again before the coffin and, wearing his best somber expression, led the congregation in a subdued rendition of "All to Jesus I Surrender."

THE FOLLOWING DAY, Evelyn returned to work. She had been employed at Atlantic Securities for eight years and after three promotions was now chief settlements administrator with her own office, albeit without a window. Her job, part of the firm's back-office operation, was to execute the delivery and receipt of assets. In order to take effect, each order that a trader shouted into a trading pit or placed with a dealer had eventually to move through the more orderly process of settlement—the actual transfer of money and instruments from one institution to another. This took place anywhere from hours to months after the initial promises had been made. Evelyn didn't make the decisions that led to the transfers, and she bore no responsibility for the loss or gain they represented, but without her approval no money changed hands.

Her first morning back, she concentrated as best she could on her screen, drawing her eyes over the initials of counterparties and clearinghouses, tapping in payment codes, her hands moving over the keypad with unthinking speed, toggling in and out of the software's fifty-odd forms. She found that her mind was able to float as she went, some well-grooved path in her brain slipping into the circle of automation. And she was thankful for that repetition; it was a kind of blessing, the way it allowed her to forget for spells of a few moments at a time.

As she was drawing up her final tallies for the day, her assistant, Cressida, knocked on her open door. She was a rather shy, single black woman, whom Evelyn had recruited from Boston College through the company's minority-outreach program. Evelyn had told her any number of times there was no need to announce herself, that she should just come in and say straight up what she needed, but Cressida had persisted in her apologetics. Having known such hesitancy in herself back when she first started out, Evelyn recognized it as the first, useless defense against criticism, one that excited precisely what it sought to deflect. There were businesses where deference would get her somewhere. Banking wasn't one of them. She wished she had it in her to drum the message home again, to set the girl straight once and for all, but she lacked the will this evening.

"It's about the house accounts," she said.

"You're going to have to remind me, darling. Come on now, sit down."

"From the Hong Kong office," she said, perching on the chair opposite Evelyn. "The unresolved trades. I'm not sure how you want me to enter them in the log." She looked at the paper in her hand as if ashamed of her admission.

At the college job fair, sitting across the folding table from her in the gymnasium, Cressida had worked so hard to strike a confident note, delivering her rehearsed lines about experience and interest like an actress unsure of her character's motivation. As a recruiter, Evelyn knew she was supposed to be sorting for focus and drive, weeding out the young men and women who seemed unsure of themselves, selecting instead those model minority students who not only grasped the rules of the presentational game, suggesting their ability to pick up the rules of games to come, but also seemed to embrace them, taking a kind of hushed, understated pleasure in the well-groomed display of their credentials; those were the ones whose obedience you could count on, their fear of scarcity already marshaled into conservative ambition.

Cressida had shown none of this, arriving in an ill-fitting pantsuit clearly borrowed for the day, her résumé on plain white paper, just as Evelyn's had been at the first bank she interviewed with.

She had wondered in the year since she'd hired Cressida if sympathy were a form of nepotism, a favoring of emotional kin. With the exception of a few mistakes at the beginning, the kind anyone might make, she had performed well. It seemed to Evelyn that her vote of confidence had done what it was supposed to do, encouraging the young woman to rise to the occasion. It was just that she couldn't dislodge the thought that she had chosen Cressida for her company as much as for her fit.

"Which trader?" she asked.

"McTeague."

She took the account sheet from Cressida and glanced quickly at its contents. Trading floors were chaotic places and in the course of a day there were always a few botched transactions that had to be placed in house accounts to be resolved once the market closed. Some traders didn't get around to working out these "fails" for a day or two. McTeague, however, often took weeks, carrying over millions of dollars in scrub positions. Because he had been put in charge of the back office in Hong Kong he was his own boss on accounting matters. All Evelyn could do was complain to him about his laxness, which she'd done several times to no avail. Nonetheless, the data on this sheet had to be a mistake; it showed McTeague's house account holding an unreported loss of three hundred and forty million dollars.

"Who gave you this?"

"Sabrina. Same as usual."

"This came out of Fanning's office?"

Cressida nodded.

Evelyn had never met Doug Fanning but she had been in the same room with him a couple of times at company functions and she had seen him operate. He got a lot of mileage with the staff out of his apparently casual approach to people, which, because of his unofficial status as second-in-command of the entire holding company, struck people as unusually egalitarian. He had championed, in prominent fashion, the renovation of the second floor as a free, company-wide gym, and was known for walking the halls after his workouts still in his shorts, setting the phones of the husband-hunters flashing with gossip. And yet for all his show it wasn't the usual cocky, know-it-all, young banker's affect that came through. There was something different about him, something Evelyn recognized: the extra effort of the uninvited. She didn't quite trust him.

Which was why, rather than call Fanning to alert him of what she'd discovered, she instead tried Brenda Hilliard upstairs in compliance. If this was a misappropriation of funds, that department would have to be notified, regardless of who McTeague reported to. She got Brenda's voice mail. By then it was after nine o'clock and most everyone had gone home, the whine of the vacuum cleaner starting up at the far end of the hall. She decided to send Brenda a quick e-mail, saying she needed to talk to her in the morning.

As she and Cressida left the sealed quiet of the lobby through the revolving doors and emerged onto Congress Street, the cooler night air swallowed them, carrying with it the hum and rush of the expressway. They turned onto Purchase Street, a few taxis tapping their horns for a fare, black women in business suits in this part of town apparently good enough for their services; ignoring them, they crossed the plaza in front of the Boston Fed and made their way into South Station.

Evelyn had never felt comfortable with co-workers outside the office and strangely only the more so with Cressida, to whom so much else might be said. Above all she didn't want to disappoint the girl by seeming weak. Cressida had been the one, Evelyn felt sure, who had organized the office to send flowers to Carson's funeral, in addition to the flowers she herself had sent.

"Have you heard anything yet?" Cressida asked, as they paused at the top of the stairs leading down to the T. "From the police, I mean."

When was it, Evelyn wondered, that she had started to believe that she had left behind the world in which such a question might ever be asked of her? How long had that particular illusion lasted? In Roslindale, her apartment awaited her, tidy and quiet; the remote placed neatly on the coffee table, her kitchen counters wiped clean.

"They have a suspect," she said. "Just a matter of what kind of case they can make, I guess." She spoke more to herself than Cressida. "I should care about all that, I suppose. Revenge, or what have you. Getting him off the street. But I don't."

Over her assistant's shoulder, she could see onto the station's main concourse, where the last of the day's travelers sat at the shiny steel tables beneath the big schedule board waiting for the commuter service west.

"If there's anything I can do . . ."

Evelyn shook her head. "Go on now," she said. "You'll miss your train."

Chapter 11

Later that same night, the head of data security called Doug to inform him that an e-mail had been sent to compliance referencing McTeague. Doug instructed him to erase it before it could be opened. He had just logged on to the bank's server to pull up Evelyn Jones's personnel file when his doorbell rang.

It would be Nate again. Over the last several weeks, he had become a regular visitor. The first time he'd appeared, at ten thirty sharp, standing on the front steps all doe-eyed and expectant, Doug had been watching a Red Sox game and he'd seen no harm in letting the kid sit on the couch beside him while he finished up his correspondence for the day. After that, Nate had turned up almost every night the Sox played, content to drink a beer and follow the score as Doug worked. When the game was over he would go on his way. Even if they didn't say much to each other—in fact, especially if they didn't say much—a few hours of having another person in the house felt all right. He wasn't the kind of company you had to entertain.

Then, a week ago, while Doug was napping through the seventh-inning stretch, Nate had reached his hand over and rested it on Doug's thigh.

A ballsy move for a kid that nervous, but then he'd had a few more beers than usual.

Years ago, down in sleeping quarters, sailors had now and then whispered come-ons or run a hand along Doug's arm as he lay in his bunk. He'd never taken up their offers. The idea of it had done nothing for him: two guys getting each other off.

But something in the tentativeness of Nate's gesture made him curious how it would play out and so he'd kept his eyes closed and let the kid's hand move up over him. The mechanics were awkward at first but having someone else jack him off for a change didn't feel half bad. Afterward, Nate had left soon enough, no reciprocation required. Which seemed reason enough to keep him around. That and his access to Charlotte Graves.

The bell rang again and Doug rose to answer it.

"You're here," Nate said.

"Yep," he replied, remaining in the doorway, letting the boy wonder if he'd be let in this evening. From that first day that he'd crept into the house, something in Nate's demeanor had goaded Doug on—his lack of defense, a vulnerability the shyest women lacked. It was a provocation of a sort, such weakness.

"Martinez is pitching," he said, hopefully. "Are you watching?"

"I'm busy," he said. "But go ahead. Turn it on, if you want."

He spent the next hour reading up on Evelyn Jones. Her performance reviews were stellar. If you believed her supervisor, she was the patron saint of settlements, but given that man's doddering liberalism Doug had no idea if he meant it or simply felt a historical obligation to praise his imagined inferiors. Doug trusted more the traders' comments, who to a man reported that she was cleaner and faster than most anyone else who had handled their work. Around midnight, he called Sabrina and told her to do a public records search. As the game was ending, he finally closed his laptop.

Nate was sitting cross-legged beside him, the sleeves of his oxford shirt rolled up past the elbows of his slender arms.

"You're not a baseball fan, are you?" Doug said.

"What do you mean?"

"Before you started coming over here, you didn't follow it."

"Sometimes I did."

"What is your deal, anyway? Don't you have somewhere to be? Out with your friends or something?"

Nate looked into the mouth of the bottle he'd been drinking from. "I like being here."

"Why?"

He shrugged. "I just do."

"Well, I got to get some sleep. Time for you to go."

"Would you mind . . . I mean, it's okay if you would, but would you mind if maybe . . . I stayed over?"

"Where? On the couch?"

"Okay," he said, his eyes brimming with fear and longing. "If that's what you want."

"Jesus. Come on, then," Doug said, leading him up the stairs to the bedroom.

What Nate wanted, and what Doug let him do once he had turned out the light, was to lay his head down on Doug's stomach and take his dick in his mouth. He had never really touched Nate before but he palmed the top of his head now, guiding his motion. It had been a long time since he'd been given a blow job and though the boy was no professional his eagerness helped.

Afterward, he couldn't sleep, not with Nate in the bed beside him. He tried for a while before fetching his computer from downstairs and starting in on more work. A box in the corner of his screen showed the Nikkei continuing to drop. Eventually, after nodding off for an hour or so, he got up and showered.

When he came back into the room to dress, Nate had woken and rolled over onto his back, his face blurry with sleep, his cheek marked by the creases of the pillowcase.

"What time is it?" he asked.

"Quarter to six. I'm going to work. You should get up."

He rubbed his eyes with his knuckles and sat upright in his frayed T-shirt and boxers, his fuzzy, unshaven jaw giving him even more of a grunge look than usual. He smelled of pot most nights and had that laconic, hangdog look that stoners wore.

"Don't you have school?"

"It's senior week," he said, yawning.

A lifetime of doing only girls and now Doug had got himself into this. A hand job or two was one thing—a convenience—but now the kid was blowing him. The way he looked at Doug in the closet mirror was almost worshipful, his need clinging in a way that a girl wanting Doug to call her never had. He felt implicated somehow, and it galled him.

"Do you mind if I ask you something?"

"What?" Doug said.

"Have you ever done this before?"

"Done what?"

"Been with a guy."

"I got an idea," Doug said, pulling a tie off the rack and quickly knotting it. "Let's skip the conversation part. Okay? Let's keep it simple."

DOWNSTAIRS, HE WAS about to open the front door when something caught his eye through the window.

"Unbelievable. Just look at that."

Charlotte Graves and her two hounds were standing beside the garage, the woman leaning down to gather twigs which she deposited in a plastic shopping bag dangling from her wrist, while the dogs sniffed impatiently at the grass. In the gray dawn, the three of them looked like figures in a dream, a nightmare in fact, as if the world had been emptied by plague, leaving only these ragged scavengers.

"Feel like saying hello to your tutor?"

"No. She's just walking them. She'll keep moving."

"You bet she will."

Doug crossed the circle of the driveway before she noticed his approach. Startled, she stood sharply upright, yanking the dogs to attention. The Doberman bared his teeth and snarled.

"What do you think you're doing here?"

"You're up earlier than usual," she said.

"You realize you're trespassing. Your property is a hundred yards that way," he said, pointing her back up the hill.

She grinned. "The interesting thing is, Mr. Fanning, not only am I *not* trespassing, but you *are*. It's a strange bit of law, but there it is—I didn't write it. You'll understand soon enough. Soon enough," she said.

"You're mad. You're totally mad."

"So I'm often told. These days, even my dogs might agree with you. But they're like you. They don't know who they are. Or rather, they're pretending to be people they aren't, which I suppose amounts to the same thing."

"Listen to me," he said, moving a step closer, causing the mastiff to start barking, saliva dripping from his black gums.

"Samuel! Quiet!" she scolded. Amazingly enough, the animal obeyed. "They're usually not so boisterous at this hour. That's why I walk them early: my mind's clearer than theirs." A light rain had slickened the grass and was slowly dampening Doug's jacket. "I can see things more lucidly at this time of day," she said. "For instance, why did you build this house? To support a belief about yourself, about the life you're living? To give that belief a concrete form in the hope the building would make it true? Isn't that the idea? And isn't it false? Wouldn't you say that honesty—not of the rule-following kind but of the clear-eyed-apprehension-of-the-world sort—wouldn't you say it requires us to give up those childish equivalencies: the doll for the person, the object for the dream? If a person couldn't do that, it might suggest a lack of inner resources, don't you suppose?"

"You have no idea who I am," he said. "You think I'm like every other person in this town living in a new house, but you're wrong. I have as little time for them as I do for you. And I'll tell you something for free—you're as obvious as they are. You just happened to get here first so you think that gives you some divine right to have it all to yourself."

As he spoke, the Doberman squatted and proceeded to dump a pile of steaming shit onto the lawn.

"Oh, I do apologize. Honestly. That's very rude of him. Bad, Wilkie! Never on the grass! I got him from the pound, you see, and he's never taken well to instruction. It's hopeless now, of course," she added. "You simply can't imagine."

"Listen," he said, telling himself to just let the dog shit go, just let it go, "this lawsuit of yours, you're going to lose, so why not do us both a favor and just drop it. I didn't come after you. But if you keep this up, I will."

Suddenly, both dogs lunged leftward, catching Charlotte off guard and forcing her into a run as they chased after a tabby cat Doug had never seen before. Their speed was too much for her and she stumbled at the edge of the driveway, her feet slipping on the wet grass, her hand and shoulder and then thigh coming down hard onto the pavement. Freed from her grasp, the dogs dashed forward, disappearing around the corner of the house.

"Great!" he shouted. "Another fucking lawsuit!"

Miserably, he walked toward her prone figure, though by the time he reached her, she'd sat up and was brushing grass from the arm of her jacket. Rain ran off her forehead, down her nose, and into her eyes. She looked utterly lost at that moment, as helpless as a child. He was about to reach a hand down to help her up when he saw Nate jogging across the circle.

"Ms. Graves, are you okay? Are you all right?"

He knelt beside her and put his arm around her back.

"Who's that?"

"Can you move? Can you move your legs?"

She nodded and as Doug looked on, Nate dipped his shoulder under her arm, put a hand around her waist, and raised her off the wet ground.

"She needs a doctor. We have to call an ambulance."

"No, no," she said. "Don't be silly. I'm fine." She pushed the hair out of her eyes and straightened her skirt. "Those beasts will get no dinner."

"You need to be x-rayed."

"Heavens, no. Once you get into one of those hospitals you

never get out." She looked shaken but appeared steady enough on her feet.

"So," Doug said, "just to be clear, you've been offered medical attention and you're declining it, correct?"

Nate glared at him but said nothing.

"All right, then. I guess Nate here will get you home." And with that he strode off, leaving the two of them huddled together in the early-morning drizzle.

As soon as Doug entered Evelyn Jones's office an hour later, he realized he'd need a plan B. Whatever the origin of her immunity—intelligence, race, lesbianism perhaps, fact-based suspicion, some combination of these—his default MO would get him nowhere here. And yet she had to be won over. A bit of bad accounting was one thing. It could be papered over once he'd got an explanation from McTeague. But throwing the compliance department into investigative mode before he knew the facts—that wasn't an option.

"You mind if I close the door?" he asked.

"Be my guest."

Memos were tacked squarely to the bulletin board, binders arranged neatly beneath a row of five clocks, each labeled for the city whose time it kept. Along the front of her desk sat two small picture frames, their backings to Doug. Sabrina's sleuthing had turned up the fact that she'd been absent for her brother's funeral just a day or two ago.

"So," he said, leaning back in his chair, his eyes wandering the lunar white boards of the dropped ceiling. "It looks as if Jim Lowry is moving over to community relations. Which will leave his position vacant. Is that a job that interests you?"

He allowed the silence that followed to stretch on a few moments.

"Vice president. For operations? Are you serious?"

"Yeah. I've been in this office two minutes, and I can tell for a fact you'd be better at the job than he is. Besides, your evaluations have it written all over them. And I know from the look on your face you know that's true. Most of those assholes out there—they're cattle, pension seekers, cowards. *Leadership,* though. That's the question, right? The one the hiring committee would ponder judiciously before taking dead aim at mediocrity and finding the mark as sure as the men who hired them. *Leadership.* How fucking debased that word has become, don't you think? Excuse my language. Seminars in swanky hotels where the lemmings take dictation from some retired guru hack. We pay for this shit too, we pay for them to fly off and learn the seven principles of how to manipulate your underlings and keep them cheerful as you do it. Millions a year."

Evelyn Jones neither nodded nor looked away, her attention even and unremitting.

"There's another thing we both know," he said. "You get a big promotion and people—not to your face, of course—say, That figures. Right? African American woman, big corporation, diversity initiative. They do the cultural math and that's what they think. Now, that would piss me off if I were you because you're good at your job. And frankly, while I know a lot of the staff around here think of me as the friendly type, when it comes to management, I don't give a shit who anyone is. I want the machine to work. Because the best parts of it, I built them. That's why I want you to have Lowry's job. And I'd make sure people understood that."

"We're being honest here, Mr. Fanning? Is that the idea?"

"Absolutely. But if you give me a second, I think I know what you're thinking: 'Last night I discover a gaping hole in one of Fanning's trader's scrub accounts and this morning he's in my office offering me a vice presidency. How easy does he think I am?' Am I in the ballpark?"

"Yes," she said, resting back in her chair. "You are."

"McTeague fucked up. Thanks to you, I spent last night on the phone figuring out what happened. It was a favor for a client. I've spoken to him about it, and it'll be worked out. Now, just to be clear," he said, "do I want compliance getting their nose in this? No. Do I read employee e-mail, including yours? Obviously. If you don't already, you will once you move into operations. You'd be negligent not to."

"So you're asking me to keep quiet about a possible loss of three hundred million, not to mention a reporting violation?"

"You're not keeping quiet. I'm his supervisor and I've been notified. What I'm saying is this is how the chairman's office wants to handle the matter. It's how I want to handle the matter. But part of you is still thinking, 'He's only here because he's got a problem and there wouldn't be any of this talk about a vice presidency otherwise.' That's not wrong, of course. It's just not the whole picture. The situation brought you to my attention, that's true, but the fact is I think the bank would make more money if we promoted you. And that's what we're here for, right? You're not a romantic about that, I hope—our purpose?"

"I'm not an innocent," she said. "If that's what you mean."

Doug leaned far enough forward to get a sidelong glance at the framed photographs. In one, a vacation shot, Evelyn and two other women smiled for the camera at an outdoor table under a parasol, a beach in the background. The one beside it appeared to be a family portrait: an older black woman in a blue dress seated in the middle, a much younger Evelyn standing over one of her shoulders, a boy of about fifteen resting his hand on the other.

"Is this your family?"

Her gaze hardened.

"No disrespect, Mr. Fanning, but I'm getting the sense that you already know more about me than I'd care to tell."

The offer of promotion had begun as a piece of improvisational bullshit but he was beginning to think it might not be a bad idea.

"I only ask because while I never had a brother—"

"Don't go there," she said. "You don't want to go there."

"Why not? Because we don't know each other? I'm not offering sympathy, if that's what you think. I just know enough to know remorse can fuck with your ambition. And you shouldn't let it."

"You're one hell of a condescending asshole."

Doug smiled at the pureness of her hostility.

"When can you start?" he asked.

He thought she might leap up and swat him across the face but instead she simply shook her head in wonder.

By the time Doug headed out for his lunch meeting with Mikey, Sabrina still hadn't been able to track down McTeague.

"Call me as soon as you hear from him," he told her, on his way out of the office.

He walked quickly up toward the Common, where the benches were full of legislative staffers and store clerks, eating their bag lunches. The gold dome of the State House glittered in the midday sun. After Manila or Seoul or New York, Boston had always appeared quaint to Doug, an unlikely town for the business he and Holland had created. The spirit of their venture would have made more sense in boomtowns like Phoenix or Charlotte. But they had worked well with the material at hand, letting the historical distinction of the place act as a kind of ambient reassurance, a patina of solidity worth tens of millions in advertising.

In a booth at the back of the restaurant, he found Mikey muttering into the wire that dangled from his ear. He was jotting notes along the side of his *Herald*, the far page of which had come to rest on a half-eaten plate of manicotti from which it sponged the pasta's thin red juice.

"You're late and you look like hell," he said. "Have a seat." Pushing the wire aside, he said, "I got an investigator following this orthodontist out in Weston. Guy owes a boatload of child support. Turns out all his money's going for OxyContin. I got to say if you met the wife you'd understand the painkillers. She's quite a human being. Third husband, fourth investigator. I'm just waiting for my guy to tell me he got the pictures of him coming out of the pharmacy."

He didn't have time for this, Doug thought, checking his BlackBerry only to find the Nikkei was down another hundred points.

All day from his office window he could see into the neighboring tower, where workers clicked away at their screens, filling their filing cabinets with endless records of prices and depreciations and liabilities likely to pay, until they no longer noticed the bargain struck between meaningless days and whatever private comforts they'd found to convince themselves the meaninglessness was worth it. But it was different if those workers were your muscles and tendons and by your will you directed their exertion, regulating the blood of cash. Then you weren't an object of the machine. You were something different: an artist of the consequential world. A shaper of fact. Not the kind of author Sabrina wanted to be—some precious observer of effete emotion—but the master of conditions others merely suffered.

That's what he didn't like about McTeague's freelancing like this. Doug wasn't in control.

"So," Mikey said, "we got this hearing with Miss Graves on Monday. You'll be there, right?"

"What for?"

"To give the victim a face," he said, waving the waiter over. "We don't want her getting a sympathy vote. Old-lady-against-faceless-enemy kinda thing. Trust me, this is what you pay me for."

"You told me it was bullshit. Now you make it sound like a tobacco trial."

"You'll be in and out in half an hour."

"I caught her trespassing this morning. Should we mention that to the judge?"

"Let her tie her own noose."

Glancing over Mikey's shoulder, Doug saw a guy at a table by the window, early twenties, dressed in expensively faded jeans and a sweater pre-patched at the elbows. He was leafing through a magazine, the white wires of his earphones trailing down into his pocket, a laptop open beside him. He saw these people everywhere now, these aging children who had done nothing, borne no responsibility, who in their bootless, liberal refinement would judge him and all he'd done as the enemy of the good and the just, their high-minded opinions just decoration for a different pattern of consumption: the past marketed as the future to comfort the lost. And who financed it? Who loaned them the money for these lives they couldn't quite afford with their credit cards and their student loans? Who else but the banks? And what was he reading? *GQ* or *Men's Health*? Some article telling him how to shave his nuts or pluck his eyebrows or sculpt his tender gut? His hair was carefully unkempt, shiny with product, a deliberately stray curl hanging down over his forehead.

"Now what do you want to eat?" Mikey said. "Pasta? Chicken Parm? What's it gonna be."

Last night, Nate had turned over in his sleep and nuzzled up against Doug, his arm coming to rest across his chest. For what seemed the longest time, Doug had remained still under that warm weight, wanting to shrug it off but unable to.

"I got to go," he said, seeing McTeague's number appear on the screen of his phone.

"What kind of a lunch is this? You just got here."

"Call me later," he said, heading back onto the sidewalk.

"Where the hell have you been?"

"I'm on vacation," McTeague said. "Finally. 'Cause you know, the funny thing is, I never took any vacation, not since I got out here. And that's the company rule—you have to take your paid vacation. Good, simple tool for risk management—make sure people take their holidays."

"Well, your timing's pretty shitty. Where the fuck are you?"

"Macao. You ever been? It's like the Chinese Vegas. Casinos everywhere. Kind of butt ugly during the day but they get the fountains lit up at night. Turn on the neon, and it ain't half bad. Some real old-time glitter. And the bird markets, you should see the bird markets. You pick one out and they'll kill it on the spot and fry that sucker up for you."

"You're drunk."

"Not really. I mean, sort of. Getting started, I guess. Or maybe I'm in the middle. They have great girls too. You should check it out when you visit. They'll suck your cock for hours, if you want. They're all saving up for college."

In the background, Doug heard the screeching cheers of some Asian game show.

"Well, I'm glad you're getting your rocks off. I spent this morning in Evelyn Jones's office trying to explain your accounting. Is one of your hedge-fund buddies out of pocket? In which case, why didn't you call?"

"Let me tell you, Doug. What you and me did in Osaka—that was great. That was classic. I mean, when you recognized that Japanese deputy dude—amazing. The mistress, she was kind of complicated actually. I don't know if I ever told you. I thought she had me figured, at first. But enough booze, it doesn't really matter what you think anymore, right? You just do what you do and it doesn't matter what you think about it. So in the end I didn't even have to ask her. I just mentioned the guy—this is after we'd started fucking, she's getting another drink—and she unloads on him, goes on and on about what a creepy shit he is and then she tells me straight up. The whole story about what the government's gonna do. You ask me, she knew exactly what she was doing—fucking him over. But what a tip? I mean Jesus. We were thirty-five percent of profits last quarter. How can you walk away from a tip that big, right?"

Doug slowed on the path back across the Common.

"What are you trying to say?"

"Listen, Doug. I swear to you. I haven't stolen a dime. If you hadn't respected me so much, taken me in like you did, maybe I would have, you know? But being in so close with you, a higher-up, taking me under your wing, giving me this stage to play on, 'Don't worry about the middlemen,' 'Call me direct.' That's what you always said."

"So what the fuck's the problem?"

"Doug. There are no clients. I made them up. From the beginning. All that money you've been funneling to cover their positions—it's ours. And it's still in the market."

He came to a halt in the middle of the pavement, forcing the young couple headed toward him to part their hands as they passed.

"You're lying," he said.

"I was in the money. Every contract. Every position. And you wanted to pull it all back. But I kept remembering what you told me: keep your eye on the big picture, don't let fear stop you, the models aren't always right. It was there for the taking. And you always said the losers were the people afraid of the risk. I was in the money, Doug. It was all profit. I was getting ready to hand you a windfall bigger than you'd even imagined, wrapped up in a bow. But when the market turned I just froze. And I had to keep asking for all that cash. To post margin, to keep the positions open. And you . . . you kept feeding it to me."

Doug tasted the remains of his breakfast at the back of his throat and then in his mouth and he leaned over to vomit on the grass. A shiny feathered rook looked on in perfect indifference. He wiped his mouth with the back of his hand.

"You're lying," he said. "Tell me you're lying."

Chapter 12

As Henry climbed the narrow back staircase of Charlotte's house on the last Friday in June, and set his bag down in the room where he had spent his boyhood summers, he realized his mistake: here nothing changed. Not the ancient lumpy mattress, not the frayed satin lampshade, not the linen square on the water-stained bedside table. At the inn in town, where Betsy had always insisted they stay during their annual visit, out there in the light of day, at a restaurant or coffee shop, his sister's predicament could be broken down, its components approached diplomatically, each of them discussed and resolved. But here? Here, Charlotte's circularities drew energy from the very decrepitude of the place. The house *was* her argument, its density of association imperative to preserve. It may have belonged to others once, to his ancestors or his parents, but it was all hers now, the physical form her opinion of the world had come to take. How could he ever change her mind while living inside of it like this?

Indeed, the initial signs were not positive. The entire first afternoon, during which he'd thought they might take a walk and ease into things, Charlotte spent conducting some half-cocked tutoring session with a sunken-eyed youth, who listened in rapt attention to a lecture that jumped from William Jennings Bryan and the gold crisis to Father Coughlin and the paranoid style in American politics. Sitting in the front room trying to keep up with the day's blizzard of e-mail, Henry marveled that a woman who'd retained this much history could nonetheless be so far gone when it came to ordering her own life.

"I didn't know you were still taking students," he said once the boy had left.

"I imagine," she said, "that he doesn't have many books in his own house. It's so easy to assume people do. But then many don't. And he's lively. I thought he was one of the usual dullards at first. But he's got promise. The world—the actual state of things—it's broken in on him. Which is moving. You have no idea what it was like at the school toward the end. How the content remained the same while the meaning of the exercise changed so entirely. From enlightenment to the grooming of pets."

Here was his sister's familiar recipe: well-meaning condescension leavened by faith in meritocracy and finished off with a dose of liberal apocalypse. She was the classic mid-century Democratic idealist, who'd lived long enough to see hope's repeated death. Raised on Adlai Stevenson, Richard Hofstadter, and redemption through rigor. It would have been easier for Henry if he hadn't agreed with her about so much. If their father hadn't stamped them at such an early age with a patriotism for process and an aesthetic revulsion at display of whatever kind.

Also, if he hadn't loved her. Ineluctably. Love tinged by an envy he'd never understood.

Practicality had been their dividing line. By choice or circumstance or fate—the lines between these seemed less discreet to him the older he got—he had been the practical one, devoted to practical functions. Not a judge of acts, not even a creator of much, but a watchman, guarding the largely unseen. She had read, studied, and taught, loved a doomed man once, and through all of it somehow retained the energy for a more or less permanent outrage at the failure of the shabby world to live up to its stated principles. She followed politics assiduously, rejecting all the while its premise of compromise. If she hadn't been so well versed in the checkered moral record of most actual martyrs, she might have allowed herself to become one, finding her single cause. As it was, she'd served and done battle with the school of a wealthy town, and apparently considered much of her effort wasted.

Henry's plan had been to evaluate the gravity of the situation for the first day or two, allaying his sister's usual fear that he'd jumped to conclusions, and then raise the subject of her moving on Saturday evening, think it through with her on Sunday, and, if all went well, perhaps even look at a few places early in the week, before the Fourth of July party at the Hollands'.

Instead, at breakfast on Saturday—which consisted of Orangina and stale bread—she blindsided him with the news that she had sued the town without the aid of a lawyer, claiming that Finden had violated their grandfather's bequest of the land.

Slipping into the backyard, Henry phoned Cott Jr. to find out what in hell was going on. The man's father had been the lawyer for the small Graves family foundation that gave to local causes, and he had inherited the job.

"I assumed you knew," Cott Jr. said. "Norberton over at the hall told me she'd filed *pro se*. Quite a piece of rhetoric apparently. But she managed to use a few of the necessary phrases so they couldn't toss it out."

"Why wasn't I told of this?"

"By whom?"

"By you."

"Ah," he said. "I'm guessing she never mentioned firing me. The truth is, Henry, the Graves Society hasn't been a client of mine for three or four years at least. We'd always sent the check over to the Audubon but Charlotte got into some kind of policy dispute with them—beaver habitats I think it was. In any case, she instructed me to cancel the donation. I reminded her that she had to give away five percent a year to someone. And that's when she removed my name from the checking account. She hasn't spoken to me since."

Thus was Saturday morning lost to a rear-guard action of intelligence gathering. Charlotte would hear nothing of withdrawing the suit and couldn't understand why he would want to. The hearing before the judge was scheduled for Monday and she would be delighted, she said, for him to join her.

"I know these sorts of legal matters have always been your end of things. But there's no reason to let that upset you. It's all well in hand."

After a lunch of cottage cheese and grapes, Henry's phone started lighting up and soon enough he'd been dragged into a conference call with his senior staff and someone over at the State Department, who had been getting reports all morning of a possible coup in Uzbekistan. Sitting at the kitchen table, watching his sister prepare a sauté of sirloin and carrots for the dogs, he listened to his deputy describe getting a call an hour earlier from the Uzbek foreign minister, who had phoned the New York Fed to request that ninety percent of his country's sovereign asset deposits be wired to a bank in Tashkent. The problems being that (1) no one was quite sure which side of the coup the foreign minster was on; (2) the Uzbek president was proving somewhat hard to reach; and (3) the State Department, unable to determine if this was an Islamist revolution or a pro-Western military putsch, hadn't decided yet whether to stand by the current dictator or throw him overboard. Eighty million dollars was an unremarkable sum for a foreign-country transfer but enough to fund a small civil war and thus endanger U.S. basing rights, necessary for the resupply of forces in Afghanistan. During a pause in the proceedings, Henry's chief counsel, Phillip Bretts, noted drolly that the man at State had been appointed only last week to the Central Asian Desk from a job at the National Cattlemen's Beef Association.

"Any chance of getting a bit of that meat?" Henry whispered, holding his hand over the phone just as Charlotte emptied the frying pan into the dogs' stainless-steel bowls.

"It's Sam who insists on the finer grade," she observed. "Wilkie was perfectly happy with the ground chuck."

By the end of the call, Henry was ready for a drink.

He took his Bloody Mary out onto the back terrace and tried to ignore the weeds coming up through the mortar of the brick. Despite his anger at Charlotte's loony behavior, he had to confess that he hadn't seen her so animated in years. Perhaps even since they were kids, now that he thought about it. Back when she'd been queen of the realm in which he'd been so happily captive. In Rye, he used to trail her for hours from the playroom into the yard and back upstairs to the inner sanctum of her bedroom, where he'd been allowed only on her capricious wish, the air there shaded in the afternoons by the giant copper beech. Even now, he could remember how the sun used to play over her dresser and the rich, red carpet and the bed where she lay reading or writing in her diary. He doubted he and Betsy had ever created a paradise such as that for their daughter, Linda. Perhaps because she was an only child. Or maybe it was just that Henry, as an adult banished from the kingdom of mystery, could never fully credit its existence for his daughter, and could only fake a belief in it for her sake in the hope that somehow, on the far side of that impenetrable divide, the garden was still damp and lush and time had yet to be invented. Impenetrable except perhaps in the most fleeting moments, together with the person you'd adventured with there once.

What was a brother supposed to do? Charlotte was happy for the moment because her outrage had found a target closer to home than the halls of Congress and she'd managed to convince herself that she had a chance to win. But none of that changed the obvious: she was barely feeding herself; the house was more of a ruin than ever; and however you wanted to describe them, her relations with the dogs had gone beyond mere eccentricity.

Sunday he drove into town to buy proper sandwiches for lunch and insisted they go out for dinner. At the restaurant he tried to make up for lost time, keeping gently at her, drawing the conversation around to the difficulties of maintaining the house on her own.

"If it would make you feel better," she said, "you're welcome to hire me a cleaning lady. Though she'd only be allowed in the kitchen."

"That's not what I mean."

"Of course it isn't. You don't mean anything you're saying. You want to ship me off somewhere so the idea of me here doesn't weigh on you. It's not like you can hide that, Henry. From your own sister. But even if I were inclined to go, which I'm not, now is the last time I'd budge. Here on the verge. I mean, just look at what's going on. Take a step back for a moment, and look at what's going on in this country, and I don't mean just the criminals at the top—they'll do their damage and stumble out eventually—I mean the last thirty years. And then tell me if you can honestly say that the intrusion of that house, the cutting down of those woods, whoever they might have belonged to once, doesn't stand for something, for a rot more pervasive. And then tell me

I'm wrong to want to take a stand. You can't. Not without betraying language, and I think you're better than that. I know you are. Because that really would be the end. To accede to that. To the notion that words mean nothing anymore. That they're pure tactics. You don't believe that."

And on she went, speechifying, close, he had to admit, to the height of her powers.

Letting go his mission for a while, he ordered another drink and let himself enjoy her company. Most of his colleagues didn't read much other than the *Journal*. Betsy had kept up with things, novels and films and biographies, but they agreed with each other about so much that at a certain point they'd stopped discussing it all. The fierceness of his sister's opinions had never dimmed. It was the spirit of their father in her, the old man's crusading energy, difficult at times for their mother to bear, but so obviously the thing she'd fallen in love with.

When the young couple at the adjacent table began arguing about their renovation, the husband insisting they fire the architect, whom the wife described as not only visionary but, in case he hadn't read a magazine or newspaper in the last year, "quite fucking important," Charlotte granted Henry a conspiratorial smile, gathering him into her fold, an invitation that in the moment he couldn't help accepting with a roll of the eyes. Who was he kidding? His new neighbors in Rye were absolute pills. Their children were deplorable in the manner of overbred dogs. The fellow being in banking, he had asked Henry over for a drink. Their house had struck him as the cross between a playpen and a corporate retreat center. But what could you do about it?

When the waiter asked if he'd like a third glass of wine, he said yes.

Back at the house, Charlotte made tea and they sat at the kitchen table. The table where their father had liked nothing better than to set out broken gadgets on a Saturday morning, a radio or toaster or lamp that had given up over the winter, and opening his tool kit begin to fiddle. Recalling such mornings, Henry, a bit drunk, felt a bone-tiredness, the kind he couldn't afford to let in too often, not in a job where the travel never stopped. It was the sort of tiredness a mind allows a body only when it knows it's home.

"So, did you manage the coup all right?" Charlotte said. "Is everyone's money safe?"

"It'll work out in the end. A few days of caution won't hurt anyone."

"Such an anonymous sort of power you wield. So far from the madding crowd. It's always intrigued me. Thinking about the people affected by what you do. The fact that they'll never know you. Sure, Daddy tried cases, but he met his defendants. There was a scale to the thing. It's not a criticism. It's just I wonder sometimes what it does to you. What it's already done to you. The abstraction. Lives as numbers. We all do it, of course. We do it reading the paper. What does ten thousand dead in an earthquake mean? Nothing. It can't. The knowledge just breeds impotence. But your abstractions, your interest rates, they change people's lives. And they'll never know who you are."

"When things get bad enough, they tend to find out."

"That's not my point. I'm talking about you, Henry. I'm sure there are plenty who simply enjoy your kind of influence, the ambitious. The ones whose power makes them furious. And there are the crypto-sadists, such an underestimated lot. But you're neither of those, however much of a fellow traveler you may have been over the years. And yet there it is—your system and other people's pain."

"It's not all pain," he said. "Money allows things."

"Of course. It's just a matter of to whom. But, then, that's not your area, is it? That's someone else's set of choices."

Sauntering drowsily in from the living room, the Doberman rested his head in Charlotte's lap, and Henry watched his sister pat him gently on the head.

"You know it's funny," she said. "All weekend, I've tried to convince Wilkie here that you're a good sport but he won't believe me, will you Wilkie? He's convinced you're a member of the Klan."

HENRY SLEPT rather poorly that night, waking more than once to what sounded like growling. *The Klan?* He could just see the expression on the face of the director of an assisted-living facility when Charlotte dropped a comment such as that into an interview. He got a few solid hours toward morning before his sister woke him, warning that they'd be late to court.

"We can't take them with us," he said, standing bleary-eyed by the rental car, as she came down the walk with Sam and Wilkie.

"Why not?"

"It's a government facility, not a kennel."

"Don't be silly. The bailiff's an old student of mine."

The county courthouse was a Greek Revival affair whose sandstone had gone gray with soot. The main hallway, adorned with portraits of deceased superior court judges, was already bustling at eight thirty: an officer showing a line of jurors into a waiting room, lawyers hunched with clients, explaining to bewildered family members the nature of their loved one's predicament, while on the benches nearby policemen killed time before being called to the stand.

Lo and behold, when they reached the courtroom door, a balding guard in his forties lit right up with a smile.

"Miss Graves," he said. "How ya been? I saw the name on the sheet and I wondered if it was you."

"I've been very well, thank you."

"I saw that business in the paper a few years back about the school and all. That was no good the way they let you go." He reached out to shake Henry's hand. "Best teacher I ever had," he said, his voice filled with wonder at the discovery of his own nostalgia.

"How kind of you to say. Now, Anthony, I was wondering. There is just a small favor I was going to ask. My dogs. I was hoping they could come along. Into the courtroom with us."

"Oh, geez," he said, clicking his tongue. "The judge. I don't know if he's going to like that. It's against rules." He considered Wilkie and Sam for a moment. "They wouldn't happen to be medical dogs, would they? To help you get around, I mean."

"Well . . . yes, now that you mention it, they do help. A great deal."

"Charlotte," Henry whispered, only to receive an elbow in the flank.

"I'll tell you what, Miss Graves. You bring them in here, and I'll just settle them down in the back row, where no one can see them. How's that?"

"Wonderful. I knew I could rely on you."

She and Henry took seats in the third row of the courtroom and stood when, a few minutes later, Anthony called out, "All rise, the Honorable George M. Cushman presiding."

"You weren't expecting *that*, now were you?" Charlotte whispered.

"Expecting what?"

"You remember the Cushmans. Mommy and Daddy used to have drinks with them all the time. That's their son, George. He would come to the lake with us. Don't you remember? Chubby George."

"Oh, for Christ's sake. This is ridiculous. You're going to embarrass us."

"My God," she said, glancing over her shoulder. "Will you look at that? He's here, the bastard. With some slickster lawyer. Just look at those pinstripes. They're an inch apart."

Turning to look, Henry saw a man in his late thirties with tightly shorn black hair and a rather barren expression. He had that overgroomed look to him that many of the younger bankers did these days, giving them, at times, an almost feminine appearance, despite all their hours in the gymnasium. Not so his companion—a pug of a man whose pinstripe was indeed immoderately wide. He chewed gum and thumbed impatiently at the wheel of his BlackBerry.

"What business does he have here? I'm not suing him."

"Gee, I don't know," Henry said. "You're only trying to take the man's house. He's an interested party. He's allowed to intervene."

Before Charlotte's case was finally called, they had to sit through two DUIs and a dispute between the country club and one of its junior members over a malfunctioning golf cart, reminding Henry that only the luckless, the petty, or the deranged wound up in court.

Reviewing his docket in chambers earlier that morning, George Cushman had a thought similar to Henry's upon noticing that he would have to conduct the hearing on the Graves matter that day. The prospect saddened him. Though they were hardly friends, he'd known Charlotte Graves for the better part of his life and said hello to her whenever they met in town. What was more, as a member of the board of the Historical Association, he would have liked nothing better than to rule in her favor. He found houses like the one that had been thrown up on that land almost as offensive as she did. No one denied that Willard Graves had given the property to Finden for preservation or that he had specified in the bequest that should the town sell or develop it, it would revert to the estate. But the rule against perpetuities as it related to conditions broken was clear enough in this state: after thirty years the right to repossess the land was no longer valid. That term having long since expired, the town maintained, quite correctly, that its title was now absolute; it could do with the acreage as it pleased. As he would with any *pro se* plaintiff, Judge Cushman had done his best to tease from the mass of verbiage in Charlotte's petition some colorable argument. But when, after six pages of single-spaced invective, she'd begun a history of her family's donations to local charities, he'd given up the effort. He would give her her day in court and soften the blow by delaying his dismissal of her complaint by a few weeks.

Straight out of the gate, however, the problems began. When Charlotte stood from behind the plaintiff's table she said, "Good morning, George. I did just want to say, I am so glad it's you."

Incredulous, the town attorney rose to object but Cushman stayed him before he could speak. The lawyer for the intervener, Fanning, however, would not be held back.

"May I approach, Your Honor?"

"No, Counselor, you may not. You will be pleased to sit down. Now, Ms. Graves," he said, "litigants must address this court as either 'Your Honor' or 'the court.' Is that clear?"

"Of course, I'm so sorry. I didn't mean any offense. Your Honor."

"All right, then," he said. "Is there anything you'd like to say in addition to your submissions in this case?"

"Oh, yes, there is. You see, after I sent you the letter I found this book in the library that had what they called model pleadings, and right away I realized that I may have somewhat obscured my central contention. The way I wrote it out, I mean. This business of the thirty years. I understand that. *Why* we have to quiet the wishes of the dead like that I'm not so sure, but there we are. I'll leave that for another day. But what I'm saying is slightly different. Would you mind if I read a quote?"

"Go right ahead," Cushman said, leaning back in his chair.

"This is from a book I came across by a Professor Duckington. He writes, 'While, in its infinite wisdom, the legislature has seen fit to extinguish the rights of *individuals* in possession of contingent remainders in real property, presumably in the interest of dusting titles clean of those cobwebs of the common law that were seen as an encumbrance to an efficient and reliable system of sale and purchase, the people's representatives were sufficiently mindful of their own prerogatives, along with those of churches and *charitable corporations*, as to exclude themselves *and the latter* from the consequences of their good judgment.' "

She closed the book, returned it to the table, and smiled proudly.

"Heaven help the man's students," Cushman said, "but it sounds accurate enough. The rule applies to individuals. But the distinction's not relevant in this case."

"Oh, but it is, George," she said. "You see, my grandfather—he was a charity."

"Come again."

"Willard Graves, before he died, he turned himself into a charity: the Graves Society. We've been puttering along ever since. My point is, if you look at the records, *he* didn't give the land to Finden. The society did. So you see, the thirty-year rule—it doesn't apply here. The conditions in the bequest are still good. Which means the land no longer belongs to Finden or to Mr. Fanning. It belongs to our family's trust. In fact, it has ever since the town sold it. The documents are all here in my file. I believe all I need from the court is the title. And then we'll be done."

For the following ten seconds no one in the courtroom uttered a word. In fact, they barely moved. Like guests at a funeral who have just witnessed the lid of the coffin come open and the corpse sit up to greet them with a smile, they stared at Charlotte in awe.

Then the shouting began.

Mikey nearly fell over the front end of the jury box, where he and Doug had been instructed to sit, as he leapt up to yell, "Approach! Approach!," taking on, in panicked violation of courtroom decorum, the voice of the judge himself, whose rejoinder was hardly audible over the fuming objections of the town lawyer, who didn't even bother addressing himself to the bench, hurling his words directly at Charlotte. By the time Judge Cushman got a hold of his gavel and began slamming it, Wilkie and Sam had scampered into the aisle and begun barking up a racket, causing everyone but an appalled Henry to turn in still greater astonishment to the sight of two drooling hounds bolting toward the front of the courtroom.

"Bailiff!" Cushman cried, standing to pound his gavel. "Bailiff!"

Order wasn't restored for another ten minutes, as the dogs were dragged snarling from the room and the lawyers, ignoring local rules, jumped onto their cell phones to offices and aides in a desperate effort to fill in the suddenly gaping void in their understanding of a case for which they had barely bothered to prepare. After denying repeated motions for a continuance, Judge Cushman declared a recess and returned to his chambers with Charlotte's file.

By the time he'd finished examining the documents, he'd been reminded that there were, after all, a few unique pleasures to his occupation. He could of course give the town time to regroup. But they had no good argument for why they deserved such a reprieve. The evidence Charlotte was relying on had been stored in their own basement. And as to the legal argument, she was perfectly correct. The donation of the land had come from a charity. The rule didn't apply. He needn't reach the question of whether the town had been willful or merely negligent in its sale. Either way, they lost.

Back on the bench, he listened with serenity to the attorneys' pleas, objections, and even their threats of appeal and motions for recusal. When at last they had exhausted themselves, he thanked them for their advice, and then, allowing himself just this once a flash of that declamatory rhetoric that as a law student he'd dreamt of dispensing but never quite found an opportunity to employ amidst the grayness of actual litigation, he began, "As the great British prime minister William Gladstone once put it, 'Justice delayed is justice denied.' " Announcing his finding that the papers presented left no room for doubt about Charlotte's claim, he continued, "The court is certainly sympathetic to the plight the purchaser now finds himself in, having built a house on land it turns out that he does not own. But the right of reentry is an ancient one, predating our own Constitution. I cannot set it aside merely because it presents an inconvenience. However, now that the subject of ownership has been settled in favor of the Graves Society, my hope is the parties can arrive at a negotiated settlement. With this in mind, I suspend for sixty days the order I hereby enter granting plaintiff's family trust title in the land."

Looking down over his glasses at the once-again silenced courtroom, he asked, "Is there anything further in this matter?"

Chapter 13

Glenda Holland had decided it was just the thing to stay put in Finden on the Fourth of July and throw a grand party for all their friends and obligations. Jeffrey had canceled their plans for Capri, the Cape house was still under renovation, and Florida was out of the question in such ghastly weather. Besides, the Harrises were staying in town, the Finches, the Mueglers, the dreary board of the Historical Association, to which she had been dragooned into writing checks, and of course her wretched son and his prankster friends, and their parents for that matter, if they wanted to come—who was she, after all, to be embarrassed by her son's failure to crawl from the tub of even a public school?—in addition to which there was the advantage that as long as Jeffrey invited clients and a few shelves of Union Atlantic's management, the whole hing-ho could be charged up on the bank's entertainment account.

It being too late for save the dates, she'd gone straight to invitations, whizzing them out FedEx and doubling up the numbers. The caterer had to be bought out of a wedding contract, the tent people bribed, and the florist threatened with boycott. But by the time the real heat commenced that weekend before the Fourth, her chief suppliers had more or less fallen into line and the phone had begun to ring off the hook.

Starting late on a midsummer party, she'd expected half her list to have other plans but it turned out people were avoiding big-city crowds this year for fear of terrorist attacks and were delighted at the invitation. The chef was talking about a fourth boar and the temp agency hired to manage the parking said the field usually occupied by the sheep Jeffrey had purchased years ago to qualify for the family-farm deduction would have to be cleared away for the overflow. It all appeared to be coming together. Everything but the fireworks.

No one could be found to do the fireworks. Local governments had the firms all tied up in annual commitments and the big corporate parties had long ago been booked. Her assistant, Lauren, had scoured New England for anyone with a match and an explosive but come up dry. Finally, only days before the event, practically on her knees in the back of a restaurant in the North End, Glenda had managed to pry a nephew off the team for the Boston Pops show for a perfectly ridiculous sum of money and a promise to allow him to indulge his creative side. By the third, the house was overrun by staff, and Glenda retreated to the chaise in her bedroom, where Lauren took all her calls, while she hunkered down with a master guest list and the table charts. Spread on the coffee table in front of her was a map of the dining tent and a basket of little white pin flags onto which Lauren wrote the names of the guests as Glenda called them out.

After resisting her plan as belated, Jeffrey, once he sensed momentum, had in typical fashion reversed course, invited everyone and their accountant, and demanded certain pairings at dinner, leaving her a phone book's worth of Korean industrialists and German bankers, her knowledge of whose social skills was a virtual black hole.

"What on earth am I supposed to do?" she said, holding up table number twelve, trying not to move her lips and thus crack the teal mud caked to her face. "Put Sarah Finch next to some Brazilian sugarcane magnate? It's absurd. I try to get a few friends together and this is what he does to me."

With Jeffrey's secretary, Martha, weighing in on his behalf via speakerphone, whole armies of financiers advanced across the map from wasteland tables doubled up by the kitchen tent to the very borders of the social center, only to be beaten back again by Glenda's Sweet Briar classmates and a protective guard of village worthies airlifted into a kind of improvised DMZ ringing the single-digit tables of note. It was close quarters for a while, with Martha insisting the head of Credit Suisse and his wife could under no circumstances be expected to make conversation with the high-school badminton coach ("Mrs. Holland, the *bank* is paying for this, you realize?"), but with a few tactical retreats, Glenda was able to keep the ranker forces of tedium at bay, setting up Jeffrey at his own table with the absolute necessaries and forcing the remainder back to the periphery. By seven o'clock, once she and Lauren had tidied up the charts and sent them downstairs to the calligrapher for place cards, she was done for. A martini, a chicken Caesar, an Ambien, and two Ativan later, she was ready for a sound night's sleep before the big day.

When, shortly after dawn the next morning, the driver delivering the mobile air-conditioning units backed his truck into the last of the six black Escalades containing EverSafe International's full-event protection team, he found himself quickly surrounded by twenty-odd men in ill-fitting dark suits and wraparound sunglasses, wielding everything from stun guns to Glock 9s and shouting at him to get out of the vehicle, put his hands above his head, and lie facedown on the freshly sprinkled grass.

A year or so later, to the Hollands' minor cost and irritation, they would discover through their lawyers, before settling out of court, that the driver of the truck, a Mr. Mark Bayle, was in fact a veteran of the first Gulf War whose nearly cured PTSD had been massively reactivated by that morning's incident, causing him pain, suffering, anxiety, and eventual unemployment. At the time, however, the accident's most immediate effect was to whip Glenda, woken by the shouting, into a kind of pre-event seizure roughly six hours ahead of schedule.

If all Jeffrey Holland had been required to explain away that morning was how he'd approved the head of corporate security's recommendation for a complete vulnerability assessment, perimeter protection, and tactical team on his property without either noticing that he'd done it or informing his wife, he would have been in excellent shape. As it happened, however, the NASDAQ had closed at a five-year low on the Monday of that week; WorldCom had announced another exaggeration of profits, placing on life support the bank's single largest loan recipient; and to cap it off, on the afternoon of the third, the Massachusetts and New York attorneys general had announced a joint investigation of Atlantic Securities' favoritism in the distribution of IPO shares. In short, it wasn't shaping up as much of a holiday for Jeffrey. By the time an outraged Glenda bolted through his study door in her nightgown shouting about the thugs in the driveway, he was already an hour into a conference call with the general counsel and half the board, trying to account for internal policies he'd never heard of, let alone read.

By one o'clock the air outside had reached ninety-eight degrees, and many in the small army assembled to feed and entertain the Hollands' guests had begun to wilt under the pitiless sun. An assistant to the chef's subcontractor for the wood-burning ovens had fainted at his station, knocking his head on an ice chest and requiring removal to an air-conditioned bedroom at the back of the house. Trying to manage both her boss and the party, Lauren had set Glenda up on a couch in the library, where she could receive emissaries from the feuding vendors without either standing up or entering the furnace of the outdoors until both were absolutely necessary. The band claimed the caterer had done them out of electricity and the florist warned that if the technician sent by the air-conditioning firm to replace the traumatized driver didn't figure out how to operate the machinery soon her creations would wither and die. These, at least, were people in Glenda's employ. The fire marshal was another matter. While he'd kindly expedited her request for a permit for the show, upon inspection and discussion with the nephew in charge he had determined that the barge from which the fireworks were to be launched was floating at an insufficient distance from the shore of the pond, which would now need to be ringed with flame-retardant tarps.

"My *God*," Glenda exclaimed, sunken into the corner of the couch. "Have you no mercy? Can't you see what's going on out there? Flame tarps? Where in creation do you expect me to find those? Not to mention the fact that they sound *hideously* ugly. Couldn't we just give it a miss?"

The man, a stolid, bearded fellow in white shirt and epaulets glanced wearily at Lauren, who started searching her phone for the town manager's number.

"If you only knew what it took me to retain that young man. When I think of what I paid him. He could send his firstborn to college. I'm begging you," she said, managing another sip of her drink. "We did invite you, didn't we? You and your wife?"

Once Lauren had led the marshal from the room, Glenda decided that, all in all, the best thing might be to nap.

Down in the field, a high schooler in red vest and bow tie pointed Evelyn Jones along an aisle of luxury sedans, and up against a barbed-wire fence. She applied her lipstick in the rearview mirror and then made her way through the parked cars toward a crowd of guests bottlenecked at the gate, where some kind of checkpoint had been set up.

"Glenda's gone too far this time," a silver-haired lady in front of her said to her husband, as security guards body-scanned each invitee with their metal-detecting wands. "Who does she think we are? Militants?"

"Believe me," the man ahead of her said, "there are people out there planning things. This here makes a good deal of sense." Evelyn recognized him from the newspaper: the head of State Street, lately plagued by kidnapping threats. Farther along, various bank employees and their spouses feasted their eyes on the chairman's estate, unfazed by the precautions. She supposed she was one of the few who wondered if she'd be allowed to pass. But they did let her through and she proceeded along the path to a set of long folding tables staffed by a team of severe-looking, young blond women who wielded their pens and clipboards like guardians of an auction for qualified buyers only, ready in an instant to lose those winning, welcoming smiles and halt the riffraff in their tracks. One of them beamed an extra beam as she checked Evelyn's name off the list and handed her a place card, her visage replete with that secret liberal pleasure of being given the chance to be kind and nondiscriminatory to a black person.

Up on the main lawn a waiter in a white jacket, sweat running down his face, offered her a glass from a tray of sparkling wines. Guests had already begun to roll up their sleeves and mop their brows with cocktail napkins. She strolled to the open end of the square formed by the back of the house and the two circus-scale tents and from there looked down the far side of the hill to a pond where several men in a rowboat were making their way toward a floating dock.

She'd known when Fanning routed her an invitation to the party not to expect barbecue in the backyard. But this was something else.

Then again, perhaps this was part of her new station. She was, after all, soon to be a vice president for operations.

Her aunt Verna had nearly fainted with joy at the news. "That's it," she'd said. "You go right on, you hear me? You just go right on." Verna had always been the pragmatist in the family, the survivor. Years ago, when she was a girl, Evelyn had asked her aunt how she managed to stay so thin all these years and she could still remember her saying, "Well, Evey, I'll tell you my little secret: there's nothing like good, old-fashioned anger to burn those calories to the ground."

What would Verna make of all this? Would she hesitate? Would she think it too much?

As soon as Evelyn had received the call from Fanning's secretary last week saying he wanted to meet, she'd expected a snow job. But a doubling of her salary? A position in management? The only other black woman in the upper ranks of the company was Carolyn Greene, a light-skinned Princeton grad, whose parents had a house on the Vineyard. At Evelyn's first minority-employee luncheon, Carolyn had asked her whose secretary she was. From the position Fanning had offered her, Evelyn could move to any bank in the country or into another line of business altogether. She could buy the house she'd long been saving for. And about one thing at least Fanning had been right: she would be better at the job than her boss.

You dream of such things with your brother fresh in the grave?

She could hear her mother's voice. Yes, she thought. I do.

Feeling a trickle of cooler air on her feet, she moved back along the tent's edge and passed inside. A giant chandelier had been dropped to encircle the main pole. Floral arrangements three feet high, bursting with red and blue, rose from the center of tables still being laid by a crew of waiters.

Nearby an older couple sat facing Evelyn, having taken refuge from the drinks tent opposite. He looked familiar, the gentleman, in his rumpled gray suit, his white hair neatly parted, his hands folded in his lap, a kindly look about him. Where was it, Evelyn wondered, that she had seen him before? And then she remembered. It had been back in the spring at the payment systems conference she'd attended down in Florida. He was the man from the Federal Reserve who had given the keynote address. She remembered it because such things were usually dull as all get-out. But toward the end of his review of the progress in securing commercial payments, this man had taken a step back from the specifics to describe to the audience the importance of their work, reminding them that while the business of keeping money flowing was a technical one, it supported and allowed millions of daily acts from the purchase of food to the paying of rent or salaries or medical bills. "Politicians argue over relative distributions," he'd said. "The market fiddles with the price of goods and labor. But all of it relies on you. You're the invisible medium. Not the hand of the market but the conduit. You touch virtually everything you see. Most of you work for private corporations. But the trust, it's public."

An old-schooler, she could remember thinking at the time. A man who sounded as if he meant what he said.

His wife—could that be the wife?—caught Evelyn's eye and smiled at her in a knowing fashion, as if they had just shared in some rarefied private joke.

Before Evelyn could say hello, the gentleman volunteered an apology if they were in her seats; she assured them that they weren't, explaining briefly about having heard him speak.

"Ah," he said. "I hope I didn't bore you. I can become rather self-important at times."

"That, at least, is the truth," the woman observed.

"This is my sister, Charlotte."

"How do you do?"

"All right, I suppose," she said. "Are you a banker, too?"

"I work for Atlantic Securities."

"Well then, you're in good hands," Mr. Graves said, with an open-faced smile, apparently not the least imposed upon by her approach. "This is quite a gathering," he added.

"It sure is. Not sure I really fit in," she said, chastising herself as soon as the words left her mouth. Why should she offer such an admission?

"For which you should count yourself lucky," Charlotte rejoined.

After Fanning's visit, Brenda Hilliard from compliance had phoned Evelyn back to ask what the issue was that she had wanted to discuss; Evelyn had prevaricated, saying there had been a mix-up, that the problem had been resolved. She had gone along with Fanning's scheme. That's what she had done.

"I didn't mean to interrupt you both," she said. "I just wanted to say I enjoyed your talk."

Mr. Graves smiled again. "You're very kind to say so. Enjoy the party."

THROUGH THE FRENZY of the day's preparations, Nate and the others had sheltered around the Hollands' pool on the far side of the house. As usual on such idle summer afternoons, they'd gotten high and entertained themselves by playing bring-me-down, a game wherein the last things you wanted to think of while baked were hurled at you by your closest friends in an attempt to defeat your buzz. Each attack required retaliation and further bong hits, the whole disordered affair not infrequently bringing Emily to tears—of distress or drugged stupefaction one could never quite tell—while the boys more often resorted to throwing objects or shoving one another into the pool.

As surrogate families went, the four of them were tight-knit, having learned early on the value of ridicule as a means of avoiding the awkwardness of their mutual affection.

The game that day had begun with the minor stuff of yeast infections, poor hygiene, and other bodily insecurities before reaching personal matters—Emily's retarded cousin, Hal's inability to attract girls. And it might have ended there but for the stuff they were smoking. Having failed to graduate, Jason, on Hal's canny advice, had thrown himself on his parents' mercy, promised to rededicate himself to studying in the fall, and suggested that what he really needed was the chance to help others for a while. Thus it was that he'd recently returned from his week of Habitat for Humanity—in Jamaica.

What little he remembered of the experience, he recalled fondly. A nail-gun injury on the second day had put him on the sidelines of the actual construction, but he'd made the most of the company. The four jumbo tubes of Crest he'd emptied and stuffed with the finest of the local crop had sailed through customs at Logan in his toiletry bag and made it safely back to the house. Life since had taken on a new texture. Jason had hacked around on an electric guitar for years but it was only after returning from this trip, after hours of practice in the soundproofed basement, that he'd begun to realize just how outsized a talent he might be. Others had not fared so well. Interlopers to the gang of four had come, smoked, required Xanax, and fled. The first girl Hal had courted since sophomore year had wept in terror at the sight of the Hollands' tabby cat and demanded to be driven home. When seriously gotten into, the new stuff was an all-hands-on-deck kind of experience.

And so it came to pass that in the late stages of this particular session, at the point where someone usually threw in the towel and began agitating for food, reprisals instead intensified. Nate, coming to Emily's defense in response to the hit on her defective relative, went straight at Mrs. Holland's alcoholism.

"Oh, that's a good one," Jason said, sitting with bare, rounded back at the end of the diving board. "That's a real good one. It reminds me, I've been meaning to ask you, Nate, how's the widow? Your mother, I mean. The one who's sitting at home right now. The one who's going to watch the fireworks alone tonight. Ever think maybe you should spend a little more time with her?"

The question stung but the line of attack had been used before, hardening him to the sharpness of it.

"Whatever," Nate said, lying back in his deck chair. "You haven't been able to ejaculate since you started those anti-depressants."

Jason leapt to his feet and came around the pool to stand over Nate, his face flushed and shiny with bakeage. "You're a liar. At least I haven't been spending my nights on my knees sucking some stranger's cock."

"Jason!" Emily shouted, leaping up from her chair. "Shut the fuck up!"

In this game, surprise was the only trump and Jason had played it. Nate had thought it would be safe to share his secret with Emily, but he'd been wrong.

"Interesting," Hal observed, crossing his legs and lighting another cigarette with which to enjoy this final round.

"I mean I knew you were queer," Jason said, "but senior citizens? Is that some kind of fetish thing? You like Daddy?"

"You are such a royal asshole," Emily said.

"Come on, tell us. What does the old man taste like?"

"Fuck you," Nate said, picking up his book and towel and heading back into the house. Just inside the door of the Hollands' solarium, he paused, listening to the whir of the engines powering the Jacuzzi and the sauna and the air conditioner, the THC in his blood still burning down the cells of his brain.

He could go home if he wanted. But things were too real there, too slow. And what use would it be heading over to Doug's? Six nights in a row now he'd gone to the mansion at ten or ten thirty and, finding the lights out and no car in the driveway, waited by the side of the garage until eleven thirty or later. Most nights the sky had been clear, the trees on top of the hill by Ms. Graves's house visible in black profile against a dome of pinhead stars. Sitting on the cool grass, he'd wondered what his father would have thought of him, waiting there in the dark for this man. Or what he would have thought about the things Nate had done with Doug already. It was a habit of late, this guessing at his father's judgment of the things he did or said. Yet no matter how often he tried it, the result was always the same: it didn't matter. Nate wanted it to, but it didn't. Imagining his father's reactions was just an end run against his being gone, his having chosen to go. As if an endless hypothetical could keep him alive. The fact was, if Nate wanted to sleep in Doug's bed, no one but Doug could stop him. He was already that free.

With no idea where to go, Nate stepped into the back hall of the house. From the kitchen, a procession of waiters in black trousers and white smock shirts appeared, sliding past him, trays of wine balanced at their shoulders. One of them, a narrow-faced redhead with thyroidal eyes, spread his bulbous glance down Nate's bare chest like a cat stalking a bird, a lubricious grin playing across his lips as he sped by, leaving Nate feeling as alone as he ever had.

IGNORING THE PARKING minders trying to wave him in, Doug sped past the entrance to the field and turned right at the intersection, and then right again, winding his way around to the far side of the property. He'd attended plenty of the Hollands' parties over the years and was in no mood for one this evening, but his business with Jeffrey couldn't wait any longer.

All weekend, he'd camped out in a conference room with the door locked and McTeague on speakerphone, as they worked through each fabricated transaction until by Sunday night he'd assembled the full picture: Atlantic Securities, and not its supposed clients, held thousands of futures contracts obliging it to purchase Nikkei tracking shares at a price hundreds of points higher than where the Japanese index now traded. As they presently stood, McTeague's positions represented a loss of more than five billion dollars. With each further drop of the Nikkei, the loss grew exponentially.

For the moment, Doug had taken the only practical step: he'd kept McTeague in place and continued to funnel him enough cash to cover the margin and hold the positions open so the losses would remain, for now at least, unrealized. But he couldn't keep Holland out of the loop any longer. For one thing, Finden Holdings was running out of money to lend Atlantic Securities and would need more from Union Atlantic as early as tomorrow. More important, they had now reached a line over which Doug had no intention of stepping alone. Setting up a single-purpose vehicle like Finden Holdings to get around regulatory limits was one thing; it skirted rules without quite violating them. But what Atlantic Securities and its parent bank would have to do now to survive was altogether different: deception of the exchange authorities and the deliberate misstatement of the company's exposure to the shareholders and the public. Doug knew well enough how the principals defended themselves in investigations of this sort of thing. They did what Lay had done at Enron—claim ignorance of operational detail. Cutting the occasional corner might have been an implicit part of Doug's job in special plans, but he had no intention of letting Holland play dumb on a scheme this size.

When he saw the lights of the party through the trees, he pulled to the side of the road. He hadn't walked twenty yards along the fence when he glanced to his left and noticed a high juniper hedge, which seemed oddly familiar to him, almost as if he'd dreamt of it. Coming closer, he recognized the gap in the bushes and the white gravel drive. It was the Gammonds' house, where his mother used to clean, where he used to pick her up in the afternoons, its brick façade smaller than he remembered it, the shutters painted white now rather than dark green. He'd never come to the Hollands' from this direction and hadn't known this house was so nearby.

The sight of it brought him up short. Picturing the old lady in her jade necklace, a moment he hadn't thought of in years came back to him, an exchange they'd had the last time he'd come here.

She had asked, as usual, how school was going, but instead of giving his standard curt reply, he'd told her what he hadn't figured out a way to tell his mother—that he was leaving, going into the navy. No one else but the recruiter had known, not even his cousin Michael. He had wanted to shock the old lady, to show her that he was more than her cleaning lady's son. But she hadn't been the least surprised. "Good for you," she'd said. "My father was an admiral, commanded the Second Fleet during the war. He always had tremendous respect for the enlisted men."

A trowel in her gloved hand, the skin of her face a fine, tan wrinkle, those heavy stones and the little silver rings that separated them hanging around her neck.

Why hadn't she given him away, he wondered now. When his mother approached, Mrs. Gammond had said nothing, made no congratulatory comment or aside, as if she'd known the news was a secret. She'd just smiled and waved goodbye.

She had been elderly back then; by now she would be dead and gone.

Putting the matter aside, he kept walking up the street, looking for a gap in the fence. Stepping into the field, he strode through the tall grass, making for the house.

Out of the corner of his eye, he saw a figure moving quickly toward him in the twilight.

"Hold it there," the man called out, "you can't come in this side." He hustled up to block Doug's path, all suited six-three of him, complete with an earpiece and a flag pin on his lapel.

"Get out of my way," Doug said.

"This is a private party, sir, if you—"

"I pay your fucking wage!" he shouted, pushing past the goon.

He found Holland coming down the steps of the terrace, a crystal tumbler in hand.

"We've got a problem," Doug said. "We need to talk."

"Well, gosh, thanks for the news flash. I've been dealing with it all morning. Bernie *fucking* Ebbers. How much money did we lend that guy? And now that showboat Spitzer is after us. Like we're the first people in the world to do our clients a favor? He's a politician for Christ's sake, he does favors for a living. But oh no, the party in the market is over, right? And the people want their sacrificial lambs. The script's as old as Teddy Roosevelt, and if we're lucky it'll be just as toothless. But they'll want cash and that's the one thing we don't have right now, thanks to you." He emptied his glass. "So yeah, you're right, we've got a problem."

"Let's go inside."

His shoulders slumping, Holland turned back up the steps and led Doug down the hall and into his study. Closing the door behind them, Doug leaned his back up against it.

"We're in trouble," he said. "More than we thought."

As Doug explained what McTeague had done, Holland's head moved up and back, as if tapped on the nose by a boxer. When it sunk forward again, his mouth was half open and he looked dazed.

"No," he said, shaking his head. "No."

At which point, the door handle nudged Doug in the small of his back and he stepped aside to watch Glenda enter. She wore a red silk dress with blue pearl buttons and across her chest a spray of diamonds.

The Adderall she'd taken following her nap had mixed with the drink to give her the novel sensation of being simultaneously drunk and highly efficient.

"Hello, Doug," she said, unsteady on her feet. "How are you? I was *so* sorry to hear about Judge Cushman's decision. But I'm sure you and Charlotte will work it out, won't you? Now Jeffrey, you need to come with me. Did you notice we have three hundred guests in the yard? Come along, come with me."

She motioned with her index finger as a parent might to a child.

"Where the fuck is Lauren?" Holland asked no one in particular, and certainly not his wife.

"She's doing her job, dear. Now it's time for you to do yours. Come along."

"Jesus, Glenda," he said. "Hold it together, would you? I'll be there in ten minutes. Just get out there and deal with it. And for Christ's sake stop drinking."

Glenda turned to Doug and smiled. "So good to see you," she said. "You really are so handsome. And my husband keeps you all to himself." She rested her limp, sweating hand on his wrist. "Be a darling. Bring him out to the party, won't you?"

Like a luxury car with poor turning radius, it took some effort for her to steer back through the door, which Doug closed behind her.

Across the room, Holland stood with his back to the bay window, his face drained, all his bluster gone. He could put on exasperation about WorldCom and Spitzer and all the other difficulties; he could even enjoy them, the way they lent him the air of the embattled leader, comfortable all the while in the knowledge that in the end the bank would take a few write-offs and move on. Companies with bloated stock prices could now and then go belly-up, but everyone knew the biggest banks just kept marching.

"We give McTeague to the authorities," he said, reaching for conviction. "That's what you do. We fire him, close out his positions, and put out a statement."

"Are you out of your mind? We'd lose half our capital base overnight. Our customers would run for the doors. Not to mention trigger a crisis. You're not thinking straight. We're talking about survival. And not just for this company. You've got a responsibility to that."

"Who the fuck are you to talk about responsibility?"

"Come on, Jeffrey. Is this how you're going to play it? Throw your hands up, get some cheap ethical high, and spend the next three years in depositions?"

"Is that a threat?"

"Don't be ridiculous. The point is, you're letting the situation get to you. That's not how it has to be."

"Oh really? And what do you propose?"

Doug had never seen him so frightened. Most all of what Holland had achieved in life had flowed from the bottomless well of his self-confidence, a great, social largesse that made everyone in his orbit feel as if they'd been selected for the bright and winning team. Contemplating a failure of this magnitude undid the premise of him.

"We keep feeding him money for now," Doug said. "We keep the positions off our books, on his phony clients. And we wait. Sell what and when we can and wait for the rest to turn around. We keep our nerve. That's what we do."

"That's your plan? Double the entire bank down on a single bet and hope for the best? I expected more out of your scheming mind."

"You have another idea?"

"Fraud. That's your answer? You're suggesting we commit fraud?

You want me to stand up at the shareholders' meeting and with all the other great news add that things are going fine and dandy in foreign operations?"

"It's your call," Doug said, wandering over to the bookcase. "We can sell. I can call Hong Kong right now. If you're lucky, you'll get to retire with some fraction of what you've got and be remembered as the guy who built a powerhouse and ran it into a ditch. And once they start digging and reporting and trying to understand what really happened—and they will—the shareholders will sue you anyway, and maybe the Feds will too. That's one option: be the upstanding guy. But that's not the advice you hired me to give you. I'm here because you wanted to win."

Doug took down from the shelf a vintage leather-bound edition of de Gaulle's memoirs only to find that the pages remained uncut.

"You know what I've been thinking lately?" he said.

"I shudder to think," Holland said.

"About how things are changing. The old compact. Between government, companies, the news. The basic assumptions about how everyone behaves. Most people have some vague sense of it. They feel a kind of undertow and they're scared by it. But they don't see how fundamental the shift is. They don't see it because they're too busy surviving or lamenting whichever piece of the old assurances they happen to be losing. So they get sentimental, wishing the tide wouldn't come in. At least that's what the losers do. You can do that. Or you can admit what we've always been up to. And then you can focus on the bigger picture."

"And what might that be?"

"Influence. Power over information. Control. Something bigger than rules or good taste. The more permanent instincts. You know what I'm talking about. You even get off on it. It's just the appearance of it that bothers you."

"You're a piece of work. You really are."

"You think you get all this for free?" Doug said, gesturing at the paintings and the antique furniture.

"Who the fuck do you think you are? Free? I was making loans before you were born."

"Sure. And every year the interest rate got better, didn't it? Government caps came off, and you could charge twenty-five percent on Joe Six-Pack's credit card, and get him to pay *you* for the privilege of keeping *his* money."

"What are you? Some kind of Socialist now?"

"I'm nothing," Doug said. "I'm just saying, you take the advantage you can get. That's how you got what you have."

"Yeah, with one difference. It was legal."

Doug smiled, leaning back against the bookcase. "That's right," he said. "And the governed have consented and all is well in the hearts of the people."

Holland sank onto the bench in the window, all his fretful motion spent. As he stared over the darkened field from where Doug had come, the two of them listened to the sound of trumpets from the tent outside, their high, shiny notes rising on the night air.

EARLIER, AS CHARLOTTE and Henry had approached the gates, they'd been confronted by the expressionless faces of the guards.

Don't be fooled, Wilkie whispered. *They're not here to protect you. And I know what you're thinking—that it's always a conspiracy with me. But just remember, they said I was paranoid, that I'd invented all that business of a plot against my life, but you know now how the FBI listened in on me, how they followed everything that went on in the Brotherhood, and I'm supposed to believe your white government didn't know there were gunmen there at the hall waiting to kill me? You've been uppity, Charlotte. You've thwarted one of their kind. Now watch,* he said. *They will take your protectors from you.*

And so they did, insisting the dogs be tied up to a tree. No animals allowed. They would be given plenty of water, they said, the more barrel-chested of the two claiming to be a lover of dogs.

You come to Sodom and leave your minister tethered at the gate? Sam asked, despairingly, his pompous head thick with sweat. *God's grace may be infinite, woman, but to think that He should give us help against sin without our asking and crying and weeping to Him for His help; to think that God should save us and we never set apart any time to work out our own salvation. What reason have we to believe such things? God is in Ill terms with you. He visits you not with His great consolations. Despite what you think of your victory, all things are against you; the things that appear for your Welfare, do but Ensnare you, do but Poison you, do but produce your further Distance from God.*

God is a character, Charlotte thought, as she handed the leashes over to the men. A well-rounded character in a well-rounded book.

And she and Henry continued on up the hill, the ministers' voices fading behind them.

Just three days earlier, after her vindication had been called out from the judge's bench for all to hear, she had taken Henry for a walk up to the nursery to pick out saplings for planting once the mansion had been leveled. But all he could summon was a barely disguised disappointment at the result, as if returning five acres to their property and nature's way were more burden than triumph. Sam and Wilkie, however, had been the larger disappointment. All spring she had calmed herself with the thought that once the strain of arguing her case was over, the dogs would relent. After all, it was for them, as well as herself, that she had fought so hard to beat the intrusion back.

Instead, their berating of her had grown incessant, their talk traitorous, reminding her that in siege warfare, it didn't matter how high or thick your city walls were if the enemy's agents were within.

And so just when she'd thought she might at last turn her eye to the future, Charlotte had found herself once more having to call up memories in defense: how quiet it had been in the woods, say, on a late afternoon in August as the thunderheads gathered and you could see up beyond the pale evergreen and birch, where against the powder-gray sky the black-and-orange wings of butterflies danced in the last shelves of light, fair creatures of an hour that she might never look upon more.

—then on the shore
Of the wide world I stand alone, and think,
Till Love and Fame to nothingness do sink.

"They were the same age, you know?" she said, as Henry glanced into the drinks tent.

"Who?"

"Keats and Eric. When they died. Twenty-six. Though of course Keats had written a good deal more and of much finer quality. But there we are. Correspondences—they keep you company."

"I don't know what you're talking about."

"No, I don't expect you do."

"Over here," he said, leading them across the way into a second, quieter marquee, this one artificially cooled and full of elaborately set tables. He pulled out two chairs for them to sit.

"Why on earth did we come here?" she asked.

"You were invited, remember? By Glenda Holland."

"Ah, yes. The woman who's trying to pull the ladder up behind her. She thinks siding with me and the Historical Association will somehow absolve her of her wretched taste."

"Why is that woman staring at us?"

"Which one?"

"That black woman over there," Henry said. "In the beige dress."

"I haven't a clue," Charlotte said.

Eventually, the woman approached. Apparently she'd heard Henry pronouncing on something or other down in the swamps of Florida.

Once she had left, Charlotte examined the place card in her hand. The number one was written on it in elaborate script. A very fine pen had been used to make such a mark, she thought, the ink strained through the nib to near perfection, not seeping at all into the crevices of the linen paper. A quick, sure stroke. You would have such place cards at a wedding. And tables like this. Eric's family being Catholic, the ceremony would have been important to them. Who wouldn't like it to look as it had for Henry that day he danced with Betsy on the parquet?

In what dim hollow of her mind, she wondered, had such fantasy never died?

Guests began filtering in for dinner. A bass drum sounded from the stage, followed by the heraldic notes of horns, as the assembled musicians struck up *Fanfare for the Common Man*.

"I've always rather liked this piece," Henry said. "You remember Daddy used to love Copland."

"I suppose he did."

"With the record player in the window. Out on the porch. You remember."

Late Sunday mornings with the newspaper and the breakfast tray and Charlotte in one of her blue cotton dresses and afterward their father would go back into his study and keep working. The never-ending work on behalf of the People. The work of justice conducted in the dependable medium of statute and brief.

The second burst of horns ceased, followed by a bar of silence and then again the low rumble of percussion.

"It's just the right sort of optimism," Henry said. "Confident without the swagger."

"But isn't it amazing," she said, "what context does. The émigré Socialist homosexual cheering on the New Deal. And yet what becomes of Copland here? Pure bombast. Congratulations for pirates."

"I'm just saying it's a good bit of music."

"Well, it's certainly a simpler world if you can cabin things like that. One discreet experience after the next."

"For Christ's sake, can't you give it a break? I didn't have to come up here, you know. It's not as if you enjoy my company."

"Oh come on, Henry, there's no need to revert. We're not playing house. I say these things because I think you understand them and most people don't. I'm sorry if it sounds like criticism. It's just conversation, as far as I'm concerned. I know you want to help me. I appreciate that."

"Then why don't you tell me what's going on?"

"How do you mean? We won. The law did what it's supposed to do. I would think you'd take some satisfaction in that."

"I don't mean about the land." He watched a few familiar faces—the head of State Street, the head of Credit Suisse—coming through the entrance of the tent with their wives. "How am I supposed to say this? You're my sister."

"Ah. I see. You think I'm losing my mind."

"I didn't say that."

"You didn't have to. You meant it."

"You're barely eating," he said. "And the way you talk to those animals of yours."

"I knew it would come to that: the old lady and her pets. But the world's bigger than you think, Henry. It always has been."

"Meaning what?"

"Do you imagine Betsy is entirely dead?"

"Charlotte, please. Give the woman a little respect."

"That's precisely what I'm doing. I'm not talking about ghosts. I'm saying she's not entirely gone. Not in you."

"Of course not. I have memories like everyone else. But as they used to say in college, that's ontologically trivial. Not to mention which, she's got nothing to do with your dogs."

"Well, there you are. You ask me what's going on but you don't actually want to know. Not unless you already understand it. There's a lot of that going around at the moment—your kind of certainty."

"Oh, come off it. Don't try to make this about politics."

"Like I said, it's a much simpler world if you can separate things out like that. History's a bit of a problem for you on that account, but then who am I to question the wisdom of the age? You're no doubt efficient."

Guests assigned to the table where the two of them had perched began arriving to take their seats, smiling cautiously in Charlotte and Henry's direction.

"Come on," she said. "Let's get this over with. Where are we sitting?"

"Table one, apparently. I suppose they've put me with Holland."

"Well then. Time to dine with your captors."

As they walked toward the center of the room, Holland waved them over.

"Henry, I want you to meet Doug Fanning, head of foreign operations and special plans. He runs everything around here. Doug, this is Henry Graves, president of the New York Fed."

For a moment the two of them beheld each other in disbelief, Henry watching his own shock reflected in Doug's face, whose eyes had gone wide with amazement.

"Do you know each other?"

Before either could reply, Glenda appeared with Charlotte on her arm and proceeded to nudge Henry to one side.

"My husband is such an awful dunce. Of course they know each other, dear. Doug and Charlotte are neighbors. Don't you listen to anything I say? Now," she said, pulling out the chair beside Doug's. "You're right here, Charlotte. I've put the two of you side by side so you can have a good long talk. If you get to know him, you'll see Mr. Fanning is an absolute sweetheart. And the fact is, Doug, that house of yours *is* a bit ugly. Nothing that a good hedge wouldn't solve."

Before Henry could intervene, Glenda grabbed him by the arm and led him around to the other side of the circle.

THROUGH THE salad course and the first glass of wine, Doug and Charlotte sat in silence, the volume of conversation around them growing steadily louder. Having got what he needed from Holland—verbal approval at least—Doug had tried to leave but Glenda had returned to drag him and Jeffrey into the yard.

How perfect, he thought now, how absolutely perfect that Charlotte Graves's brother should be the president of the New York Fed, elected by a club of his colleagues, half from his alma mater no doubt. What could be more establishment? It made sense of her hubris—imagining herself a guardian of good order.

Before that courtroom charade, she had been an irritant. Now she was a problem. Judge Cushman's order couldn't be allowed to stand. Doug had already talked to Mikey about how to proceed. According to the public record, the Graves Society was a financial mess. They would attack the charity. If they could kick the struts out from under that, her argument would crumble. But they would need documentation faster than she would ever produce it.

"So!" she said, addressing herself to the silver-dipped roses at the center of the table just after their dinner plates had arrived. "Where is it you suppose you'll go come September? A neighboring state, perhaps?"

Emptying his second glass of wine, Doug lifted his fork from the table, wondering how quickly she would bleed out from a stab to the heart.

"You were a schoolteacher, right?"

"That's none of your business. But yes, I was."

"Do they have mandatory retirement these days? Or was there some other reason you had to leave?"

"It's incredible to me, Mr. Fanning, that a person could be quite so transparent as yourself. One imagines that adulthood comes with some minimum of complexity. You had one of your minions look back over the local paper, did you? Learned of my travails? How intrepid of you. Perhaps you already know, then, that my subject is history. Most of my fellow teachers, and the textbooks for that matter, presented the material as if it were a simple record, a kind of newscast to be placed in front of the young, for what reason these days no one's particularly sure, beyond a few nostrums about not repeating ourselves. But that's not the tack I took. I was a little more opinionated than that. I had the temerity to suggest that certain developments in human society were better or more dangerous or more evil than others, and I'm not talking about your standard twentieth-century horrors, the ones they throw in for free. I'm talking about people like you. The despoilers. The patriots of capitalism. Given the ubiquity of your type these days, is it any surprise they forced me out?"

Doug took a breath to calm himself and said, "I'm going to take a wild guess and say that you knew the Gammonds."

"Herb and Ginger?" she said. "Of course. They were lovely people. Have you bought their land as well, then?"

"No. When I was a kid I knew them. My mother used to clean their house."

"Is this some kind of joke?"

"No. I grew up in Alden."

"I see," she said, examining his face in earnest, considering this new fact. "I know what you see when you look at me. An old whatsit crying, 'Not in my backyard.' That's what you say to yourself about what I'm doing. A crone who wants her trees back. Which I do. But I have to take my stand where I can. You probably won't believe me when I say that it's not personal, but it isn't. I suppose I have allowed myself to think of you as a villain, but really it's not you I despise. For all I know you're a Democrat. It's just what you stand for that I can't abide. And I'm not so naïve as to think that running you off that land will solve the bigger problem, but at least I will have done that.

"I wonder, Mr. Fanning. If you were to see a lone soldier fighting an army, what would you think of him? That he is a fool? Or that he simply believes in his cause?"

"Neither. I'd say he was going to lose."

"Right. Because that matters more than anything to you, doesn't it? Dominance. That's the childish pleasure you people can't get enough of. You get your fix dressed up in a suit, but it's no different than a drug. You're angry. And once the men like you start this war of theirs, people will die by the thousands to cure that feeling in them."

"In my experience, killing doesn't cure much."

She raised her head, turning her ear to listen to something over the din of the party. "Do you hear that?" she asked. "Do you hear barking?"

"You need to understand something," he said. "You haven't won anything. You just haven't lost yet."

"What have they done with them?" she cried, standing abruptly from the table, straining to hear some phantom noise. "Henry," she called out, bringing a halt to the table's conversation, the bankers and their wives staring at her in polite alarm. "Henry, where are they?"

Relegated to the children's table, Nate and the gang had waited what seemed an eternity before the fat-slathered pork and spareribs finally arrived. They set to gorging and in no time at all their plates were clean and cleared and peanut-butter parfait topped with American flags on toothpicks appeared in front of them.

"I can't take this music anymore," Jason said. "We need to get out of here." He rose without pushing back his chair, causing his knees to slam against the underside of the table and spill multiple water glasses before he fell again into his seat.

Eventually, they roused themselves and headed out through the broiling kitchen tent, past a swarm of short, dark people scraping half-eaten dinners into heaping garbage pails, the taller black waiters staring blankly at the tips of their cigarettes, as the head man popped the corks of the champagne. "On the trays!" he shouted, as the four of them slipped through an opening by barrels of melting ice.

"It's hotter than a jungle out here," Hal said.

Spotting a guard lounging at the gate in his shirtsleeves, they tacked rightward toward the trees in front of the house. That's when they heard growling and the rustling of chains. Jason jumped sideways, falling into a rose border.

"Dogs," Hal said.

Walking nearer, Nate recognized Wilkie and Sam. "Weird," he said. "They're my tutor's."

"That's deep. What do they teach you?"

Their bowls were empty and they looked up at Nate with sad, gaping eyes.

As the others drifted off, he untied their leashes and shooed the two of them up onto the terrace and into the house. Adjacent to the kitchen was a kind of cat apartment with carpeted walls, wicker bassinets, and in one corner a forest of dangling string. Way too large for this feline retreat, Wilkie and Sam knocked about like vandals in a child's room, their bulky heads clearing windowsills of teak brushes and padded collars, Sam ripping strands of twine from the mobile with an impatient yank of his jaw.

"Chill out there," Nate said, looking through the cabinets of tinned salmon and prescription drugs for something more substantial. Finding nothing, he opened as many tiny cans as he could into the miniature bowls before the dogs shouldered him aside to get at their supper. He fetched them water and sat for a moment on the chair in the corner, watching their glistening tongues lick the steel clean.

And then their heads were up again, eyes still brimming with hope.

"That's it, guys. Sorry."

They sniffed at the cat baskets, rummaging in search of their inhabitants.

"Stay here, okay? Just stay."

He pulled the door ajar and crossed back through the kitchen, heading out into the front hall, wondering where Ms. Graves might be. Here and there on decorative chairs and benches guests had taken refuge from the heat and the crowd, an older couple dozing upright on a chaise longue, a Japanese businessman in a tight black suit tapping away at his BlackBerry, while a few feet behind him a gaunt woman in a sweat-stained silk dress ruminated on a painting over the fireplace.

Heading up the stairs, Nate paused on the first landing, from which three hallways ran off into different wings of the house, each painted a different color, one beige, one pale blue, one dark red. The others had likely retreated to the third floor, back up to Jason's room, which could only mean more bong hits and combat, a prospect he didn't relish just now given how forcefully his retinas continued to pulse to the beat of his heart.

Stilled there on the landing for a moment, he found himself slowly drawn to the pattern on the wallpaper of the blue hallway. Little indigo diamonds were set on an azure background and surrounded by tiny gold stars each in turn ringed in a halo of silver, the design stretching on uninterrupted by picture frames or light fixtures, as if decoration of this particular wing had gone unfinished.

Coming closer, he could see another pattern beneath, stamped in outline onto the paper itself: hexagons contained within octagons contained in circles, which were themselves woven of figure eights, each figure only an inch wide, the stamp repeated a thousand times over. Moving from background to foreground and back, his eyes roved up and down, left and right, searching in vain for a place to rest, for something to comprehend or analyze, but he could find nothing, no larger, central figure or meaning, forcing him eventually to give up and simply let the pattern enter him unconceptualized, the whole ungrasped, which strangely enough, after a few moments, produced an oddly pleasurable sensation, a kind of relief from the responsibility to understand, at which point he moved in a step closer losing all lateral perspective, as when he'd lost himself in the endless zigzag of the houndstooth check of his father's overcoat as he was carried half asleep from the backseat of the car up to his bedroom as a boy, pressed against that endless repetition. The sudden memory of which he now condemned as sentimental. Thus covering self-pity in self-punishment, both of them equally false, both of them walls thrown up to block the view of something hopelessly vaster.

He kept on down the hall, coming to the open door of a bedroom done up in nautical style with powder-blue curtains and a navy bedspread and a replica of an old ocean liner set in a glass box on a table between the windows. At the bedside table, he picked up the cordless phone and dialed.

It rang three times, as it always did, before his mother answered, her voice rising gently on the last syllable of "Hello?"

"It's me," he said. "I'm over at Jason's. I told you, right? His mother's having this party."

"Is she? Oh, good. Have they given you supper?"

"Yeah. They've got these tents set up and everything. Are you going to watch the fireworks?"

"Oh, I'll probably put the TV on later. I suppose they'll be starting soon. It's a good night for them."

"I'm sorry."

"What for?"

"That I'm not there."

"Don't be silly. I'm fine. I'm just catching up on the paper. There's a wonderful piece about walruses with the most amazing pictures. Such odd-looking creatures and they sing these incredible songs to one another. I'll cut it out for you."

"I could come home if you want."

"Nate, don't be silly. I'm fine. Are you staying the night?"

"I might."

"Well, enjoy yourself."

"Did you put the air conditioner on?"

"Oh, no, it's so loud. I hate the sound of it. I've got the windows open and there's a bit of a breeze."

"Mom, you should turn it on. It's broiling."

"It'll cool down."

"Well . . . I guess I'll see you tomorrow?"

"All right, then. Good night, dear."

He put the phone back in its cradle, aware all of a sudden of the quiet.

"Nate? What are you doing here?"

He turned in wonder to see Doug already halfway into the room.

"Jason Holland," he finally sputtered. "He's my friend."

"Jesus. What a mind-fuck this party is. Where the hell did Glenda put the bathrooms? I've been looking all over."

"There's one right there," Nate said, pointing to the far end of the room.

When Doug had gone inside, Nate instinctively rose to shut the door to the hallway, his heart sprinting, imagining what would happen if Jason or one of the others were to wander in here now. Slowly, his breathing came under control. He tucked his shirt into his shorts and ran a hand through his hair, wishing he'd had the chance to shower after swimming and sweating out in the yard with the dogs. In the mirror, the fabric bunched now at his waist looked queer so he untucked his shirt again and tried pulling his shorts lower on his hips.

When Doug stepped back into the room, Nate noticed that he was pale, as if he hadn't slept. Strangely, the exhaustion seemed to have removed from his face a layer of his usual indifference.

"So you know the Hollands?"

"Yeah," Doug replied. "I know them."

"I stopped by the house a few times. Have you been away?"

"I've been busy."

The thrill of being alone in a room with him again seemed to make everything else fall away. What would it matter if someone did come knocking at the door? This—between them—this was about what they wanted. Not who the desire made them.

Trying to hide his erection, Nate took a seat on the edge of the bed.

Doug paused to inspect the replica of the ocean liner.

It was the SS *Normandie*. Just over a thousand feet, according to the brass plaque. As long as an aircraft carrier, with a draft as deep, and likely capable of a similar speed, thirty knots or so, complete with the ballrooms and the luxury suites. Such a classy, elegant profile, she had, the stuff of postcards. Capsized dockside in the Hudson, if Doug remembered correctly, and sold for scrap.

"Glenda's crazy," he observed. "She thinks she's some kind of duchess."

"Mrs. Holland? Yeah. She's a weird cook too."

"Let me guess. You're high as a kite."

"No—I mean, not really. We smoked earlier but—"

"I need a favor," he said, examining the fine thread braided into a miniature length of rope and coiled on the ship's foredeck. "In the old lady's house. There are papers, records, lots of them, I'm guessing. I need as much about the case as you can get. Are you going to do that for me?"

"I thought it was over."

"No. We're just in a new phase."

He came over to stand in front of Nate. A couple of weeks earlier he'd gone so far as to agree to go to a movie with the kid, even though he knew it would only feed his fantasy of the two of them as actually together. Nate had dressed up in pressed chinos and an ironed shirt; he'd even polished his shoes.

To be that innocent, he thought.

He looked up at Doug with such tender hope.

"What do you want from me?" Doug asked. "You want me to fuck you?"

Nate blushed. "Why are you being so harsh?"

"That's what you want. Right?"

When he tried to stand up Doug put a hand on his shoulder and pressed him down again; he turned to face the wall. Looking at the kid's profile, it occurred to Doug how easy it would be to take his head in his hands and with a quick twist of the neck, kill him.

"I swear to God," Vrieger had said to him once, "I wish I had stabbed every one of those passengers to death. At least then I'd know what we did to them."

"You think I'm an idiot," Nate said. "You think just because I keep coming to your house you can say anything you want to me. I'm not as weak as you think. I've been through stuff."

"Okay. Fine. But here's the question: Are you strong enough to tell me what you want? That's the test, in the real world. I told you what I want. I want those papers."

He reached out and cupped the back of Nate's skull in his hand, pressing his thumb and forefinger into the taut muscles of his neck.

Slowly, reluctantly, Nate leaned forward, letting his head come to rest against Doug's stomach.

"What if I want to tell you that I love you?"

"You don't love me. I make you hard, that's all. Which is fine. The rest is daydreaming. But don't worry," Doug said, running his hand through Nate's hair. "I like you."

"Really?"

"Sure. Why not?"

DAISIES AND MILKWEED and high summer grass scratched at Charlotte's ankles and shins, catching on the hem of her dress as the crickets and frogs all about her in the field sang in endless oscillation.

They can't have gone far, she thought, how far could the dogs have gone? Lights from the party died away at the woods' edge.

"Samuel!" she called into the blackness, dotted here and there by fireflies. "Wilkie!"

Mosquitoes swarmed at her head and along her bare arms she could feel the tingle of gnats. The air itself seemed to sweat, the pores of every living thing opening wide, sap bleeding from the pines, the bushy arrowheads of the grass stalks bursting to seed, the whole warm earth breathing in the darkness.

Her temples still throbbed from the receding cacophony of voices and music. She'd focused as best she could talking to Fanning, as she always tried to in the presence of others, holding fast to the teleological mind, that once broad current that flowed past the lacuna of doubt and random transport. But those organizing arguments dropped away again here.

Stepping into the woods, she reached her hand out and felt the smooth bark of a birch.

"Come along," she called out to them. "Come along."

She could barely see her hand in front of her face, the darkness molten now like a closed eyelid's slow swirl.

Why search? Such pedants and moralists Sam and Wilkie had become. Yet as soon as she imagined being without them the feeling of loneliness bit at her. She had been nearly cured of that disease before they had come along. She had been content in solitude. Her soul kept alive by the leaps of incandescence that now and then hallowed intervals otherwise inconsequent: the rhythm of words singing off a page, a sonata turning time into feeling, a landscape on a canvas so caught as to grant one brief respite from the fear of total neutrality. These were the body and blood of her faith in the world. What the utilitarians and the materialists and the swallowers of all the cheap scientism would never understand: that the privilege of walking by the river in nature's company owed as much to a mind trained by poetry and painting—of Protestant plainsong or Romantic largesse—as to any quiddity of nature's own. You walked through the painting. You saw through the poem. Imagination created experience, not matter alone.

"Wilkie!"

If they went too far they might reach the road, where they could be hit by a car or cut their paws on glass.

Somewhere in the distance, she heard a young woman's cry. She turned, seeing nothing but darkness behind her. All of a sudden, there was a terrible beating of wings and she felt the stiff tips of feathers brush against her arm as a bird took off right beside her, a crow by the sound of the call it made as it veered up and away. She began walking more quickly, her breathing growing heavy again, the back of her dress soaked through with sweat. Roots protruding from the ground and the low branches of the pines made the going hard. Just as she saw what she thought were lights up ahead, she felt a sharp nick on her leg and shifted to her right to avoid it only to feel another stab on her wrist. Frightened, she reached her arms out in front of her, and started moving faster still.

THE GUESTS, stuffed and drunk, had at last been herded out onto the lawn for the fireworks, the flush-faced town collegians on break from summer internships grabbing their third or fourth glasses of champagne as the foreign investors trailed after them remarking to themselves that no matter how weak the dollar or poorly managed the public fisc, really you couldn't beat the States for all the sights to see. And there, teetering on a riser overlooking the pond stood Glenda Holland soused to the gills, trying to shush the players who'd already struck up the opening largo of the *1812 Overture*.

Hal, for reasons he couldn't later recall, had been in search of twine and a shovel when, at about this time, he flipped the switch on the garage-door opener. The panicked sheep fled as if from the abattoir, waddling at a clip across the drive, bleating as they went, only to be penned again between the tents, driven into the rear of the gathering crowd, who turned in astonishment at this sudden outbreak of the agrarian. When an EverSafe Security employee drew a semiautomatic from under his jacket and held it down toward the shaggy, neglected creatures, a vegan sophomore from Vassar standing nearby cried "Terrorist!" at the top of her lungs. No sooner had she uttered the word, than champagne flutes were tossed aside and crushed under foot as the guests toward the front, blind to the nature of the threat, were sickened by the sudden knowledge that their decision to avoid city crowds had failed to deliver them from danger, and with no other direction to go they hurried down the slope into the grass, scattering toward the woods and the pond and roadway. Others closer to the incident merely returned to their tables, baffled as to the origin or meaning of the episode. For a while, mild chaos reigned, Glenda trying desperately to conscript the guards as shepherds, while some of the younger and more inebriated guests, amused at the folly, began feeding the sheep the remainders of the peanut-butter parfait. Nerves shot, the animals began shitting profusely, on the grass, on the dance floor, on the feet of exhausted partygoers, who sent up new cries, the stink thrown off by the steaming piles mixing with the stale scent of the machine-cooled tents to give what remained of the gathering the air of a barnyard in autumn or early spring.

Emerging onto the terrace, Nate encountered a ewe working a drainpipe loose with the scratching motion of her tubby white flank.

"You!" a man in a baggy gray suit called out. "Have you seen my sister?"

"Shit," he said, recognizing Ms. Graves's brother from one of his visits to her house. "I'll find her."

It seemed to take forever to wade through the milling crowd. Eventually, he managed to circle around to the parking area, where by the gate he finally saw her. She walked stooped forward and with great effort. When he reached her he saw she had bright-red scratch marks lined all up and down her arms and legs and one across the side of her neck.

"Ms. Graves, the dogs, they're inside, they're fine. It's my fault. I wanted to feed them."

Tears welled in her eyes, though her kindly, pained smile never faltered.

"These people don't clear their underbrush," she said. "There's a nasty patch of briars in there. A few hours with the clippers is all I'd need."

Lending his arm for support, he walked her slowly up the path.

"What on earth are you doing here?" she asked. "Don't tell me these people are your friends."

No sooner had he found a chair for Charlotte back up on the lawn than Mrs. Holland once more ascended the little riser, waving her arms and calling out to whomever remained to please, please, hurry up and watch. The bleary faces of a few stalwart celebrants turned just in time to see the barge on the pond explode in one single, hammering burst, the flames from the blast shooting twenty or thirty feet into the air before dripping back into the water like burning fuel, and so too over the dry grass, which began at once to burn.

Chapter 14

The heat kept on through July. On the Finden High playing fields, soccer-camp kids drilled from steamy morning to hazy afternoon, and the unfortunates remanded to summer school sweated it out in the same remorseless classrooms they'd tried all year to avoid. Mold flourished in unfinished basements and in the trunks of parents' old cars littered with sodden swimsuits and damp towels smeared in suntan lotion and the remains of spilt beer. The moisture dampened even the sound of traffic, which in the normal course of events would have lessened once the semester ended, but school exchanges had been canceled in the wake of 9/11 and family vacations to Europe called off. Parents told kids to get summer jobs and pulled back from the promise of cars for college. You heard stories of people's moms and dads being laid off from office jobs that if you'd ever bothered to contemplate seemed eternal in their boredom. The town put out the usual flags, and the flowers beneath them bloomed. And for all the worry shot down the cable wires, for all the jokes about duct tape and the town police cordoning off the baseball diamond to detonate a gradeschooler's lost knapsack, for all the hours of news spooling tape on the dirty bomber and Saddam's vast arsenal and the tall, smiling Satan eluding our might in the mountains of some hopelessly foreign country, the drama club still had its bake sale and the library still sold books out on the sidewalk from noon to three on weekends, and you still wished for a clarifying rain at the end of each sweltering day.

Such a rain arrived on the Friday afternoon two weeks after the party, just as Nate was getting to Ms. Graves's house. She led him into the living room and took a seat in her usual spot on the couch. In the stifling heat, the room's disarray was strictly oppressive, the mounds of clutter like plants rotting in a jungle. None of this would ever be cleared away, he thought, not as long as she remained rooted here.

Her voice lacked its usual force and she often paused in her meandering discourse, which contained no more breathless jeremiads. She spoke awhile of Dewey and the spread of primary education, but he could tell her thoughts were elsewhere.

"You needn't worry," she said after a particularly long silence, during which he'd noticed the scabs still visible on her shins. "I know you aren't studying for your exam anymore. You've been good to indulge me like this. I know I've bored you."

"That's not true," he said, gnawing at the blunt end of his pen.

She gazed past him out the window.

"I've been thinking of birch trees for along the riverbank. What do you think? Perhaps a mix of things would be better."

On his way over, Nate had tried telling himself that the documents wouldn't matter, that she had already won her suit. But the excuse seemed thin now; Doug wouldn't want the files if he couldn't gain something by them.

"In any case, I'll make us some tea."

As soon as she left the room, he began darting from one pile of paper to the next, keeping a close eye on the door. He gathered bank statements, tax records, notarized letters, and anything else from that mass of print which seemed relevant. On a stack by the fireplace he saw a manila folder labeled "Society Minutes" and he shoved it in his knapsack along with the rest. His only thought as he went about his task was a disavowed one: that losing his father permitted him this moral lapse. As if, in some grand ledger, his loss had earned him a pass or two.

Ms. Graves returned carrying a tray of tea and biscuits.

"I've been returning to Whitman," she said, as she poured them each a cup. "He's right about most things. But if you take him to heart, you can't always read the poems in your favor. He has this way of looking back at you. Here's one I came across this morning. 'To a Historian.' "

She put on her reading glasses and recited the lines in a slow, reflective voice.

" 'You who celebrates bygones, / Who have explored the outward, the surfaces of the races, the life that has exhibited itself, / Who have treated of man as the creature of politics, aggregates, rulers and priests, / I, habitan of the Alleghenies, treating of him as he is in himself in his own rights, / Pressing the pulse of life that has seldom exhibited itself, (the great pride of man in himself,) Chanter of Personality, outlining what is yet to be, / I project the history of the future.'

"Bracing stuff, no? The question is, can you chant personality without devolving into solipsism? Can you trust the pulse of life without becoming Mr. Fanning? Because he is the future. One way or the other. His kind of rapaciousness, it doesn't end. It just bides its time."

Later that evening Nate stood in the middle of Doug's kitchen watching him spread the files across the counter. He'd gone home first to shower and change but on the walk back he'd sweated through his T-shirt again.

"Does this mean she's going to lose?"

Doug fingered an envelope, glancing at the return address.

"She was always going to lose," he said. "It's just a question of when."

"She's not evil, you know."

"You feel bad, huh?"

"Wouldn't you?"

Doug flipped through another folder, ignoring Nate's question. "This is good," he said. "You've done well. There's beer in the fridge if you want it."

Taking one, Nate wandered down the hall, through the first empty room, and into the space where the TV stood in the corner. Here, binders and files now covered a large portion of the floor. Two laptops, their power cords running several yards to the wall sockets, were set up on the kitchen table, which had been brought in and placed beside the couch.

Doug followed him in and turned on the Sox-Yankees game.

"The fact is, she was obliged to give us copies of those papers weeks ago. That's the law. So you can relax. It's not on you."

They watched as the designated hitter, Ramirez, struck a ball deep into center field, driving home the runner at third and bringing the crowd at Fenway to its feet.

It wasn't too late to walk back into the kitchen, Nate thought, to gather those papers up and leave. "You were wrong about the baseball thing," he said. "I did watch it before I met you."

"You're a weirdo."

"Yeah. So are you."

"Why don't you go upstairs. Go ahead. Take your clothes off. I'll be up in a bit."

Nate's heart thudded against his chest. "What if I don't want to?"

"Suit yourself."

The bed hadn't been made. Nate pulled the sheets up and tucked them in, arranging the cotton blanket at the foot of the mattress and putting the pillows back in place. He wondered if he should keep the lamp on but decided not to, leaving only the light from the bathroom. He folded his trousers and put them with his shoes and belt on the floor in the corner. The nights he'd stayed over they had always been under the sheets together, Nate getting Doug off, never the other way around. He had never even been naked in front of him.

He waited there in his underwear, terrified at the thought of what kind of person he was for wanting this. He waited ten minutes and then another ten. He could hear the television still on downstairs, switched to a different station.

Eyes closed, trying to forget everything—his life and the world outside this house—he sensed that for all the highs he'd experienced while stoned in the back of Jason's car or tripping by the lake, for all the cares that such forcings of the brain had displaced, none would free him from himself as this might.

To be pressed down into the bed by Doug's full weight, the last remnant of the minding self rubbed into oblivion. To be taken over and used up and made to go away. A body as strong as Doug's could do that to you.

At last the sound of the TV ceased and a few moments later Doug came through the bedroom door. He walked to the window and leaned against the sill.

"You're not taking your shirt off?" he asked.

"I don't look like you. I'm not muscular."

"That's fine. You're more like a girl that way."

"Is that how you think of me?"

"I'm just saying, you're fine. Go on. Take your shirt off. And the boxers."

Nate pulled his T-shirt over his head and laid it on the bed beside him and then he slipped his shorts off, his throat tightening, just a thread of air reaching his lungs.

Pushing his shoes off and unbuttoning his shirt, Doug approached the bed.

"My God, you're young," he said, taking Nate's chin in his hand. "You really are."

Withdrawing from his touch, Nate lay back on the bed, covering himself with one hand.

"I've never done this," he whispered.

Making no reply, Doug picked Nate up by the rib cage and turned him over onto his stomach.

"Just close your eyes," he said, shifting onto the bed. And then Nate felt Doug's knees pressing against the inside of his own, spreading his legs apart. He'd been self-conscious about his body for so long, for so many years, and yet he'd still never known the sensation could be this intense, as if, perversely, by enacting the fantasy of self-forgetting the self only grew stronger and more ineluctable than ever. He heard the drawer of the bedside table open and close.

"Here. Up on your knees."

Doug's hands grasped him at the waist, pulling him backward. He turned his head to look up at him but again Doug told him to close his eyes. A thick warmth pressed up against his ass and then, after a moment of struggle, he felt a sudden, sharp ring of pain coil up through his body and into his head, making the blood beat at his temples and forcing him to gasp for breath.

"Don't worry. I'm not going to rape you."

That he would lose control of his bowels seemed certain but when that sensation ended he found himself able to breathe again, breathing and sweating, still in great pain but a pain that moved too fast along the tips of his nerves to make him want to stop.

He felt Doug's pelvis flat against him and the muscles of his back and neck released and he let go, the vigilant self finally fading as the thrusting began, the shock of it driven into him over and over.

From the base of his spine some liquid locked deep against the bone released and burst up into his skull, heating his brain to the edge of fainting. Leaning down on his forearms, his forehead to the mattress, he held on for another few seconds and then came without touching himself, his head jerking sharply backward, his shoulders contracting down his back.

A few strokes later Doug pulled out of him and rolled flat on the bed.

Nate stood and headed quickly for the bathroom, closing the door behind him.

"You all right?" Doug called out a few minutes later.

"Yeah," he said, leaning against the tiled wall of the shower, the old dread of discovery and the basic penal shame washing back over him with the scalding water.

Part Three

Chapter 15

From the window of his office on the tenth floor of the Federal Reserve Bank of New York, Henry Graves looked down over the crowds rushing westward along Liberty Street and up Nassau toward the Fulton Street station. Those who hadn't already been let out early for the Columbus Day weekend moved with more than their usual haste toward the buses and subways that would drain them from the city by the tens of thousands, emptying them into Jersey, Westchester, and Long Island, where supermarket inventories had already dropped a few points and the local banks had balanced their sheets for the week and sent their people home.

Downstairs, the Open Market Desk would trade Treasury bills for another half hour but the volume would be light. Soon Fedwire would settle, clearing everything from corporate bond sales to the credit card purchases of the secretaries and mutual fund salesmen hurrying now along the street below. Over the weekend when these people went to the movies or the mall they would swipe their cards through magnetic strips and thus do what for centuries had been the sole province of kings and parliaments: they would create money. Short money to be sure, but money nonetheless, which until that moment had never appeared on a balance sheet or been deposited with a bank, that was nothing but a permission for indebtedness, the final improvisation in a long chain of governed promises. And as they slept, the merchants' computers would upload their purchases and into the river of commerce another drop of liquidity would flow, reversing their commute, heading back into the city to collect in the big, money-center banks, which in the quiet of night would distribute news of the final score: a billion a day shipped to Asia and the petro states.

Behind him he heard his secretary, Helen, enter and turned to see her carrying a bouquet of lilies in a crystal vase. A beam of the expiring sun shot through the globe of water in her hands, spraying light across the dark portraits over the couch and dancing briefly on the paneling.

"Who on earth are those from?"

"Me," she said, clearing a place on the coffee table. She was a tall woman and had to bend nearly to a right angle to adjust the stems, her hand reaching up to brush her graying hair behind her ear. Most women her age at the bank had cut theirs short and wore skirts and jackets of a uniform blue or black. Helen, who was English, looked more like a tenured scholar in some branch of the humanities, dressed in formless cotton trousers, a turtleneck, and a red cardigan.

"What for?"

"It's your birthday."

"Oh. I suppose it is. That's kind of you. Unnecessary, certainly. But kind."

"They were supposed to arrive hours ago but they should last awhile," she said, stepping back to appraise her arrangement. The phone on her desk rang and she returned to the other room to answer it.

Down below, the last rays of sun passed over the heads of the pedestrians to fall evenly across the wall of a building at the corner of Liberty and William, which until recently had displayed a mural of Seurat's *La Grande Jatte*—a set painting for, of all unlikely things, a Hollywood movie shot in the financial district. They had left it up after the production and Henry rather enjoyed having the mural there to remind him of the original, a painting he tried to visit whenever business took him to Chicago. One habit of his, at least, of which his sister would approve.

Two months ago, back in August, Charlotte had found a new cause for her paranoia: what she claimed to be the theft of documents from the house, as if they hadn't simply been swallowed up in the general chaos. She'd gone so far as to call the police to request an investigation, which they quite reasonably declined to open, this in turn only heightening her sense of persecution. Concerned that her rate of deterioration was increasing, Henry had got in touch with a neighbor, whom he'd asked to phone if she saw anything awry. The woman had called four times since. First it was a dozen saplings delivered in burlap wrap and left to die in the sun; then branches stacked at the end of the driveway to prevent cars reaching the house; after that, the collapse of one section of the barn roof, through which rain now poured; and finally, the dogs howling at all hours. Last week, he'd gone ahead and hired a home aide. While at a conference in Basel, he'd got a call on his cell phone from her saying Charlotte had barred her at the door and told her never to return.

"You don't have a lot of options," his lawyer had told him. "If she gets violent, we can talk."

"Are you expecting someone?" Helen called from the other room. "There's a woman downstairs. She says she made an appointment."

He knew there had been a reason for him to tarry here on a Friday afternoon but he hadn't been able to recall what it was.

"Yes," he said. "That's my fault. I forgot to mention it."

A few minutes later, Helen showed Evelyn Jones into his office.

With some reluctance, she placed her handbag on the coffee table and, flattening the front of her skirt onto her thighs, perched on the edge of the couch.

"Can we get you something? Coffee, water? Or something stiffer for that matter?"

"Oh, no, I'm fine, really." She looked about the room with what struck Henry as genuine marvel. "It's not what I was expecting," she said. "This building."

"Yes, it's a bit unusual for the neighborhood. It's modeled on a Medici palace. You saw the wrought iron? Rather fanciful, I suppose. But the idea of a central bank was still new back in the twenties. I think they wanted to make a statement. You're sure I can't offer you anything to drink?"

"No, thank you. I know you're busy. I'm probably interrupting."

"No, just wrapping up the week. I'm not traveling for once, which is a blessing."

He remembered now that when she first left a message a week ago he'd guessed it was an inquiry about working at the Fed, which while a rather direct approach wouldn't be unheard of and would account for her nerves. But noticing her rigid posture and pursed lips he wondered if there wasn't something more than that to her visit.

"We get them from the Met," he said, following her eyes to the paintings. "We loaned them a bar of gold back in the seventies for some show or other and they've been kind enough to let us borrow from their basement ever since. The one problem being my predecessor decided the appropriate policy would be to hang only paintings by artists from the Federal Reserve's Second District, a somewhat limiting condition when it comes to the history of art. But there we are."

"I shouldn't be here," she said. "I shouldn't have come."

"Not at all," he said genially, beginning to perceive the outlines of the thing. "Do you have another appointment after this?"

"No," she replied, surprised by the question.

"So you're not in a rush?"

She shook her head.

"I tell you what. Since this is your first visit here, allow me to show you something."

He stood up before she had the opportunity to decline, holding his arm out to guide her back through his office door.

"Helen, I'm just going to take Ms. Jones downstairs. We won't be long." He led her along the arch-ceilinged hallway, their footsteps silent on the thick carpet. "Did you fly down?" he asked, as they stepped onto the officers' elevator.

"No, I took the train."

"Yes, it's far more civilized than a plane these days." He allowed a few floors to pass before observing, "When they built this place they dynamited their way a few stories into the bedrock of the island. It was one of their great precautions. Turns out it was the only foundation strong enough to bear the weight."

The elevator doors slid open and they made their way down the windowless passage to the security officer's desk.

"Charles," he said, "are the tours over for the day? I was going to show this young woman around."

"It's all yours, sir," he said, leading them through the ten-foot, cylindrical airlock and into the antechamber. "Will you need any help with the stock, sir?"

"No, I think we're fine," Henry said. He unlocked the inner gate with his own key and ushered Evelyn into the vault, clicking the gate shut behind them. At the center of the room stood the metal scales still used to test the purity of the gold. Beside the scales were two pairs of magnesium shoe clips worn to protect the officers' feet lest they should drop a bar in transit and crush their toes.

"We're eighty feet below the sidewalk here. Thirty feet below sea level. Go ahead," he said, gesturing toward the rows of floor-to-ceiling metal cages that lined the walls, numbered but otherwise unmarked. "Have a look."

His guest glanced at him first, inquisitively, as if an elaborate trick might be afoot, but then succumbing to curiosity she approached one of the cages containing dark-yellow bars ten feet high and twenty deep. After a moment, she turned to look down the aisle, taking in the sheer number of separate compartments.

"It's the largest accumulation of monetary gold in the world," he said. "In fact, it's a decent-size chunk of all the gold ever mined."

"And all this belongs to the government?"

"No. The Treasury keeps our reserves at Fort Knox and up at West Point. The vast majority of what you see here is owned by foreign central banks. Most countries in the world deposit with us. We're just the custodians. When governments want to do business, they call up and we move the gold from one cage to another."

"They trust us that much?"

"For these purposes, yes."

She passed on to another compartment and gazed at the wall of shining gold.

"The tours come to the outer gate here every day. I think last year we had twenty-five thousand visitors. People love to look at it. It reminds me of something Galbraith said: 'The process by which banks create money is so simple the mind is repelled. A deeper mystery seems only decent.' I suppose this is what's left of the mystery. And yet this," he said, indicating with a sweep of his hand the whole contents of the vault, "barely matters. Add it up and it's no more than eighty or ninety billion worth. The wires clear more than that in an hour. All anchored to nothing but trust. Cooperation. You could even say faith, which sometimes I do, though it's certainly of an earthly kind. Without it you couldn't buy a loaf of bread.

"Of course as my sister never fails to remind me, the bigger ethical question is what people—what governments do with their money. Whether they buy medicine or food or arms. But there are conditions of possibility for doing any of these things. Whichever choices we make. The system has to work. People have to trust the paper in their wallets. And that starts somewhere. It starts with the banks."

Her fingers curled around the bars of the cage she stood before.

"I guess you know why I'm here," she said.

"Yes. I think I do."

At the end of August, Evelyn had paid $390,000 for a shingle cottage on a tree-lined street out in Alden. The kitchen at the back was a bit dark in the mornings but it had a view of a dogwood and a rhododendron in the yard. Upstairs was a bathroom and two bedrooms with dormer windows that made the rooms feel smaller than their dimensions but comfortable nonetheless. She'd always pictured moving into such a place with a husband, but with Aunt Verna's encouragement, she hadn't allowed that image to stop her.

On the new commute home, she passed a video store and often stopped to pick up a DVD, a comedy or romance, which she'd watch with dinner.

Years before, in college, she'd taken a literature course and they had read a lot of James Baldwin, among others. Though she couldn't remember what book it came from, one line in particular had always stuck with her. People pay for what they do, Baldwin had written, and more, for what they have allowed themselves to become. And they pay for it simply, with the lives they lead.

On the one hand, this sounded harsh, as if people were forever letting themselves go, as Aunt Verna would say, and being punished for it with their own misery. That was one way to hear it. But there was a democratic spirit to it as well, a sense that life consisted of the distance traveled, for good or ill. In which case, her guilt at having all that she did while her brother had got nothing lacked a purpose. Experience provided its own justice. From where it would come, no one could predict.

Two weeks ago at church, she'd stayed after for coffee. There, she'd seen a boy of nine or ten, thin with a high forehead, whom she had noticed back in June passing out programs at Carson's funeral. She'd noted him at the time because she didn't recognize him and she'd wondered who had placed him there at the door if not a member of the family. He appeared afraid when she approached him and said it wasn't the minister who had invited him to help that day.

"I came on my own," he said. "Did I do something wrong?"

She assured him that he hadn't. She was just curious, she said. Had he known Carson?

"He used to let me hang out with him. When he had calls to make in the park. He'd ride my scooter sometimes. The thing is . . . see . . . the thing is, I seen him shot. I was across the street when they did it.

There was two of them. And then quick-like, there was people calling the ambulance and all that. But I seen him lying up in there before they came, his face all shot up, and all these bills on the floor, I don't know why they hadn't taken the money or nothing, but there was all this cash, his I guess. But when I came back a couple minutes later it was gone, so I guess someone musta took it."

Yanked from the dimensionless efficiency in which she'd dwelt since the day her brother died, Evelyn had seen vividly for the first time the image of her brother's corpse, of his shot brain smeared on the tile.

The next day she didn't go to work. In fact, she ended up staying out half the week, in that new house of hers, in which she suddenly felt herself to be a stranger.

Coming to see Henry Graves, she'd known that eventually he would ask her why. Why was she telling him what she knew?

He put the question to her once they had ridden the elevator back upstairs and returned to his office.

"I must tell you," he said, "in all my years here I've never had someone come through the door to report their own institution. I confess I'm curious."

Evelyn drew herself up to deliver her piece. But what came to mind were not the words she'd prepared but the look on her aunt Verna's face when she'd told her about her latest promotion, how her eyebrows had risen, her eyes brimming, her whole face opening up as her shoulders let go, as if for all the world she'd been told, as in a dream, that she were free from a burden she'd never thought to imagine gone. It was a look Evelyn had seen before, at each stage of her accomplishments, and each time it nearly broke her. She could never tell Verna how routine her job was, how bureaucratic and spiritually thin. That would be cruel. But then so, in its way, was coming here to blow the whistle. Once the lawyers got involved, who knew what would count for the truth? She had pieces of evidence about what McTeague and Fanning had done but she wasn't, after all, the person in charge. As best she could tell, the protections for a person in her position weren't worth the paper they were written on. It wasn't only *her* hopes she was jeopardizing by being here.

Henry Graves's welcoming expression had been replaced by a more sober, businesslike concern.

"I can't say for sure," she said. "You're probably wondering if it's because I have some grudge against Fanning. I don't care for him but that's not why I'm here. Maybe I'm just tired of worrying."

"My staff is going to need to debrief you," he said. "If it's okay with you, I'd like to do that right away."

She nodded and he reached for a phone on the side table. As he talked with his deputy, Evelyn looked about the office again. It was smaller than many occupied by the senior executives at Atlantic Securities and without the views. Perhaps she was only imagining it, then, this sense of imperturbable calm and yet it seemed manifest to her sitting there encased in those heavy stone walls, the gilt-framed paintings looking down from the wall, as the grandfatherly white man in his jacket and tie took the situation in hand.

She wondered if this were the feeling that so many people out there in the country hungered for: a sense of continuity, gone or never present in so many lives.

Give me one thing that won't change. Just one.

Daddy will take care of the money.

The dealers whose henchmen had shot Carson knew the need for this feeling as well as anyone, and they used it every day. But here in the undying realm of the central bank no violence was required. Here the aristocrats of bureaucracy guarded money's permanent interests. Part of her wanted never to leave this room with its promise of the cessation of all struggle. And yet to recognize this longing was to see herself as a traitor. To what, she wasn't entirely sure. Life perhaps. Or the belief in it.

"We're all set," Henry said, putting down the phone. "Are you ready?"

Chapter 16

"Where are you?" Sabrina asked.

"I don't know. Twenty-eight, maybe. Twenty-nine."

"Wow," she said. "If you're not careful, you might actually become interesting."

From the office where he had wound up, Doug could see over Four Point Channel and across the corner of the harbor to the new federal courthouse with its slanting glass façade and a row of flags out front, fluttering in the breeze.

"So here's the deal," Sabrina said. "Holland wants you at the Ritz for the deal closing with Taconic; McTeague's called three times; you've got a message from Mikey to contact him ASAP; the guy you hired to erase our e-mails says someone's messing with his program; some official-sounding Chinese guy from the Singapore Exchange wanted to confirm your mailing address at eight this morning; Evelyn Jones is on vacation; and some kid named Nate called to say he was waiting for you 'in the room.' Which I'm not even going to touch. You think just *maybe* you could turn your phone on?"

In the last few weeks, Doug had begun to wander like this. Using the stairs, he'd head down to floors of the tower he'd never visited before, the reception areas distinguishable only by the pallor of the ferns and the colors of the abstract paintings hung over the leather chairs. Departments whose staff he could once have recited by name had doubled or tripled in size, filling whole floors. Nodding at the smiling secretaries, saying the occasional word to the middle managers surprised in the corridor, all of them as ignorant as could be of how untenable the bank's predicament had become, he'd wind up in the office of someone down in consumer credit or government relations who was out for the day, and there he'd sit in the quiet with the door closed and his phone off, trying again and again to order his thoughts.

Through July and August the Nikkei index had shed another twelve hundred points; the Japanese Ministry of Finance, criticized for their earlier intervention, had done nothing to prevent the slide. McTeague's losses had ballooned. They were larger now than the value of Atlantic Securities itself.

But then again, hardly anyone knew. If some deputy department head occasionally bothered to e-mail Doug, inquiring about loans from one division after another to an obscure subsidiary named Finden Holdings, he didn't bother to reply. Even Holland seemed to have voided the problem from his mind, entertaining clients at Red Sox games and the Boston Pops and now finalizing the stock-only purchase of Taconic, the bank that had fallen on hard times back in the spring.

Union Atlantic's customers still drew on lines of credit and made payments on existing loans. The insurance subsidiary still wrote policies and, after initially projecting large, 9/11-related losses, looked as if it might actually show a modest profit. People all over the country still opened checking accounts and paid bills and withdrew tens of millions in cash. On the Asian exchanges, there were rumors of a huge bet on the Nikkei but people figured it was a hedge fund in Connecticut or London, because, after all, banks wouldn't expose that much of their own capital.

Indeed, the larger the problem grew the more routine the management of it had become. What had started as a crisis had turned into a condition. And then, just as the condition surpassed any previously imaginable level of acceptable seriousness, it seemed to vanish altogether, as if too big to see.

"You there?" Sabrina asked.

"Tell Holland I'm on my way."

"What about the rest?"

"Tell that computer geek to work his shit out. I want those e-mails gone."

"So dramatic. Can I shred something?"

"Piss off."

"Maybe I'll become one of those cooperating witnesses. I could write a memoir. I'm so sick of Franco. I had this whole idea about how to generate a subtle, almost perverse sympathy for him, but it all seems ridiculous now. I slept with this schlep in Watertown the other day. I tried taking his grandmother seriously, but in the end she was just an old Fascist. Who knows? My therapist says—"

Doug pressed End. He hadn't moved his gaze from the courthouse façade. He had been in the building only once, with the general counsel for a hearing in a shareholder suit. Washington had spared no expense for the judges. From the marble floors to the courtrooms rimmed in arabesques of pink-and-blue pastel, you could be forgiven for expecting exhibitions of modern art rather than juries and sentencings.

To check the markets, he switched on the television in the corner, searching for the business channel. But before he reached it, he came upon those images that were constant now on cable news: the satellite photos of the Iraqi desert, still after still of warehouses and outbuildings surrounded by nothing but sand. Like all of them, this report was being narrated by some retired member of the brass paid to opine on the nature of the weapons hidden beneath all those roofs and tarps. Soon the screen cut to B roll of aircraft carriers and naval destroyers, as the old soldier described the slow but steady buildup of hardware in the theater. The segment ended with a shot of a tanker moving low in the water, as the news anchor, in a voice that somehow managed to blend excitement and resignation, reminded the audience of America's vital interests in the region.

Lately, Doug couldn't sleep for watching this stuff. And he knew Vrieger would be watching it too. Watching the endless repetition of facts and speculation and probable lies, the consumption of which at least partially numbed the helplessness of seeing it unfold at such distance and so inexorably. The two of them had spoken the previous week and Vrieger had told him that he was all set, headed to Virginia soon for training, the invasion apparently scheduled for March but plenty of contractors needed already for logistics and security, hundreds of them flowing into Kuwait each week.

In the small hours of the morning, Doug would lie awake staring at the maps with the fancy graphics of arrows sliding toward Baghdad from north, south, and west, as the commentators prattled on: neocons smugly suffering lesser minds, while their opponents expressed incredulity at the ignorance of the American people for supporting the idea of such a war; and then there were Doug's favorites, the young, pro-war liberals, so fresh-faced and eager to prove they weren't weak or queer. But whoever the commentators were, the reports seemed always to return to the endless stock footage of tanks kicking dust and missiles blasting hot off the decks of cruisers. Which carried Doug back, over and over, to standing on the deck of the *Vincennes*, that furnace wind blowing off the fouled waters of the Gulf, clogging the ship's every pore with sand, and to the cursing of the Iranian thugs in the speedboats spit over the radio waves, and to watching the coordinates of the jetliner's altitude rise across his monitor.

In the hours before dawn, when he finally managed to turn off the news, a mild delirium often took sway, a semiconscious but still-unresting state, in which unremembered moments floated up into his senses, strangely complete in air and texture, almost dreamlike in their exactitude. Like sitting on the vinyl backseat of his uncle John's station wagon between his cousins Michael and P.J. with the windows rolled down, thrilled to be out of his mother's apartment and on the way out to the Cape, the voice on the radio calling the game as the miles of scrub pine blurred green across his eyes; and later, the deep, ineffable happiness of returning to his cousins' house, a beautiful dusk place full of shouting and motion and the clutter of sports gear and toys, his uncle and aunt's orders barked and ignored, Michael not turning off the hose but letting the water run all the way to the bottom of the drive, where they built their hurried dams for the pleasure of watching them overrun, glimpsing in his cousins' casual disregard of their father's rebukes the freedom that came with bossy parents—to resist, to push back against a strength and solidity your petty acts could never overcome.

Or waiting out in front of the apartment, out in the cold air for his mother, after snow had fallen, wanting not to be late again to Mass because then everyone would turn to look at them; making a snowball with his bare hands as he waited for the sound of her footsteps on the stairs; watching her walk to the car in her black wool coat and blue dress, her once-a-week face made up with blush and lipstick; his hand burning on the frozen pack in his fist, seeing her breath and his, wishing his snowball were hard enough to smash the windshield but knowing it wasn't; and then entering the car, going back into that silence that wasn't even punishment or rebuke but simply her way of getting by, the air from the whining defroster cold on his face at first, its stale plastic scent soon erased by the sharper smell of his mother's cigarette.

Like taunts, these memories were, the past trying to claim him back at his weakest moments.

If he could just sleep, he kept thinking, then his concentration would return. He could switch off the news and his brain would stop shaking loose these useless recollections and he could focus again on the problem at hand.

He headed down into the lobby and out to the car waiting to take him to the Ritz. On the way there, he dialed Mikey.

"I don't know how you got those papers," Mikey said, "but they did the job. You won. That Graves Society's a joke. She stopped making donations three years ago. And their taxes—anyway, the court tossed Cushman's order out. Charlotte Graves isn't getting title to anything."

"Does she have an appeal?"

"To God, maybe."

"Good. I want you to call the broker and get the house listed."

"Didn't you hear what I said? You beat her."

"Yeah, I heard you. But I need it listed. I want the asset in cash."

"I just won your fucking appeal for you! I spent a year building you a house for Christ's sake. You picked the investment, we cleared the land, you got your mansion. Now just live in it for a few years, would you? Turn a real profit."

"I appreciate all you did. I'll have Sabrina handle the broker if you want."

"Who the hell *are* you?"

"I'm your friend, Mikey. But the situation, it's changed."

From the hotel window, Nate could see a young couple down at the Arlington Street gates in shorts and sun hats. They paused to consult a map as their children ran ahead to gawk at the statue of General Washington mounted on his horse, his bronze eyes casting a permanent gaze up Commonwealth Avenue. Beyond the gates, in the Boston Public Gardens, the branches of the weeping willows swayed over the edge of the pond.

As he watched the man drop down on one knee to photograph his wife and children gathered beneath the statue, Nate dialed Emily's cell phone again, impatient for her to answer. Two months ago, she'd left for college and they'd spoken on the phone most weeks since. But for the third time that day her line went straight to voice mail. As he was about to hang up, his handset beeped and he saw that she was calling in.

"So you're on it as well?" she said. "The other two have been calling me all day telling me how deeply important all our friendships have been, Jason waxing on about how much he loves me all of a sudden. It's so mid-nineties. They've never been to a rave in their life. You guys are all going to wake up depressed with jaw aches."

"I'm not on Ecstasy. I'm not with them."

"So what's with all your calls? What's the emergency?"

"Nothing," he said. "I was just checking in, seeing how it's going up there. Is your roommate still a hassle?"

"I don't believe you're not in a crisis, but whatever. We can talk about that in a minute. To answer your question, yeah, she's definitely a problem. The whole vegan, bisexual, anti-NAFTA, Nader-voter situation I could more or less deal with if she'd just keep it to herself. You'd think she'd at least shut up when she meditated, but no, that's when she *chants*. And she has the gall to warn *me* about the false consciousness of cynicism. She's a cross between a Hari Krishna and a Stalinist. It's obviously just an aggressive formation against whatever void of boomer parenting she suffered, but I don't see why I should have to cope with it."

"I need you to cover for me," Nate said.

"Cover for what?"

"I told my mother I was going to visit you. I've been gone a bunch lately and I think she's starting to suspect. I just don't want her to worry, you know?"

"Where are you?"

"The Ritz."

"Oh, my God. You're with him! That is *so* hot. I mean I should probably be worrying about you as a friend or whatever, but that guy is smokin'. It's so much easier for you guys. The boys in my art history class don't even look at me they're so busy checking each other out. They were comparing underwear brands yesterday. But what's with the hotel?"

"He's negotiating some kind of deal. They stay here all night."

"And he asked you to come with him?"

Nate hesitated, not wanting to disappoint Emily by upending the image behind her playful envy. Besides, what sense could he make of his circumstance if it didn't conform in part, at least, to other people's more ordinary arrangements? How could he explain to her that despite all he and Doug had done they had never actually kissed?

"Do you miss Jason?"

"That drooling pothead? Maybe. I did meet this one guy in Intro Psych. He's German, so at least he knows how to have a conversation. I don't know. This English professor last week, he handed out the syllabus and told us we'd be reading nineteenth-century novels with heroes and heroines our age or not much older, and he asked if we thought our feelings were important enough to write books about. So this one kid said, how could his feelings matter if they didn't have any consequences, like marriage or kids or your reputation? Of course, he looked like he was on meds, but it riled my roommate up enough to insist our feelings about politics mattered. Which I sort of agree with. But who wants to read a novel about some vegetarian's journey to an antiwar stance?"

"Doesn't it depend on how intense they are?" Nate asked, a little jealous that Emily got to spend her time considering such things.

"What do you mean?"

"Your feelings. I mean if they're intense enough, they have consequences, right?"

"You're really gone on this guy, aren't you?"

Just then he heard a knocking at the door. "I gotta go," he said. "He's back."

"Okay, lover boy. Take care of yourself."

When Nate opened the door he was dumbfounded by the sight of Mr. Holland. For a moment the two of them beheld each other in bewildered silence.

"Nate. Hi there. This is Doug Fanning's room, isn't it?"

"Yeah," he said, unable to conceive of any reason he would be staying at the Ritz-Carlton on his own dime.

Stepping past Nate, Mr. Holland entered the room, looking about with a befuddled expression, which fell away as he took in the unmade bed and the clothes on the chairs and Nate's knapsack lying on the floor.

Unlike Mrs. Holland, who rarely managed to hide her aggression toward Jason's friends, Mr. Holland had always greeted them warmly. He seemed cheered by the idea that his son had friends at all, as inattentive parents often were, relieved by some vague notion of their child's social success. He was friendly in a general way. But he suffered from no lack of focus now.

"Is Jason with you? Is he in the hotel?"

Nate realized he was being offered an escape route. If he could rope Jason into the story somehow and then get to him before his father did, he might save himself. But he couldn't put the pieces together quickly enough.

"Actually . . . I know Mr. Fanning. From Finden."

"From Finden? I see."

He glanced at his watch, as if recalculating the odds on a particularly complicated bet. Nate understood that he wouldn't be asked to explain himself any further, and that this was probably a bad thing. "Well," Mr. Holland said, "I need to see Doug. So if he drops by, maybe you could tell him I'm downstairs."

He was already back through the door when he turned, as if halted by the belated awareness that their acquaintance required some parting pleasantry. "Anyhow," he said, "say hello to your parents for me."

As THE CAR came to a stop in front of the hotel, Doug's phone rang.

"Are you in the building yet?" Holland asked.

"Yeah, I'm here. Are we closing the deal with Taconic?"

There was a pause and it sounded as if Jeffrey were holding his hand over the receiver. "So, yeah," he said. "Good that you're here. Just sit tight, another forty-five minutes, an hour maybe. I just have to go over a few more things with the lawyers and then we'll all meet in the ballroom."

"What's going on?"

"Nothing. The deal's fine. I just want you close at the end, that's all."

A liveried bellhop opened the car door and Doug passed through the revolving glass into the lobby. Beyond the elevator bank, to the right of the front desk, two heavyset white guys in navy-blue windbreakers were talking quietly to the hotel manager. They had wires in their ears and walkie-talkies on their belts. They weren't secret service and they didn't look private. FBI, maybe. Definitely federal.

Doug considered walking back onto the sidewalk and hailing a cab. But if they were here for him, how far would he get? Not today or tomorrow, but next week or next month? He would need time to arrange things, on his terms.

As soon as he entered the room upstairs, Nate came up off the bed, all eagerness and alarm.

"I kept trying your phone," he said. "I didn't know where you were."

Doug tossed his briefcase on the couch and crossed to the window. Nothing unusual down on the street. No squad cars or agents. He regretted now having let Nate come here but when he'd told him he would be staying in the city for a while, he'd practically begged. He had arrived with a suitcase and a bag of books, as if they were on vacation together.

As a practical matter, Nate had been expendable as soon as he'd delivered the files back in July. And yet in the months since they had spent as much time together as ever. Doug had kept telling himself that getting off helped him sleep. That Nate was just experimenting, and he was just killing time. But the more he used the boy's body, the more frustrated he'd become.

"You shouldn't be here," he said.

"Why? Is something the matter?"

The collar of his faded blue polo was tucked under on one side and his hair, as usual, was a mess.

"What did you do?" Doug said, sliding his thumb down Nate's smooth cheek. "Shave?"

"Yeah. You think I'm too scruffy. It's my Ritz-Carlton look."

He took hold of Doug's hand and guided it down to his hip. "You look good in that suit," he said, stepping in close, their faces just a few inches apart.

His gall rising, Doug turned Nate around and pushed him forward onto the bed.

"After this," he said, "you're leaving. You understand?"

When Nate had removed his shirt and jeans, he rolled onto his back.

"What are you doing?"

"I never get to look at you," Nate said.

Doug grabbed him by the backs of the knees and pressed his thighs to his chest, bending him open. Holding him down like that, he fiddled with his own belt and trousers, amazed and repulsed by the endlessness of the boy's need. He spit in his hand and entered him with a single jab. Nate winced, his eyes watering, but Doug kept going. This was the thing—why he had kept him around. To tackle a male body, one like his own boyish self, to push it and get at it, his dick and this fucking just a means to the end. To fuck weakness, to pummel it.

Even as he seemed about to cry, Nate kept his eyes open, staring straight at him. Doug reached his hand down to cover the eyes, but with surprising force Nate peeled the hand back and kept looking. It was unbearable. He jabbed harder, pushing air from Nate's lungs, forcing him to gasp for breath. And still he wouldn't look away. A surge of nausea rose up through Doug's body as he hovered over him, threatening to drain all his energy, making him wish for a moment that those eyes were the barrels of guns that would finish him here and now. But time kept on and he was sweating and Nate came on his chest and stomach and Doug emptied himself into him and pulled out. And then Nate, spread-eagled on the bed, arms out to the sides, looked once again as he had before, like a lamed foal awaiting its owner's merciful bullet.

Doug wiped himself off and pulled his trousers up, watching Nate rise from the bed and disappear into the bathroom. The ringing of the shower water blended with the ringing of his phone, which he ignored.

Nate was quiet when he returned, dressing with his back to Doug, who flipped on the TV in search of news.

A few minutes later, from over his shoulder, Doug heard him say, "I got you something."

"What do you mean?"

"A present."

"What for?"

"I don't know. I felt like it." Coming around to Doug's side, he handed him a small wrapped box. Doug removed the gold ribbon and tore away the paper. Inside the case was a pair of black-and-silver cuff links.

"You've got all those cuff shirts. But you always wear the same links."

Doug closed the case and put it aside.

"This game," he said, "it's over."

"It's not a game to me."

"You don't know what you're talking about. You're a kid. You think that what you feel matters."

"It does."

"I'm doing you a favor. You can't see it now, but I am. You want to be defenseless all your life? You want to be the chump? You like sleeping with guys—fine. But take your heart off your fucking sleeve."

Standing up, Doug grabbed his jacket and briefcase from the couch and walked out of the room, slamming the door behind him.

At the entrance to the ballroom, a security guard asked him for ID.

"You're not press, right? There's no press allowed."

Teams of lawyers were arrayed around an enormous oblong table, their seconds seated behind them like congressional aides. The young associates whispered in their bosses' ears, as a guy in suspenders at the head of the table read aloud from a paragraph of the contract projected on a screen behind him.

Save for occasional naps on their hotel beds, the lawyers had been in this room for three days straight, fighting over the details of the acquisition, down to the last indemnification.

At a desk in the far corner of the room, Holland's secretary, Martha, was typing furiously on her laptop.

"Where's Jeffrey?" he asked her.

"Doug," she said, seemingly alarmed by his appearance. She pointed to her right. "It's the second door down. Good luck."

Another security guard, this one a man Doug recognized from the office, opened the door for him and he entered the windowless antechamber. The two men from the lobby, still wearing their blue windbreakers, sat on folding metal chairs. They stood as he entered; he heard the door close behind him.

"Douglas Fanning?" the older of the two asked, as his partner removed a pair of handcuffs from his belt.

"Yeah," Doug said. "That's me."

Chapter 17

Across from Henry, Holland rested his elbows on the table and leaned forward, interlacing his meaty fingers, the extra flesh of his neck pinched by his shirt collar.

"First guy I ever worked for," he said, "could rattle off every loan on his book, quote you the rate, and tell you who was past due, all without so much as glancing at a balance sheet. Sean Hickey. Manager for Hartford Savings. He told me to forget whatever they'd taught me and learn to read a man's face. That was the training. To sit beside him in meetings with the local entrepreneurs and give him my thumbs-up or thumbs-down. I picked the ones with the flash—the talkers. He rejected every one of them. You're thinking short, he'd say. You want steady. All that seems like a hundred years ago. It's a trader's game now, a pure trader's game."

The Bierstadt canvas hanging on the wall behind Union Atlantic's chairman and CEO depicted an untouched Yosemite in early fall or late spring, the verdant grass and mountain lake beneath the peaks struck by columns of sun descending from a gap in the clouds. Half Dome was capped with snow melting into falls that ran off the lower cliffs, the fine mist emanating from the cascades of water giving the painter away for the Romantic he was, that mystical, German idealism struck here in a grander key on the subject of the American West.

Thirty-eight million, Henry thought. That's what Holland had earned last year. And if the board forced him out, he'd collect twice that.

Through the doorway into the private dining room, a waiter in a black suit and tie approached, a plate in each hand.

"Cracked native lobster tails, gentlemen, served with poached organic eggs, papaya salsa, and Old Bay hollandaise sauce. Fresh ground pepper with your breakfast, sir?"

"No, thank you," Henry replied, unfurling his napkin.

"I appreciate you coming here this morning," Holland said. "I don't know if I ever told you, but I voted for you back when I was at Chase, when I was on your board. We were glad to have you for the job."

Henry had known as much. Holland would have preferred the appointment of a colleague from the private sector, someone more instinctively friendly to the industry's interests. But once others had coalesced around Henry, he'd taken a friendly approach.

"You worry in the right way," he said. "Which is important."

If the FBI and the U.S. attorney's office had had their druthers, they would have staked out Union Atlantic for months in order to build their case all the way up to Holland. But given the size of the problem, Henry hadn't been able to wait. He had come through the front door, as it were, only forty-eight hours ago, and straightaway Holland had offered Fanning and his trader up on a platter. The bank had been running its own internal investigation, he claimed, which showed Fanning involved in rogue activity and attempts to cover his tracks. Given that Holland's lawyers were themselves former federal prosecutors, former banking regulators, and former IRS commissioners, he knew the drill well enough: hide nothing, or at least appear to hide nothing.

In the months and years ahead, at a cost of millions, the matter of Holland's own culpability would be the subject of multiple lawsuits, civil and criminal, with teams of his attorneys vetting every discovery request of every party, the lives of associates in some corporate firm devoted to nothing else, billing thousands of hours as they went, as the perfectly straightforward question of what he had known and when was fed into the numbing machinery of modern litigation, there to be digested at a sloth's pace. Young lawyers would buy condominiums or town houses with their bonus checks, employing architects and builders and decorators who would, in turn, spend a little more themselves on cars or vacations or flat-screen TVs, though that particular trickle from the economy of distress would barely register against the job losses bound to come with the restructuring of Union Atlantic Group.

But all that was for later. Personally, Henry suspected Holland had approved of the Finden Holdings arrangement and the proprietary trading scheme it had facilitated as a way to save his share price. But it would serve no practical end to indulge in an airing of his views. What Henry needed was a functioning institution capable of playing its role as the situation unfolded. If Holland was the man who could deliver that, then so be it. Others would decide his fate.

"It's a sad case, really," Holland observed. "Doug was a bright guy. If anything, I probably promoted him too quickly. I blame myself for that. Obviously the pressure got to him. He lost his judgment. I don't know if you heard about the other stuff . . . I hesitate to mention it. But it seems he might have gotten into some trouble with this kid, a boy actually, might even have been underage, I'm not sure. Surprised the hell out of me. I'd never seen any indication of that. But I guess it fits the pattern. You deceive people in one part of your life, and if you get away with it, it just takes over."

He paused here, trying to gauge his progress with Henry. Apparently doubtful of his headway, he pressed on.

"Off the record," he said, "there's a good chance this'll make your sister's life easier. I don't think Doug will be out there in Finden much longer. He'll have to pay his lawyers with something."

This had occurred to Henry, though he had said nothing about it to Charlotte. Only a few days ago she had learned that her legal victory had been reversed. The news had struck her hard. Winning that case had at last justified her crusade, not only against Fanning and the town but against her larger enemy: that general encroachment of money and waste and display. Having it taken away had crumpled something in her. Her hectoring voice had grown subdued. When he'd once more mentioned the idea of moving, she had made none of her usual protests. Knowing that he was going to be in Boston, he'd asked Helen to set up an appointment at the assisted-living home that Cott Jr. had recommended, and he and Charlotte were scheduled for a visit there that afternoon.

What good would it do now to share the news of Fanning's downfall? It would only give her false hope. Even if the man were forced to sell, the house itself wasn't going anywhere.

He took a bite of lobster, letting his lack of response to Holland speak for itself.

"Fanning's not my concern," he said eventually. "Perhaps we could proceed to business?"

"Of course."

"Let me start by saying that if you or your board is under the impression that Union Atlantic is too big to fail, you're mistaken. There's no question here of a bailout. If you go under, the markets will take a substantial hit, but with enough liquidity in the system we can cut you loose. I hope you understand that."

This, of course, was a bluff. Henry had already begun receiving calls from the Treasury Department. The secretary was confident, his deputies said in their transparent euphemism, that the Federal Reserve shared his concern about market stability. Translation: the White House is watching this one. The administration, while opposed under free market theory to the government rescue of a failing corporation, didn't want to see Union Atlantic fall apart. There were perfectly prudential reasons for this, many of which Henry agreed with, but the chatter coming out of the executive branch at the moment suggested another concern: the argument for the invasion of Iraq was hitting its stride now, and an event of this size could change the domestic and congressional equation. They didn't want distractions. That was the gist of it. By all means avoid the appearance of rewarding speculators—no moral hazard—but now's not the time for stringency.

Would he feel the satisfaction of justice done if an operator like Holland were brought to heel? Of course. Who wouldn't? But whatever spleen the liberals liked to vent on the captains of industry, there were certain hard facts that had little to do with individual actors. Five hundred points off the Dow was one thing. Disruption of the credit markets was another. Dry up the lending system and the losses would no longer redound to the investor class alone. The man working for the Texas theme-park company that had been bought out with leveraged debt it could no longer service would lose his paycheck soon enough. As a general matter, particularly in the mouths of politicians, Henry disliked the use of personal anecdotes to illustrate the workings of the economy. They were almost always a distortion, a falsely simple story of cause and effect. Truth lay in the aggregate numbers, not in the images of citizens the media alighted upon for a minute or two and then quickly left behind. Currency devaluations created more misery than any corporate criminal ever would. What the populist critics rarely bothered to countenance was the shape of things in the wake of real, systemic collapse. In Argentina, the middle class was picking through garbage dumps. The failure of Union Atlantic wouldn't deliver the country there, but then again, these were uncertain times. And whose risk was that to take?

"I don't think anyone's talking about a bailout," Holland said. "We're talking about capital injections. I think you'd agree, the brand has value, not to mention assets. All we're looking for is a way to reassure potential investors."

"You're talking to the Emirates?"

"Among others, yes. We've got some interest in Singapore as well. The issue is the timing. I've got seventy-two hours to make a margin call. That's not very long to roll out a sales pitch. If Citi or Morgan or someone of that scale were to come on board, even in a symbolic way, it would make a big difference."

Holland dipped his head to one side and gave a slight roll of the eyes, a gesture that combined genuflection with a modicum of fatalism. He was nothing if not a good actor. His fellow CEOs, who thrived on their relative appeal in the eyes of various corporate boards, were circling to watch the kill, despite what would be in the enlightened self-interest of their own companies—that is, to prevent a broader crisis. Meanwhile, the big foreign investors sensed opportunity but didn't want to be taken for fools. What Holland needed was Henry's back-channel cajoling and if not the Fed's cash, at least its imprimatur on the deal to save the bank. The loan he wanted was one of gravitas and prestige.

"And what if we say no?" Henry said, setting his silverware down on his plate. "What if I get on the phone and instead of suggesting the 'community' rally around to protect one of its own, what if I tell them you're an awfully bad bet and that in the end the market will do its job and decide what you're really worth? And if that's a dollar a share then so be it. What then?"

For the first time since they had sat down, Holland's big politician's guile fell away and he leveled at Henry a cold stare, his act of forthrightness and contrition gone.

Henry's instinct had been right: Fanning was too close to this man for Holland not to have been involved. He had been Holland's instrument.

"What then?" Holland echoed, in a slower, more deliberate voice. "Well, I guess I'd wonder if that was the outcome our government actually wanted."

"Really? Are you suggesting the Fed lacks independence? Are you suggesting we take our marching orders from the political branches?"

Holland leaned back from the table. "Come off it, Henry. I've spoken to Senator Grassley's people. I know what you're hearing from Treasury. So what's with the civics lesson?"

In his mouth, the phrase sounded almost dirty. Incredible, Henry thought. Here he was, Henry Graves, the gray pragmatist, accused of naïveté. It made him wonder. Could it be that despite all the legalized venality he'd witnessed over the years, despite even what he would have said of himself not ten minutes ago, that he actually was naïve? That some kernel of protest had survived in him? What would that even mean? That after forty years he should stand up and say to the system he'd spent his life protecting, I disagree? Stability doesn't save anyone. Regulation is just a ruse to cover up organized theft and it convinces no one but the public. He didn't believe this. And yet like some wide-eyed undergrad, like the philosophy major he'd once been, he felt an urge. A longing even. One he barely recognized.

A secretary appeared and handed Holland a note. He read it in a single glance and then crushed the paper in his fist.

"Make that forty-eight hours," he said, shoving his plate aside. "Singapore wants its margin Thursday morning."

Holland stood and signaled for the waiter to clear the table.

"Is that really what you want, Henry? You want to see us fail?"

IN THE CAR on the way out to Finden, Helen phoned to update Henry on the calls he'd missed during his meeting: two from the FDIC, an agency terrified of a bank the size of Union Atlantic winding up on its books; another from the Office of the Comptroller, whose examiners had been caught flat-footed; and two more from Treasury.

"And the chairman phoned," Helen said. "He spoke to the chief of staff over at the White House about an hour ago."

"I'm sure he did."

"What am I supposed to tell him? That you're unavailable? It's rather implausible, under the circumstances."

"Just buy me a few hours. I'll be on a plane by four."

He directed his driver through the center of Finden and out Winthrop Street to the house. As they came up the driveway he saw his sister wielding her clippers on a fallen branch of the old apple tree in the front yard. She didn't notice the car at first and turned only when she heard his door closing. Fragments of leaves covered the front of her fleece sweater and some had caught in the strands of her hair.

"What on earth are you doing here?"

"I called you about it—our appointment. Over at Larch Brook. I told you I'd be coming."

The dogs trotted over and sniffed at Henry's waist.

"We had a tremendous rain last night," she said. "This all came down in the wind. Sounded like a shotgun being fired. Woke me right up. You used to climb this tree, do you remember?"

"Charlotte. We're supposed to be there in twenty minutes. Wouldn't you like to change first?"

She set her clippers down. Crushed and rotting apples lay all about her on the grass.

"This was the tree you wanted to build your fort in, but Mommy thought it would be an eyesore. Which is why you built it down by the river. Did I tell you there were still planks of it left when they cut down the woods? The dogs and I went by it every morning."

"No, you didn't mention it," he said. "We really should be going. I've got the car here waiting."

"I have an idea. Why don't we go for a walk? There's something I want to show you."

"We don't have time."

"It'll only take a minute."

Closing his eyes momentarily, he tried to marshal his patience. Every hour counted at this stage of the crisis. The markets were relentless, the system more fragile than most people imagined. Duty called now more than ever. But Charlotte . . . she had something to show him.

And so he followed her, around the far corner of the house, past the woodshed and into the garden. For years, she'd maintained the bushes and flower beds and small trees that their grandparents had planted. Recently, however, her attention had wandered. Thistle had taken root along the foot of the evergreen hedge and the beds were covered in ground ivy. A bench where his father used to sit and read the paper on August evenings rotted at the edge of the path down which they walked now toward the rear of the garden.

Henry wanted to be gone from here, once and for all. To be done, at long last, with the decay of this place. How Charlotte could stand living here all these years, he'd never understood.

When they reached the field at the back, Charlotte led him down the far side of the hedge, through the dead grass, and came to a stop in front of a skeletal bush six or seven feet high and quite wide, a collection of upright, arching branches, its leaves and flowers long since gone.

"What is it?"

"It's a lilac," she said. "The funny thing is, after all this time, I only discovered it a few years ago. It had been hiding here behind the hedge. It's the same shape as the one we had at home in the yard. In the springtime, don't you remember? You used to love to play inside it. To chase me. To listen to me sing."

How insupportable, he thought, to remember in the way she did. The present didn't stand a chance against such a perfectly recollected world.

Just then, to his shock, Charlotte stepped toward him and taking his face in her chapped hands touched her lips to his. Smiling, her watery gray eyes impossibly close, she said, "I'm not going to visit that place, Henry."

He tried to speak but she put a finger to his lips. "Listen. My life here, it's not your fault. And I want you to know, I don't regret it. None of it. I want you to understand that. I know I haven't made it easy on you. That I've been a burden at times. But I'm all right. And listen . . . Daddy, he would have been proud of you. Strange to say that after all this time, but it's true. He would have been proud."

"There's no need to be maudlin," he said, stilling a tremble in his throat.

"You sound like me . . . We've done all right, the two of us," she said, squeezing his arm. "We have."

His phone rang in his jacket pocket.

"It's okay," she said. "These people—they need you. Go ahead."

"This is not the end of this. You can't stay here."

"I know," she said, turning them back toward the garden. "I know."

AT JUST AFTER six o'clock that evening, Henry stepped from his cab onto Liberty Street and passed through the black gates of the New York Fed. Upstairs, in a conference room, his team had assembled and were already well into discussions with the exchange authorities in Hong Kong and Osaka. On Henry's instructions, the Bank of Japan and the Japanese Ministry of Finance had been notified of the likely sell-off of Atlantic Securities' massive position in Nikkei futures. Meanwhile, the head of open-market operations in New York was reviewing plans for the coordinated provision of domestic and international liquidity in the event it was needed in the days ahead.

"You decided yet what you're going to recommend?" Sid Brenner asked, as Henry took a seat at the back of the room and pulled out the notes he'd written on the flight into LaGuardia. At his imploring, the assistant U.S. attorney assigned to the case had seen to it that Fanning and McTeague had been taken into custody as quietly as possible, but news of the arrests had begun to get out, shortening his time for maneuver.

"Treasury's views are clear," Henry said. "They want Union Atlantic saved."

"And you're thinking otherwise?"

"They took the mandatory reserves of the third-largest institution in the country and essentially walked them into a casino."

"You don't have to convince me. You could lock these people in solitary and they'd find a way around the regs."

"So what would letting them go look like?" Henry said.

"A bloodbath. They've got business in a hundred countries. Counterparties up and down the food chain. They're ten percent of the municipal bond market. They've got more credit cards than Chase. And they're overweighted in mortgage securities. They're the definition of systemic risk. And we're barely out of a recession. It'd be malpractice to let them fail. You know it as well as I do."

"You're usually the skeptic."

"Just 'cause a body's got lung cancer doesn't mean you can take out the lungs."

Henry called Helen and told her to contact the CEOs of the major commercial and investment banks and inform them that their presence would be required at a meeting in the boardroom the following morning.

The last time Henry had orchestrated a private-sector rescue was when Long-Term Capital Management, a Greenwich hedge fund, had blown up during the currency crisis in the late nineties. At the time, the chairman of the Fed had publicly distanced himself from Henry's actions, suggesting the market ought to have been left to settle the matter.

Tonight, however, when Henry phoned down to Washington, he received no such objection. Before Henry even made the request, the chairman granted him the board's authority to employ loan guarantees should they be needed to cement a deal.

"Everything I'm seeing suggests it's isolated," the chairman offered. "A rogue-trader situation. The worst I've seen, certainly. But it's important to remember the specifics. There'll be some posturing on the Hill. They'll want to score points with the press, but it'll die down, eventually. We just don't want to give anyone too much of a platform on this." He paused, wheezing slightly. "You think Holland knew?"

"Yes."

"Well," he said, passing over the answer, "you've got whatever backing you need."

By the time Henry had finished his calls and spoken with his counterparts in London and Tokyo it was after midnight. Helen had reserved a room in case he didn't want to make the trip to Rye and back and he decided to use it. He walked the short distance up lower Broadway to the Millenium Hotel through emptied streets, past the shuttered shoe stores and fast-food restaurants. The air was unusually muggy for October and full of dust kicked up by a wind off the Hudson. Plastic grocery bags and the pages of tabloids rolled along the sidewalk and into the intersection, where the cross draft lifted them into the air like tattered kites, yanked and spooled by invisible hands.

Realizing he had eaten no dinner, he ordered a sandwich from room service and ate it sitting at the desk that looked down over the pit where the twin towers had stood, the ramps and retaining walls and construction-company trailers floodlit the whole night through.

The last city of the Renaissance. That's what Charlotte had called New York on the evening of September 11, when he'd phoned her from Basel to let her know that he was all right, that he was out of harm's way. "Banking and art. They've been growing up together in cities for five hundred years. And they're bombing the pair of them."

He'd thought it generous, that she should link their worlds up like that, as if in peril, at least, they might stand side by side.

A few weeks ago, speaking to Helen about his sister, she'd

suggested he consider bringing Charlotte to live with him in Rye. Rather than paying a facility, he could hire someone to help. It was the town they had grown up in together, after all. She would say no, he imagined, but still, he would offer. Tomorrow, after his meeting, he would call her and suggest it.

Early the next morning, he returned to the office. Despite the secretaries' protests that their bosses' jets couldn't possibly take off on such short notice, by midmorning the heads of the nation's eight largest banks had collected in the boardroom on the tenth floor of the Fed, just as Henry had requested. There he let them wait, these men who waited for nothing and for no one.

"They're not a patient bunch," Helen said, returning to Henry's office from her walk down the hall to tell the captains of finance it would be a little while longer before the meeting began.

"Best to keep them nervous. Is Holland downstairs?"

She nodded.

"And our friend, is he here yet?"

"He's right outside."

"All right, then. Show him in."

Henry stood to welcome his guest. Prince Abdul-Aziz Hafar wore a double-vented tweed jacket of a fine English cut, along with a dark-red silk tie and a red paisley pocket square, giving him the appearance of a dapper country gentleman, more likely in the market for a yearling than a bank. He greeted Henry with a handshake and a slight bow.

"You've timed your troubles well," he said in his lilting British accent. "I'm here to see my son for his fall break. That's what you call it, no?"

"Indeed," Henry said, showing him to the couch.

"My cousin tells me Citibank's the one to buy into, but then he would say that, given how much of the damn thing he already owns. We're not as freewheeling as we used to be, you know. Now that we've set up our sovereign funds. We have all sorts of advisers. So I do hope you haven't invited me to a charity event."

"No," Henry said. "I think you'll find there are still things of value here."

He had just handed the prince an outline of the arrangement he envisioned and that he would soon lay out for the men gathered at the far end of the hall, when he heard the phone ringing on Helen's desk. A moment later, she knocked on the door.

All color had left her face. "You have to take this," she said. "It's about Charlotte."

Chapter 18

You been misled, Wilkie's stentorian voice proclaimed. *You been had. You been took. And now you're trapped. You're double-trapped. You're triple-trapped. And what are you gonna do? You gonna sit-in? You gonna picket? You gonna march on Washington? Or are you gonna stand up and make some justice happen?*

Light from beneath the shade illuminated his dull black coat; it was morning and he was hungry.

For years, the two of them had slept in the living room. But no longer. They did as they pleased now, climbing on furniture, the bed even, waking her at all hours, there whenever she opened her eyes.

See it's like when you go to the dentist and the man is going to take your tooth. You're gonna fight him when he starts pullin'. So they squirt some stuff in your jaw called Novocain to make you think they're not doing anything to you. So you sit there, and 'cause you got all that Novocain in your jaw you suffer peacefully. Blood running all down your jaw and you don't know what's happening. 'Cause someone has taught you to suffer peacefully, law-abidingly—

their rules, their game—and you're surprised they win every time? Is your mind that weak, that soft? What you need is a do-it-yourself philosophy, a do-it-right-now philosophy, an it's-already-too-late philosophy.

He approached the bed and as he stretched his jaw open Charlotte could see down the minister's pink gullet.

I've said it once and I'll say it again: Extremism in the defense of liberty is no vice. Moderation in the pursuit of justice is no virtue.

"Quiet," she pled. "There's no need to convince me."

For days she'd meant to get to the store to buy herself and the dogs some food, but having no appetite herself she'd forgotten, there being no room left in her mind anymore, it seemed, for anything but her single purpose.

Stepping out of bed, she crossed the room, the dogs following her to the closet. A dress didn't seem appropriate for this day. Something more practical was in order. She chose a pair of gardening corduroys and a pullover she'd patched at the elbows.

Sam started in where he'd left off the night before, shaking his head with that self-satisfied disappointment of his. *I see that the devils are swarming about you this morning, like the Frogs of Egypt, here in the most retired of your chambers. And yet, like the sinner you are, you welcome them.*

Slave owner! Wilkie shouted. *White devil! Get your filthy paws off the woman's conscience. She's seeing at last that it's time for action. Time to swing up on some justice.*

The Blood of the Soul of this poor Negro here lies upon you, Sam said, not deigning to speak directly to his dark companion, *and the guilt of his Barbarous Impieties, and superstitions, and his neglect of God, if you are willing to have nothing done toward the salvation of his soul. Despite what you think, to convert one Soul unto God is more than to pour out Ten Thousand Talents into the Baskets of the Poor.*

You listen to me, you cracker spook, Wilkie said, *I'm not going to be taken in by your love-thy-servant nonsense. If a man speaks the language of brute force, you can't come to him with peace. Why good night, he'll break you in two, as he has been doing all along. You have to learn how to speak his language and then he'll get the point. Then there'll be some dialogue. There'll be some communication. There'll be some understanding.*

Oh, who can tell, Sam called out, his indignation rising, *but that this Poor Creature may belong to the Election of God! Who can tell, but that God may have sent this Poor Creature into your hands, Charlotte, that so One of the Elect may by your means be Called and by your Instruction be made Wise unto Salvation! The Blackest Instances of Blindness and Baseness are admirable Candidates of Eternal Blessedness. Though it be caviled, by some, that it is questionable Whether the Negroes have Rational Souls, or no, let that Brutish insinuation be never Whispered any more. They are men not beasts. Withhold knowledge of the Almighty from them and they will be destroyed.*

At her heels they raged, traipsing after her down the hallway, down the back stairs, and into the kitchen, to the window above the sink full now of dishes.

Over the grass a morning mist hung. Its tendrils stretched under the maples and down the hill. Ten minutes or more she stood there waiting, until at last she saw Fanning come out of his front door, dressed not in a suit today, as he usually was, but in jeans and a sweatshirt. She watched with relief as he got in his car and drove up to the road. She was not, after all, in the business of killing.

Yesterday, after saying her goodbyes to Henry, she had seen in her mind's eye the mansion burning, and felt, in anticipation, its heat on her skin, the heat she remembered from the bonfires they used to have in the back field when they came up for Thanksgiving and dragged the fallen branches out of the woods and burned all the raked leaves, only how much greater would the heat be when it was an entire house consumed, wood and nails and glass and a thousand substances besides? Again now, she saw the fire, and then the charred frame and then that, too, crumbling, and from the blackened earth saplings rising, drinking sun and rain, thickening in nature's time to the testaments of endurance that trees became, shading again the river and the trout, the cardinals and the blue jays and the orange-winged butterflies flitting through a summer dusk, when she and Henry had played by the riverbank before being packed in the car and driven back to Rye, only years later to discover, at night in her dorm room, Milton's pentameter describing what the two of them had lost:

. . . whereat
In either hand the hastning Angel caught
Our lingering Parents, and to th' Eastern Gate
Led them direct, and down the Cliff as fast
To the subjected Plaine; then disappeer'd.

She let the tap water run until it chilled the bones of her fingers and then she filled a glass for herself and the dogs' bowls. They lapped them quickly dry and were back at her side in no time.

They say overcome your enemies with your capacity to love. What kind of an idea is that? Wilkie asked. *He's not going to be overcome by your love. I've never called on anybody to be violent without a cause.*

There is a court somewhere kept, where your pride shall be judged, Sam warned. *And it is not here in the False Church of this earth.*

"I have not for one day believed in your God."

No, sure. And so in Great Folly you shall one day wander down to the Congregation of the Dead.

She took a box of matches from the ledge of the stove and beneath the sink found a canvas bag.

Sam and Wilkie followed her into the breezeway.

To concentrate just once more, she thought. That's all that it would take. And indeed, as she stepped down the ramp onto the floor of the barn, she began to feel as she'd imagined she would, reading those stories in the papers over the years of the environmentalists and the anti–free traders who broke the law in the name of some greater justice, the anticipation of the act clarifying experience, rescuing it from the prison of language, the inward purpose blessing the otherwise desultory with meaning. And yet, for that very reason, she'd always considered such extremism adolescent. Too simple. Willful in its ignorance of the world's complexity. And so deadly earnest. And yet how judgmental she had been. What, after all, was wrong with earnestness? Weren't Fanning and his kind earnest? Weren't all the polluters earnest, the physical and the cultural? And did anyone ever impugn or mock them for it? No one ever thought to. Avarice was never shackled by a concern for authenticity. It didn't care about image or interpretation.

The sit-down lawn mower, its paint cracked and axles rusting, stood where the family Jeep once had. Beyond it was the ladder to the loft, where the wooden tea crates full of Eric's books were still stacked, having remained there ever since they'd followed Charlotte up from New York. She didn't come in here much anymore, and for good reason.

Along with the cans of primer under the back shelf, she found tins of turpentine that she'd purchased a few years back, intending to call someone about doing the shutters and trim. She placed them in her bag with the matches.

My second wife, my dear friend Elizabeth, died of the measles on the afternoon of November 9, Sam started in again.

"For heaven's sake, can't you shut up!"

Ten days after giving me the twins, Eleazer and Martha. Oh, to part with so desirable, so agreeable a Companion, a Dove from such a Nest of young ones too! Oh! the sad Cup, which my Father appointed me! And when five days hence my maidservant succumbed, I tested the Lord's patience by imagining the malignancy to have gone up over us. Then the twins died. The sixth and seventh of my children to be taken up by the Almighty. And when a week later Jerusha too fell sick I begg'd the Lord for the life of my dear pretty daughter. I begg'd that such a bitter Cup, as the Death of that lovely child, might pass from me. But she too went to our Savior. And I died in life unto this world as all sinners must preparing for the world to come, knowing the Lord is in thy Adversity! Fifteen children I fathered. Thirteen I buried. Such a record of woe as no man should have to bear, my cross but a dry sort of a tree. But never did I despair of the Lord's infinite wisdom or cease in the business of Worship. And you stand here aggrieved by the bitter fruit of one sinful lust? One loss of a man not your husband?

"Damn you!" she shouted, pushing him aside with her knee.

Why it is useless for you to deny that it is in the shadow of his going that you have arrived here at this foolery, allowing your spirit to shape itself thus. What, after all, are your great Politics but a woe without end? What is your pessimistic liberal blather but the Bible's own warning of the Apocalypse shorn of the just Consolation of Heaven? You have decried this world as any of the Lord's preachers might, and lived as if in the End Times, yet every day you have succumbed to the pride of earthly wisdom, the pride of thinking of yourself as above the Savior's flock. And in your condescension you violate your own philosophy of tolerance. Yes, yours is a metaphysical pride. The pride of human knowledge.

"Your children must have died of boredom," she snapped, beginning to tremble.

How stupid to have no food in the house! Surely the weakness in her limbs came from hunger. Sam rubbed his wet nose at her waist, slobbering.

Among the rusting tools and old flowerpots she looked about for an implement in case she had to force a window. She found a trowel and added it to her supplies.

There are but a few sands left in the glass of your time.

Don't listen to that old bigot, Wilkie said. *Now's your time to act.*

Pushing the barn door open, she tried keeping the dogs blocked behind her, but they were too strong and they forced themselves by, running ahead down the driveway. The mist had cleared but overhead the sky was still a low ceiling of cloud, the nimbus of the sun visible only as a brightening patch of gray on the horizon.

Don't go, he said.

Slowly, she turned, the membrane porous, time's order shuffled.

Eric sat on the weathered oak bench by the ladder, leaning forward, his elbows resting on his knees, as young and beautiful as the night she'd met him.

Don't go, he said. Stay here awhile.

"But if the man comes back . . . I'll lose my nerve."

You never did. You've always been beautiful to me, in that way. You never lost your conviction.

"I kept thinking of you."

I know. I heard you. You were heard. And Nate, you were good to him. You have to remember: our love isn't the only kind. You have loved, my darling. You have loved so much. I see it. I see it in you now. You're beautiful.

"No," she said. "Look at me. Look at what I'm about to do."

But you won't. I know you won't. It's okay. Close the door. Sam and Wilkie, you can let them go now. They'll be all right.

"But there's no one to feed them."

Someone will feed them.

She feared he would disappear if she stepped closer. And so she remained still, blessed now, she understood. The dearest thread in that old fabric of being had loosened, letting him pass back through to her. And so at last she could tell someone, "It's not the dogs' fault—the things they shout. They're in me, the ministers. The puritans and the slaves. God help me," she said, tears leaking from her eyes. "I tried to love my country."

As it should be loved.

"But weren't we fools?"

Yes. Loving fools.

She wiped at her dripping eyes. And when she looked again he was gone.

She stood motionless, gazing at the bench, at its bleached wood, still as stone. A mute object. Eternal in the perfection of its indifference. For the first time that morning, she noticed the clouds of her breath visible in the bitter air.

Heading back up the ramp, she crossed the breezeway, and stepped back into the kitchen. The fridge door hung open, its shelves holding nothing but a jar of pickles and a few bottles of soda water. In the drawer, greens rotted in a plastic bag. A sack of sprouted potatoes lay on the floor between the fridge and the counter. The counter itself was barely visible beneath the clutter.

Proceeding into the living room, she wondered how it was that she had never seen the mess. How long had she been living in this ruin? When, precisely, had the storm struck?

She sat on the one cleared spot of her sofa. She could hear the dogs barking at the door, clawing at it, trying to get back in, to get at her once more. Even at this distance, their voices reached her. They were no longer distinct and yet louder than ever. A roar that nearly drowned out the litany in her head, the one she'd lived by and with, her litany: Henry II and Magna Carta and Gutenberg and Calvin and

Milton and Kant and Paine and Jefferson and Jackson's rabble and Corot and Lincoln and Zola and Dickens and Whitman and Bryan on his cross of gold and the patterned fabrics in the paintings of Matisse and Walker Evans and Copland and Baldwin and King in Memphis, the chorus exploding in her, the ideas all that were left, a pure narrative drive using up the last of her.

It had to stop, she thought, reaching into her canvas bag. She could make it stop. She could at last exercise her will over history's reckless imagination of her.

The open-faced books on the coffee table soaked up the turpentine like arid soil.

She thought to close her eyes as she struck the match and dropped it, but then that wouldn't be right. She would watch.

Chapter 19

The press conference announcing the discovery of trading fraud at Atlantic Securities was held at the U.S. attorney's office in lower Manhattan one morning in late October 2002, shortly before the opening bell on Wall Street. Minutes later, Jeffrey Holland, solemn but confident, stood before another lectern at Union Atlantic headquarters in Boston to inform the public that the authorities would have the company's complete cooperation in investigating the matter. Risk-management safeguards had clearly broken down and would be overhauled with the help of an independent advisory committee chaired by a former head of the SEC, whose recommendations would be followed to the letter. After consultation with the board, it had been decided that the role of chairman and chief executive officer should henceforth be separate. In the months ahead, Holland would step aside as CEO to focus on the larger, strategic issues facing Union Atlantic Group.

A consortium led by JPMorgan Chase and the sovereign wealth fund of Abu Dhabi had agreed to purchase a twenty-billion-dollar stake in the troubled bank to secure its capital base, while the Dutch bank ING would be acquiring the Atlantic Securities division for a nominal sum in return for assuming a portion of its debt.

In early trading, the stock plummeted thirty percent but it began to recover soon after the Federal Reserve Bank of New York issued a statement saying the plan had the Fed's full backing and that it stood ready to provide liquidity as needed in the event of serious market disruptions. The Treasury Department followed with a statement of its own.

When asked to comment on the mismanagement and near collapse of one of the largest financial institutions in the nation, the White House press secretary disagreed with the characterization of "near collapse," saying it appeared to be a case of a few bad apples. The president, he said, was glad to see that the private market was responding appropriately to maintain its own stability and had full confidence that the regulatory authorities would continue to monitor the situation.

Doug watched these announcements unfold on a television mounted behind the counter of the diner in Saugus, where he had come to purchase a new passport. In order to make bail, he'd been forced to surrender his at the arraignment, along with the title to his house. After the hearing, the government had made it clear that McTeague and Sabrina were already cooperating. Which meant all Doug's efforts at concealment were now evidence against him. If he stuck around for the two or three years it would take them to prosecute the case, and by some miracle managed to drag Holland down with him, he might get eight to ten, depending on the judge's mood. But he had no intention of going to prison. Not in the name of bureaucratic punctiliousness about where to draw the line between aggressive investing and fraud. If other fools wanted to take the fall for that nonsense then let them. Doug had violated the spirit of the law years ago, if that's how you chose to understand it, by commencing mergers not yet permitted. But then the law had changed, the profits had rolled in, and Holland had become a business hero. And now Doug was expected to do time for a bad bet on the Nikkei? You'd need to be a true believer or have a wife and kids to put up with that.

Opposite him in the diner booth sat a friend of a friend of Vrieger's whom he'd been put in touch with about getting new identity documents. The guy was in his mid-fifties, dressed in a khaki fisherman's vest, bifocals dangling on a chain around his neck. After he'd finished his milk shake and scrambled eggs and nattered on about the Patriots for too long, he handed Doug a thick, white envelope. "I hope your memory's good," he said, signaling for the check. "If you can't remember who you're supposed to be, you're finished."

On his return to Finden that morning, as he made the turn onto Winthrop, Doug was passed by a column of fire trucks. As he crossed the river, he saw flames coursing from the downstairs windows of Charlotte's house on the hill; they had caught on the overgrown bushes and on the dry shingle, setting the whole side of the house on fire. He pulled into his driveway and jogged up the slope, watching smoke billow from her front door. As the firemen unwound their hoses, a fuel tank or gas line exploded in the kitchen, sending a ball of orange flame shooting across the back entryway and into the barn. The panes of the upstairs windows began to pop. The fire was consuming the ancient wooden structure like kindling, the whole edifice starting to crackle and sag. By the time the water had been tapped from the hydrant it was too late to do much more than contain the blaze.

"Was she in there?" Doug asked the fire marshal, who stood beside one of the engines in full protective gear, issuing the occasional order from his walkie-talkie.

"Her dogs seem to think so," he said, at which point Doug realized the sound he'd been hearing all along was their howling. "Curtis," the marshal called to a police officer, "get those animals in a squad car, would you? They're driving me crazy."

"Do you know what caused it?"

The man shrugged. "These old places burn fast, but not this fast. My guess is we'll find some kind of accelerant."

Up on the road, traffic had clogged as passersby stopped to marvel at the sight.

"Did you know the woman?"

"Yeah," Doug said. "A bit."

"Anything unusual lately? Anything we should know about?"

Before Doug could answer, a voice from the dispatch squawked an indecipherable bit of news over the marshal's radio and he moved off toward a group of firefighters standing closer to the blaze.

Doug remained there for some time, standing beside the truck, watching as the flames crested and then slowly diminished, the house turning to ash and scattering into the dry air.

This, then, was her moment. Less public than the monk immolating himself on the street in Saigon, but a protest nonetheless. He didn't feel pity. His neighbor had never sought that. A lone soldier against an army. That's how she'd described herself to him. And a professional one, it turned out, choosing a battleground grave over the dishonor of retreat.

He stayed until after most of the trucks had left, leaving behind them only a few charred posts and the crooked, blackened tower of the chimney.

Of all the news he watched in the weeks that followed, of UN weapons inspectors and the sniper menacing the suburbs of the capital and the rise in housing prices and criminals being released onto the streets of Baghdad, the story Doug couldn't get out of his mind was the one about the pilotless drones flying over the Empty Quarter, a vast swath of western Yemen, off whose shores the *Vincennes* had once sailed. Intelligence services wanted to know if the operatives of various radical networks had secreted themselves among the nomadic tribes, who were the only people to traverse that portion of the Arabian desert. Cable news made only a few mentions of it but on the Web he found more and lying in bed or on the couch downstairs he watched over and over the various clips of aerial footage that people had posted.

In that nowhere place, so appealing in its way, mountains of sand razor-backed by the wind enclosed barren valley floors covered with hundreds of identical hillocks each swept to a point. Shots from higher elevations revealed a broader pattern: lunar white pockmarks spread over the flats between the sand ridges which stretched across the landscape like the wrinkled hide of some beast too large for the human eye to see, its skin slowly ulcerating in the sun.

Finally, the time for him to leave town arrived. The night before he left he took a drive, setting out along the golf course and then down a bit past the Hollands' and beyond them the Gammonds' old place, continuing on through the village past the green and the Congregational Church and the shops with their painted signs, turning at the intersection onto Elm and heading out to the state route.

There, uninterrupted woods ran either side of the highway for the first three or four miles until he reached the liquor store that still stood on the far side of the traffic light across from the muffler shop. It had begun to rain and the red of the traffic signal slid down his windshield in rivulets quickly cleared by the wipers, only to blur again as the signal turned green and he crossed the line back into Alden.

He glided through one light after the next, by the glowing signs for discount meals in the parking lots of the fast-food chains and passed the cinder-block furniture warehouses and the box-store plazas that they had knocked down the old malls to build, until eventually he reached Foley Avenue and turned off the strip. Half a mile down at the intersection with Main darkened storefronts stretched from one end of the block to the next: an insurance office, an empty showroom with a FOR RENT sign in the door, a beauty salon whose faded posters advertised hair styles of the eighties. Across the street a convenience-store awning was illuminated by the bright yellow sign above the check-cashing office next door, its metal grate locked to the sidewalk.

Christmas decorations already littered the front yards of the ranch houses along Howard, the glowing Santas and plastic reindeer arranged like inflated toys on outsize playroom floors. As he reached Eames Street, the rain softened to a drizzle and then stopped. Up ahead he could see low traveling clouds, their yellow underbellies lit by the strip that lay just on the other side of the creek and the fences. Single-family homes petered out toward the end of the block where he noticed Phil's Pizza had been replaced by a Brazilian restaurant still serving at this late hour.

The triple-deckers began on the other side of Miller, big clapboard rectangles with three front porches, stacked one atop the other, the angles on most of them no longer right, their posts sagging into the worn corners of the decking. Trash cans were lined up along the chain-link fences that fronted most lots beside the gated parking spaces. There were Christmas decorations here as well, string lights flashing slowly on and off in windows with the shades pulled and farther up Mrs. Cronin's old wooden crèche, its figures two feet high and illuminated in front by a row of bulbs sheltered under a weathered strip of plywood.

He pulled to the curb and cut the engine. Up on the third floor of number 38 the lights in his mother's apartment were still on. He pictured her as he had a thousand times: she would be into her second bottle by now, watching the evening dramas while whatever she'd managed to make herself for dinner lay half eaten on the table in front of her.

To climb those stairs, he thought. To take a seat in the chair opposite and let her pour him a drink.

She had done that sometimes the year before he left, because she'd wanted to keep him in the room with her, he being the only audience for her silence, the only person who might ask her to break it. Which he never had, having learned the power of reticence from her.

Whenever he'd been tempted over the years to get in touch with her he would recall what it felt like on those summer nights in the apartment when he'd sit shirtless across from her, his chest moist with sweat, able to clock almost exactly how long it would take before she would let slip some half-muttered remark about how fit he'd become, his baby fat all gone. Her son, the only romance she'd ever had, all grown up. And then he would remind himself that she had a phone if she wanted to call.

And yet here he was, drawn back by something, by the residue, perhaps, of all his dreams of her.

He drank a few of the beers he'd brought with him in the car, gazing into the street where he used to play hockey at dusk with his cousin Michael and the Fischer boys and Dave Cutty from up the road until his mother came out onto the front porch to call him inside.

THE DOOR TO the building had never been kept locked and wasn't locked now. A new rug carpeted the stairs but the steps still creaked beneath his weight as he climbed them. On the third-floor landing, the same worn cable rug lay in front of his mother's door, the same black umbrella stand there beside it.

He'd expected to have to wait a few minutes after knocking, his mother needing the time to rouse herself. But the door came open almost right away and he was confronted with a bearded man in his early sixties with a thatch of dark hair and a nose veined at the tip. He looked out at Doug through large, owl eyes that were clearly long since done being impressed. An ex-hippie, Doug thought, or an old biker.

"Is there some kind of problem?" the man asked, when Doug offered no greeting.

"It's just someone I knew—she used to live here."

"You talking about Cathy?"

"Catherine. Catherine Fanning."

"Yeah. She lives here. What do you need with her?"

"I want to see her."

"She's out. You some kind of salesman? We're not interested if you are."

"No," he said. "I'm her son."

The man cocked his head back, eyeing Doug skeptically. "You don't say? You're with that bank, aren't you? We saw something about that on the news."

Doug nodded. Somewhat reluctantly, the man stepped aside to let him enter.

As if in a waking dream, Doug followed him down the hall, entering a living room he hardly recognized. The old corduroy couch and chair were gone, replaced by a dark-green upholstered living-room set and a glass-top coffee table. The carpeting had been torn up and the wood floors refinished. Walls whose paper had once been stained by the steam leaked from the heating pipes were now painted a clean off-white. There were no stacks of old newspapers. No piles of magazines. In fact, there was barely any clutter at all.

"You live here?"

"I do," the man said, leaning against the kitchen doorjamb, his arms crossed over his chest. "I've lived here ten years."

"Ten years?" But how could this be? Ten years?

"Where is she?" Doug asked.

"At a meeting," the man said, the slight, righteous emphasis on the last word leaving little doubt as to the kind of gathering he meant. "You want coffee?"

"No."

Turning to look behind him, Doug saw that the wall to his old bedroom had been torn out. A dining table now filled the space where his bed and bureau used to sit.

"She must be getting on better with the landlord than she used to," he said. "He hated us."

"She bought the place. Awhile back. Before I got here."

Doug couldn't help laughing. "Bought it? With what?"

"She keeps books for a construction firm. She's done all right."

"So what are you?" Doug said. "The dry-drunk freeloader?"

The visible portion of the man's heavily bearded face squinched, as if he were swallowing something tart.

"I figured you were probably an asshole," he said. "Personally, I don't give a shit what kind of mess you're in. But you should know something: your mother's got fourteen years sober. She's doing just fine. You coming here like this—that's the kind of thing that can screw a person up. So if you're here to cause some kind of trouble, you might want to think about leaving."

He was about to make himself clear to the man, when he heard the front door open and then his mother's footsteps coming down the hall. Standing where he was, all the way into the living room, she didn't notice him at first. And so for just a few seconds he was able to watch her as she put down her suede handbag and removed her gloves, the indelible oval of her face aged and yet no different, a face too familiar to ever actually see anymore than you could see your own.

And then her eyes followed the man's to Doug. She stood motionless.

"Douglas."

"Hi there, Mom."

"Cath—" the man began, but she interrupted him.

"It's okay," she said. "Why don't you go out."

"I can stay right—"

"It's all right," she said. "Go."

He lifted his leather jacket off the back of one of the dining-room chairs and before disappearing up the hall, paused to place a hand on her shoulder, leaning in to kiss her above the ear.

After the sound of the door latch closing, his mother slowly unbuttoned her coat and turned to hang it on a mirrored rack that stood where Doug's bedroom bookcase once had. She straightened the front of her blouse and tucked her hair behind her ears. At last, she looked straight at him. Under the blaze of her unvanquished eyes, he heard a ringing in his ears and felt his whole body go suddenly weightless, as if he'd lost sensation in everything but his head.

"You look well," she said.

"So do you."

"Will you sit down?"

"I'm okay," he said.

How was it, he wanted to know, that after nearly twenty years she could seem younger than the day he left? Her black hair was silver and black now, the skin about her eyes had grown looser, the backs of her hands mottled. But to look into her face, to meet the green eyes that she had given him, sharper than he'd ever seen them, to see the color in her cheeks, was to witness an uncanny thing, as if in his absence she'd shed not gained the weight of time, a younger spirit living now in the older body.

"I should say . . . about Peter. He's a good person. He's been good to me."

"Glad to hear it. Seems like you've done okay."

"What I have," she said, her voice careful and measured, "it's enough."

How often had he imagined her here, drunk and alone? How long had that vision turned at the back of his mind, a wheel never grasping the other gears, a ghost seeking its way back into the machine?

"I've been in Massachusetts awhile," he said.

"I know."

"This last year . . . this last year, I've been over in Finden."

She nodded calmly, even gracefully, qualities he'd never even imagined in her before.

"Why don't you come into the kitchen?"

He followed her there, keeping his distance, observing as if from afar her motions as she took a filter from the box and placed it in the top of the coffeemaker and poured the grounds into the holder. From the cabinet she took down a packet of cigarettes and offered him one. He declined and she lit hers with a match from the stove.

"I quit," she said. "It's just now and then . . ."

If only she had been here on her own. If only she had been on the old couch, by herself, he thought.

"I want you to know, the reason—"

"Don't," he said. "Don't."

She straightened, and then stubbed out into the sink the cigarette she'd just lit. One hand gripped the counter while the other floated up across her chest to grasp at her arm.

"I never wanted to trouble you. You going—I understood that. I wasn't well." She clutched her arm more tightly. "Won't you at least sit down?" she said, pleading with him now.

He shook his head.

"Please."

"I can't stay."

His brain had begun to numb, the light and sounds of the apartment hitting on a dullened surface.

Through the door to the other room he could see a sideboard standing where his desk had once been. A lace doily rested on its polished surface beneath a large bowl of fruit.

He had built the house in Finden for her. He saw this now. He had built it so that he could come here and rescue her. Drive her back across the town line, this time for good. What other purpose had the house ever really had? But the woman he'd come to save—she had left before he arrived. Replaced by someone different.

He watched her pour him a cup of coffee and edge it down the counter toward him, her shoulders slightly hunched, her breasts hanging a bit lower on her chest, her hips a bit wider than before, but the color in her face, the new life—it was unmistakable. She was happy.

"I came to say goodbye," he said. "I never said goodbye before."

"In the fridge . . . there's meat loaf . . . I can make up a salad."

"I have to go."

"Or a pasta . . ." The tears leaked from the corners of her eyes as she spoke.

Doug walked from the kitchen into the hall, hearing her footsteps behind him.

I carried you, he wanted to say. Down this passageway, from our couch to your bed when you couldn't walk, I carried you.

At the door, he felt her hand on his shoulder and he turned out from under it.

"Don't," he said.

"But where will you go?"

"It doesn't matter." In the doorway, he paused. "My place in Finden. It's over by the golf course. A mansion along the river. You can't miss it. You should go see it sometime."

And with that he stepped back onto the landing and quickly descended the stairs.

Chapter 20

The bright fluorescence in the foyer of Emily's dorm hit Nate like the glare of dawn and he squinted to avoid it. He heard Emily and her friends spill through the doors behind him, laughing. It was two in the morning and they'd been drinking since before dinner, roving through parties on campus and off.

"You can't sleep *there*," someone shouted, calling Nate off the bench where he'd taken a seat. He rose, trailing behind the others. Emily was toward the front of the group whispering something to her friend Alex. He was a slender boy, a bit shorter than Nate, his hair slicked up in the front with gel. Though he wore vintage T-shirts and hipster jeans and had that well-groomed dishevelment about him that suggested a perfect nonchalance, he'd seemed anxious to Nate ever since they'd met a few months ago, when Nate had come for his first visit, sometime before Christmas. Anxious in a way Nate recognized. Emily's other friends had welcomed Nate as a part-time member of the scene, but Alex had mostly avoided talking to him.

Now he knew why. This evening Emily had told him that Alex had asked her what Nate's status was—gay or straight, available or taken. "You're fair game," she'd said as they left the dining hall. "You might as well live here."

Her dorm room was a social hub of sorts from where her hall mates came and went with their laptops and iPods and the occasional textbook or novel, which they would glance at between the trading of notes and music and IMing with friends across campus, attending to assignments in the down moments between jokes and gossip. They were like a troupe of nervous dancers working earnestly on their poses, shifting quickly from one to the next, until the weekend came, when they'd drink enough to undo all that practice.

On the third floor, people started splitting up, heading back to their rooms, someone calling out a reminder that they had to be up by eight to catch the chartered bus to New York for the protest. When Nate eventually pushed through the doors onto Emily's hall, she had already slipped into her room.

"You coming with us tomorrow?" Alex asked. He was standing by his door, feeling in his pockets for his key.

"I guess so," Nate said, his head moving gently forward and back in search of balance.

Less than forty-eight hours ago, he had been sitting in the back pew of Finden Congregational at Charlotte Graves's belated memorial, listening to one of her colleagues, a former teacher of his, talk about how dedicated she had been to her students. And he'd listened to her former students as well, four or five of them, a woman who'd become a literature professor, a man who worked for the Geological Survey, people in their thirties and forties and fifties, all of whom spoke of how hard she'd been on them and how thankful they were for it. And when they were done, Charlotte's brother had got up again and said how moved he was that the church was full and how Charlotte wouldn't have believed it.

Ms. Graves would want him to go to the protest, he thought. The march to stop the war.

"Do you want a beer?" Alex asked.

"I should go to bed."

"You're welcome to come in if you want."

Alex was trying to play it cool but the tightness in his voice gave him away.

Faggot, Nate thought, weakling. With a flick of his tongue he could murder some small piece of this boy. The little power gave him a sickening little thrill.

"So you're inviting me in?" he asked, almost coyly, giving nothing away.

"Yeah. I am."

The walls of his room were surprisingly bare. Just a few postcards tacked over the desk. Nate had expected art posters and political slogans but there was none of that. Books that didn't fit on the overstuffed shelves stood in stacks along the floor and in piles by his computer. Above the bed was a small picture of Kafka.

Alex walked to the stereo and put on some Radiohead before getting them each a beer from the mini-fridge.

"Here," he said, pulling out his desk chair. "Take this." He sat opposite, on the edge of the twin bed. For a minute, the two of them sipped their last wasted drinks of the night, looking away at the walls and the floor and the bright vortex of the screen saver with its endlessly morphing patterns.

"I guess Emily probably told you that I asked about you. She's not a big one for secrets."

"That's for sure."

He wondered if he had appeared to Doug as Alex did to him now: bold and terrified at the same time.

"It's okay," Nate said. "It's cool."

"We don't have to do anything if you don't want to. I wasn't angling for that. You just seem like a sweet guy. And I think you're kind of cute, too."

Nate examined the spines of the novels on the bookcase, amazed his legs were still capable of trembling after all he'd drunk.

"Thanks," he said, taking another swig. Queer, he thought. Coward. Predator. Weakling. Monster. Only he couldn't tell to whom the words were directed, Alex or himself. All he knew was that the derision moved in his blood like venom.

Just then he heard the music as if for the first time. As if his ears had been plugged and now the stoppers had come loose. The singer's words were hard to make out beneath the wash of sound, but the plaintive tone was unmistakable, calling out through the dark orchestral swirl, the voice promising nothing but itself, no reassurance or escape, no comfort or caress, just testament to a longing that mere touch would never satisfy, the resonance of it reaching so much deeper into the past than touch ever could and so much farther into the future, calling the aching spirit from its hiding place, at least for a moment. And Nate saw then, in his mind's eye, the form of his father's corpse laid out on the floor in front of him, his garroted head resting to one side, his neck bruised from ear to ear, the poor, dear man. And lying there beside him, Ms. Graves, in her flannel skirt and cardigan, her gray hair brushed down over her ears and her eyes closed, the two of them hovering in the netherworld between the living and the forgotten dead.

“Can I ask you a question?”

“Sure,” Alex said.

“Is it okay if we kiss?”

Alex nodded, and Nate stood, stepping through the shadows at his feet to cross the space between them.

Chapter 21

At night, from his hotel balcony, Doug watched the Jaguars and Porsches cruise up and down Arabian Gulf Road blaring pop music as they glided by the armored cars that had appeared recently at intersections all over Kuwait City. According to the concierge, the American schools had announced an unscheduled six-week vacation and the expats not here for the war were leaving with their children by the hundreds. But in the evenings along the promenade the Kuwaiti families still picnicked on the grass, enjoying the mild winter air and the views of the glittering towers up and down the waterfront, leaving their trash on the ground behind them for the municipal workers to collect—the Filipinos and Pakistanis, who came by in their minivans and green jumpsuits to spear the crumpled plastic bags and date wrappers and empty soda cans tipping and rolling in the breeze.

When he couldn't sleep Doug walked the city, whose citizens seemed to stay up all night shopping in the twenty-four-hour supermarkets. There were American sailors about as well, up from the naval base for their sober nights out on the town. He did his best to avoid them, though he knew his chances of being detected here were small. He'd been careful, at first, sounding out other guests at the hotel about which contractors might be hiring, thinking he needed to avoid the firms working directly with the State Department. But soon he'd realized how far the demand for people outstripped the supply and just how many of the men here were themselves not so interested in anyone knowing much about their past. If you were an American and a firm wanted you, the background check was often skipped lest it prove inconvenient.

Passing through the streets of low-rise apartments he'd reach Al Taawun Street from where he could see over the resorts and the private compounds to the coast, the lights of skiffs and police boats mingling with the more distant signals of tankers headed south with their American escorts for the Strait of Hormuz.

In all his life he'd never had this much time on his hands; such idleness was a menace to him. In the hotel room, he felt caged but out walking there was nothing to do but think. Seeing the young sailors in their dress whites moving in packs along the sidewalks put him in mind of when he'd left for the navy and what he'd imagined lay ahead of him back then.

He'd ridden the commuter train into Boston with his suitcase and knapsack and crossing the dingy concourse of South Station boarded a Greyhound that had taken the better part of two days to carry him up to the Naval Station Great Lakes, there along the western shore of Lake Michigan.

Through the dead of night on that trip, as the other passengers dozed, Doug had put on his Walkman and watched the fencing alongside the highway tick by in the headlights, the flat expanses of Ohio and then Indiana stretching out in every direction, the farmland parceled into one forty-acre field after another, as dark and empty a landscape as his Eastern eyes had ever seen. With the signs for Gary and Chicago, lights appeared and soon the streets were bright with lamps above the barren parking lots and block-long warehouses. As the bus bounded over paved gorges of underpasses and empty surface roads, a panorama that made the Alden strip seem like little more than a candle's light came into view: acre after acre of oil tanks and cylinders connected by masses of strut work and pipes running this way and that, white smoke jetting from valves up and down the tangle of steel, lit by thousands of naked yellow bulbs lining ladders and catwalks and above this vast tract of works, a giant orange flame billowing from the tip of a steel column like some temple fire undulating against the pale-yellow sky.

Before that trip, he'd never slept more than a single night away from home. He had signed up for the navy without ever having set foot on a boat. His first day out on a training vessel he kept thinking of the movie he'd seen on television as a kid about the sinking of the *Bismarck* and how when a ship was attacked and started taking on water, the sailors' orders were to seal off the flooding compartments along with the men trapped inside them. When the whitecaps came up on the lake and the boat began rocking, he grew so nervous he thought he'd be sick. But then the boy next to him threw up. Doug watched with fascination the disdain in the eyes of the training officer as he handed the kid a brush and pail and told him to scrub. Gripping the rails, the others had looked on as their fellow recruit got down on his hands and knees, reaching for the streaks of his own vomit running over the deck.

He'd seen then that fear was a question of balance. As long as he saw more of it in the faces of those around him than he himself displayed—that is, as long as he had confidence—he would do more than survive. He would gain. Or so he'd imagined.

Kuwaiti civilians were no longer being allowed into the northern part of the country. Only the farmers and their foreign laborers were permitted to remain. The highway leading up to the border was said to be clogged with American convoys. It wouldn't be long now, people agreed. During the day the government ran drills for possible Scud attacks and at the hotel restaurant in the evenings there were stories of UN staff departing and civilian contractors moving onto the American bases for protection.

Finally, Doug got the call from his new employer informing him of the date for his team's departure. That night, he dreamt he was in the back row at St. Mary's in Alden, listening to Father Griffin deliver his sermon, the congregation fixed in their seats and silent. All except his mother who sat in the front pew beside Nate. She leaned over to whisper words in the boy's ear and Nate nodded in agreement. Then, as the sermon continued, the two of them stood and walked back down the aisle together passing Doug without so much as a glance. Right past him and out the doors of the church. Father Griffin kept speaking and the people kept listening and no one appeared to take any notice.

Walking through Dasman Square the next day, he thought he saw Nate among a group of sailors, and he followed them for a while, waiting for a chance to get ahead of them but when he did he saw that he'd been mistaken and that their faces were all as blank and remorseless as his own. Again in the evening, on one of the narrow streets by the vegetable market, he became convinced that a kid in jeans and a sweatshirt making his way through the crowd up ahead must be Nate. And yet for all his certainty, the person turned out to be a man in his late twenties, Scandinavian or German, a reporter or photographer who when Doug grabbed him by the arm wheeled about looking wide-eyed with terror, as if he expected at that very moment to be stabbed.

On the appointed morning, he took a taxi to the port, where alongside the warehouse that the security firm had rented a few GIs stood leaning against their Humvee, chewing tobacco and eyeing their older civilian charges with a mixture of envy and contempt. Inside, the armored Suburbans were being loaded with food and equipment. The drive to the border would take about two hours, depending on the convoy traffic. Each of the eight men—four Americans, two Brits, a Chilean, and an Australian—signed their final waivers and were issued satellite phones.

Doug traveled in the lead car, which kept a hundred yards back from the Humvee that led them speeding up the six-lane highway. For miles they saw nothing but sand and limestone gravel and the occasional paved lot of rusting oil drums. As they reached the outskirts of Al Abdaly, rows of greenhouses came into view, hundreds of them shimmering in the sun, and beyond them fields full of oblong tanks, which the driver said were filled with tilapia, grown here by the thousands using the same groundwater that irrigated the strawberries under all that glass.

"Fish in the desert!" the guy beside Doug said. His name was Bill Gunther and he was from Tennessee. He had three kids in grade school and said he was being paid more than he'd imagined possible.

They arrived at the border truck stop and could see across the line into Iraq, past the unmanned checkpoint and the demilitarized zone, where a UN watchtower stood empty. It would be six or seven hours before they crossed, just after nightfall. They kept close to the vehicles, listening to the distant grind of earthmovers working up and down the line of control, flattening the dirt berm to make way for the first wave of the invading army.

At dusk, they began to hear jets streaking overhead. Moving off, away from the others, Doug wandered over the road and down a path that led past a diesel station to a shipping warehouse, its lot empty and its cargo doors shut.

Along this stretch the electric border fence still stood; behind it were coiled rows of concertina wire set in front of a wide, deep ditch in the sand. The empty highway beyond these defenses ran from here to Safwan: the highway of death, where the American planes had made of the retreating conscripts a smoldering graveyard back in '91.

Soon, thankfully, the idleness and the thinking would end and the present would once more absorb all Doug's attention. As the sounds of the impending blitz grew louder, the image of his young mother came to him once again, the person he remembered, the person he'd kept close, walking back down the aisle of the church with Nate. He could make no sense of it.

"You coming with us or what?" Gunther called out to him. He'd been sent by the team's leader to find their stray member. "Looks like the show's just about started."

To the north, a massive cloud of dust hung suspended above the roar of the advancing troops, artillery rounds starting to flash within it like lightning revealing the shape of a distant thunderhead. Soon would come the earsplitting shout of bombs.

Checking the holster of his flak jacket, Doug fingered the metal of his gun.

Under the rules established by the firm, none of them knew the identity of their client. They had been told only that it was not a government but a private entity, one that was paying top dollar. There were documents and a computer in the offices of the oil depot at Umm Qasr and someone wanted them secured.

A NOTE ABOUT THE AUTHOR

Adam Haslett is the author of the short story collection *You Are Not a Stranger Here*, which was a finalist for the Pulitzer Prize and the National Book Award. He has received fellowships from the Guggenheim Foundation, the Rockefeller Foundation, and the Fine Arts Work Center and is the recipient of a PEN/Malamud Award for accomplishment in short fiction. He lives in New York City.

A NOTE ABOUT THE TYPE

This book was set in Bembo Book, a Monotype revival of the original Bembo typeface. The font was cut for the celebrated Venetian printer Aldus Manutius by Francesco Griffo, and first used in Pietro Cardinal Bembo's *De Aetna* of 1495. For hundreds of years, Bembo has been among the most admired type designs ever created. Sturdy, well-balanced, and finely proportioned, it is a face of rare beauty and great legibility in all of its sizes.